The creativity of Abigail K.C. Sterling gave birth to Alistair Strange, the titular hero destined to save his not only his own fictional universe from an ultimate evil, but save Casey's life as well. Her series of Young Adult novels topped the bestseller lists. The screams and adulations of her legion of fans, called Strangers, made her book signings harken back to the 1960's British Invasion. Hollywood made billions adapting her novels for the silver screen. She lived the life every aspiring novelist dreams of living. Then she vanished... like a fart in a whirlwind... becoming a recluse.

But the Strangers did not give up hope that there would yet again be another "Casey For Christmas", yet the years stretched towards a decade without her delivering a fifth novel in the series. Then her publisher did the impossible... the unthinkable... they published another author's Alistair Strange novel without her permission. Plucked from the obscurity of the seedy fan-fiction underbelly, Alex K.C. Silver would be destined to save the literary universe from the ultimate evil: Casey's reclusivity.

Little do the Strangers realize that those of Team Dracarys (those loyal to Casey) and Team Griffindico (those who prefer Alex) would choose sides in fight on blogs, message boards, and social media in an all-out Fandom Civil War!

Readers of novels love to throw themselves into books about a variety of glamorous professions so that they can vicariously live through them.

- Police procedurals champion the homicide detectives, the crime-scene investigators, the vice-squad, etc.
- Legal thrillers document the prosecution or the defense of sensational court-room battles.
- Medical thrillers excite readers with diseases, operations, and plagues.

Has there ever been a novel written about the writing of a novel? Has a novelist ever been the protagonist of a novel? What kind of plot would suit the novelist as protagonist? What conflict could there be in the writing of a novel? What suspense would keep the reader on the seat of their pants? Could a novel be written that educates the reader on the steps of writing a novel? Robert Dwight Brown sought the answers to these questions and more in *Alistair Strange and the Fan-Friction*.

FANDOM

Alistair Strange and the Fan-Friction

CIVIL WARS

THE WAR OF THE WORDS
WITH ORIGINAL MULTIVERSE ENDING

ABIGAIL KC STERLING
& Robert Dwight Brown

Allonymous Books

This novel about writing a novel
is dedicated to the sheer number of writers I call friends:
C.E. O'Grady, the novelist
Cory Moosman, the playwright,
Tony Moffeit & Kyle Laws, the poets,
& John Micheal Petric (requiēscat in pāce)

Allonymous Books
A Division of Chi Xi Stigma Publishing Company, LLC

ISBN 13: 978-1-931608-58-9 (**The War of the Words Edition**)
ISBN 13: 978-1-931608-67-1 (**Make Love, Not War Edition**)
ISBN 13: 978-1-931608-76-3 (**The Invisible Man Edition**)

Copyright©2018 Robert Dwight Brown

Contact: **secretary@chixistigma.org**

"The ending is nearer than you think, and it is already written. All that we have left to choose is the correct moment to begin."
—Alan Moore, *V for Vendetta*

Chapter One

Page 1, Chapter 1
Word 1...

Not every novel has to begin with immortal words that timelessly carry itself across the generations. "Call me Ishmael." "It was the best of times, it was the worst of times..." Too many writers struggle over how to begin their novel. They try so earnestly to compose the perfect first sentence, but not every novel has to begin with an immortal opening line. For the writer to begin writing an entire novel, the novel just has to begin with word one.

Most readers, standing in the aisles of the bookstore or library, will give the writer more than just the first hopefully immortal line, they'll give the writer the first page or first chapter to capture their attention enough to be willing to part ways with their hard-earned money.

How many times does the nascent writer (or

even the most experienced of ones) rewrite that first chapter? The cliché that has been spouted since, probably, the days of Homer and the warrior-poets, is to begin in the middle of the action. If the first chapter is confusing or disconcerting to the reader, because they have to orient themselves to who the main-character is, what the situation is, what the genre the book is trying to be, will the reader put aside a book if have no idea what situation they have been dropped into? So. Back. On. The. Shelf. The. Book. Goes.

Does one begin at the beginning? And where is the beginning? Isn't there always some backstory to the story, even if begins at the beginning. Few books actually begin at the beginning with little to no backstory to speak of. I believe the Holy Bible and the book of Genesis is truly the only story to begin at the beginning: *In the beginning God created the heaven and the earth* (Gen. 1:1). Even a "Once Upon A Time" story doesn't actually begin at the beginning.

Movie trailers have the ability to draw from scenes throughout the motion picture to craft an enticing and anticipatory experience. The author only has their synopsis or summary written on the back of the book, any quotational blurbs, and the first few pages of the book.

The synopsis has to completely summarize the book, yet be vague enough not to entirely give away the story. I, personally, adore the synopsis. I love going to the bookstore and reading these backcopy (or inner-flap) synopses, intrigued by what ideas struck this particular writer as worthy of devoting the time (in some cases years) and energy (often immense expenditures of energy) into writing. I don't have the time and energy to read every book that is published (I am far too busy writing my own books), but I find that I can consume a dozen or more synopses each trip to the bookstore. It is delightful to see all the wondrous stories being told. The more stubborn reader will not even get past the synopsis. So. Back. On. The. Shelf. The. Book. Goes.

The blurbs have to be from famous enough authors so the reader will respect the quotation. The more stubborn reader does not see a famous enough author, or an author they personally like, or an author they even recognize the name of. So. Back. On. The. Shelf. The. Book. Goes.

And the first few pages of chapter one, well, that can be the real deal-breaker. Since, in most cases, the reader, unlike the movie-goer, actually can read the first several pages. The movie-goer can't simply buy a ticket, watch the first five minutes, walk out, then demand a full refund. The reader, standing in the aisle of their favorite bookstore, can read the first line, the first page, the first chapter. The author has to compel the reader to: Carry. The. Book. To. The. Cashier. And. Spend. Real. Cash. Money.

Or Back. On. The. Shelf. The. Book. Goes.

The author simply needs to begin page one, chapter one with word one. When a writer sits down with pen in hand, or at the typewriter, or in front of her computer screen, she is confronted with an almost impossible Sisyphean task. There is a blank page or screen with a blinking cursor staring back at her. Dismissing the struggle to compose the perfect opening line, there is an entire blank page to fill with words. But that is not the Sisyphean task of the writer. No matter how many pages she fills with words, with sentences, with characters, with story, there is a seemingly endless number of blank pages that follow. Each subsequent chapter begins with the bottomless blank page. The author has to conjure these words, these sentences, her characters, this story out of the ether in such a manner that this impossible struggle to write ends up being a effortless pleasure to read.

Here I am, Diary, trying to write my first novel, desperately trying to write my very first novel, the first chapter of my very first novel, and I'm stuck on crafting the perfect opening line. Why am I doing this to myself, Diary? Why am I so obsessed with composing the perfect immortal first line, when I am depriving myself of the shear unmitigated joy of writing my very first novel? I just can't seem to convince myself that after writing the entire novel, *then* I can go back and craft the perfect opening line last. If I'm ever going to get this thing written, I just got to start writing—

—My diary has always been a constant in my life. As a child,

I wrote stories for my once and future bestsellers in her pages. I wrote half-thought ideas that I dreamed of or those two ideas from the swirling collective-consciousness that bumped into each other and I thought: "There's an idea." But soon, I turned to her for advice on boys. I wrote to her about this boy or that boy and how do I get this boy to talk to me or how this girlfriend is being catty or how to keep that nerdy-boy from crushing on me. Of course, that was all foolishness, hindsight being twenty-twenty.

And now?

I'm beginning to think of her not just as a Diary, but more of a Muse as well. This is a place to not only record my thoughts, like in a diary, but also my aspirations. Now, that I have the freedom to purchase the books that speak to me through their covers, their little blurbs, the freedom to read in the open, at the cafe, at the park under a tree, or in my own living room, my own imagination has begun to give birth to... something. The more I read, the more original stories are starting to creep into my consciousness.

My own imagination has been awakened, but something else has been awakened as well. It seemed at first almost demonic. It spoke to me in my mind. It spoke to me through images, through characters, through stories. I don't know what to make of this personality that seems to be calling me, speaking to me.

At first I couldn't abide the concept of a Muse, it smacked of prostitution and polytheism. My father, a devout religious man, a devoted family man, had preached from the pulpit telling horror stories of heathen artists, the painters, the sculptors, the musicians, the actors of the world, who enslaved women as their "Muses" to serve their wanton lusts: the lusts for fame, the lusts for fortune, the lusts for the flesh. Who were these women that inspired the greatest works of creativity and art? Why did they devote themselves to being the inspiration of great artists? And where could I find a muse of my very own?

As for the spiritual Muses, these goddesses, the daughters of the Zeus and Mnemosyne ("Memory" herself), I was strangely drawn to them because they governed different aspects of creativity that I am more and more drawn to: epic poetry, history, lyric poetry, comedy and pastoral poetry, tragedy, dance, sacred poetry, and astronomy. How could something, someone, that inspires such beauty and creativity be heathenish, pagan, and evil? If they aren't pagan goddesses, if they aren't angels, if they aren't patron saints, then perhaps they are just aspects of human creativity given an anthropomorphic form that is personable, that is more relatable. These are the Muses that I think I can have a intimate relationship with.

There appears to be no Muse for novel writing. I don't know exactly when novels were invented. (I read somewhere that Cervantes' *Don Quixote* was the first novel or others say it was *The Tale of Genji* by Murasaki Shikibu, so I don't know.) The novel is certainly a rather new phenomenon considering how old poetry is. Poetry is the eldest child in my little metaphor, followed soon after by theater, while novels are the middle child, and the twins, motion-pictures and television are rather late-in-life accidents. I don't think humans ever spoke poetry in our everyday lives. Haven't all spoken interactions been in prose? The earliest stories recounting mammoth hunts by our Cro-Magnon ancestors surely were told in prose or their everyday speaking language, which is what prose essentially is. These stories were exciting prose, perhaps grandiose, exaggerated prose, but prose nonetheless. How or when the warrior-poets like Homer made the transition to from prose to poetry or song is probably unknown and unknowable. So I'm going to believe that Calliope is the Muse that is whispering to me in the quiet of the night as stories swirl around my mind, as I daydream at work unable to escape the creep of stories distracting me from my duties as a waitress. She is the Muse whose devotion and inspiration will fire my creative spirit. I have already begun to listen to her.

Sorry, Diary, when I was a child, I understood the world as a child, I had the experiences of a child, therefore I wrote as a child, but to become a published author, I need to put away childish things. I write instead to you, O! Muse.

O! Muse,

I found the most wonderful book at the bookstore. It says that you can write a novel in thirty days! An entire novel from start to finish in a month! How exquisite is that? There is even a National Novel Writing Month (or NaNoWriMo) held every November. Can you imagine all of the support you would get from all the other authors who are also on their own thirty day journey to a finished and completed novel?

But unfortunately, it isn't November yet, so I'll have to tackle this novel on my own. :(

I've decided to start at the beginning of the next month (thankfully it's one with exactly thirty days). Knowing that at the end of the month is also the day my novel will be finished will keep it all straight in my head. This will give me a little time to settle on which story idea I want to go with.

I've also put in for some vacation time, so I can settle into a routine without having to worry about working a nine-to-five for at least the couple of weeks.

All I have to do is follow the steps outlined in the book and in thirty days I'll have a finished novel that I can begin sending to agents and editors the world round.

There are, thankfully, some plot ideas to get me started. I definitely need to have an idea, a premise for the novel. That needs to happen on day one, or even before the thirty days officially begins. There is a day-by-day worksheet for the first week. There are tips for time management.

The author explains I need to set writing goals: word-count goals, chapter goals. To write an 80,000 word novel (which seems totally doable, right?) I need to average 2,666 words per day for the entire thirty days (I've done the math), or I need to average just under 20,000 words a week, and then I get an extra two days. All I have to do is keep my quota each and every day and I'm gold. Totally doable. Right?

I've got an important decision to make: whether I should outline or shouldn't outline. To plot or go with the flow. I don't know how inflexible an outline would be, or could be, or would I be limited by what is or isn't in the outline. Or am I too afraid to just wing it? How intimidating would it be to not have at least an idea of where the book is going each step of the way?

Oh, Muse, there is a thirty day calendar to keep you motivated. I have set my daily and weekly goals (beyond that of simple word counts), checkpoints if you will, when I can reward myself with small rewards: nice semi-expensive chocolates or special coffee at the cafe or a meal at a slightly nicer than usual restaurant, a two hour break to see a movie in the cinema. These little rewards are just as important as the reward of a finished novel.

You are advised on how to write your first scenes. How to assemble your cast of characters. How to follow the three-act structure. Techniques to keep the story moving forward. How to deal with writer's block. How to write a climax. What a denouement is and why it is important. And once you are finished with the first draft hopefully by Day Thirty: how to rewrite it into a manuscript worthy of you. How to find an agent. How to get an editor to publish your book. How to publish the book yourself if you so desire.

It is wonderful. I can't wait to get started.

O! Muse,

I have been a fool. I AM a fool. How could I have been tricked out of my money so easily? My money is precious to me. My time is precious to me. I believed the author when she said that I could write a book in thirty days.

This is an impossible task!

You can't get anywhere near a finished novel in thirty days. As the days started to slip by and I wasn't able to keep up with her timeline, what was expected of me as a writer, I started to descend into a deep depression. I couldn't keep up with 2,666 words a day to maintain my quota on a 80,000 word novel. Within days, I couldn't keep up with 1,666 words a day to write a 50,000 word novel. Wouldn't it be better to have a shorter finished novel, at least? I couldn't even do that!

Every night I cried myself to sleep, because I was getting so far, so very far behind. I wouldn't be able to catch up. It is not humanly possible. Even having vacation time, I couldn't keep up. Then I *had* to go back to work. I had to make my tips. I had to pay rent and buy groceries. Even with my precious laptop and being able to write anywhere I wanted, I just didn't have the time! Who in this fast-paced modern world that buzzed by at the speed of light has the time to write a novel in thirty days? There isn't a magical 25th hour so you can squeeze another hour out writing. No, the hours turned into days, turned into weeks, and before I realized it, my month was GONE! And I have nothing to show for it. NOTHING!

O! Muse,

I do not know what it truly feels like to be a writer. Had I written words? Yes. But that alone does not a writer make.

To some this is an elitist belief. If you have a story in your head, that makes you a writer, doesn't it? It does not! To be a writer, you need to have written your story down. This is in the very definition of the word "writer". I may not be a published author, but I believed I had definitely earned the distinction of being a writer.

Only I hadn't. I *believed* I was a writer. Just as *believed* I could write a novel in thirty days. Both of these assumptions have been proven false. I couldn't write a novel in thirty days. Hindsight being twenty-twenty, I discovered I hadn't even *begun* a novel in those thirty days.

I sat cozied up in bed with a printout of my manuscript propped up on my laptop. I had been crying all week due to my failure to have a finished manuscript prepared to wow the entire publishing world. Now, I wanted to know what I had accomplished in those stressful, painful thirty days.

Now I wanted to look at my precious novel as if I were an agent looking for another writer to represent. Was I willing to devote the energy away from other published authors to sell a book by an unpublished first-time author? Was I willing to send this book to editors I had cultivated a trusted relationship with? Was I so convinced in the saleability and profitability of the novel that I would put my on reputation on the line for someone who hadn't even published a short-story?

I needed to read the manuscript with an editor's critical eye. Was I willing to devote hundreds of thousands of dollars toward the designing, printing, and marketing of this novel? Was this a book that would attract an audience to a first-time author that no one had ever heard of and had no previously installed fan-base? Was there the potential to spawn a series of novels that would build bigger and bigger audiences?

I started reading, for the first time with sense of clarity, my novel.

It. Is. Awful.

It truly is. There is no spark of imagination. There are no characters that leapt off the page. There is no story to speak of, whatsoever.

There. Are. Only. Words. On. The. Page.

And that a novel does not make.

Why wasn't I SMART? Why wasn't I specific, measurable, attainable, realistic, and time-bound? While I was too specific, wanting to finish the blasted novel in 30 days, and I measured myself in word-counts, my goal was neither attainable, realistic, and I had bound myself in a time-frame that wasn't even theoretically doable.

I need to set realistic goals that align with my life. On days that I work ten hour shifts, do I need to reach that 2,666 word goal? Or can I make up for those lost words on my days-off? And if I'm called into work on those days, does my goal of finishing the book by the end of the year begin to slip farther and farther away? Should I really try to stay up all night writing, when I get my best work done in the morning, before work?

Realistic goals, Casey. Realistic. Goals.

Don't circle that date on the calendar that says, "You can start looking for an agent now!" Stop the stopwatch now. The book will take to write however long the book takes to write.

O! Muse,

Is this my "practice novel"? Is this the novel that is destined to never sell? Will I write a second "practice novel", or a third, or fourth, or *Ugh!* a fifth that never sells? Or will I be one of the select few debut authors to sell their literally first book ever?

I wonder about other writers. The ones that have been writing since their school years. The writers who not only began and finished their first and second and third novels, but also submitted (and published?) dozens of short-stories to magazines over their formative years as young writers. Do they look back at their early writings and shudder as I just have? They have no doubt grown as a writer. Always learning. Always improving. Do they even look at their first, second, and third novels anymore, preferring to hide them away in boxes or the bottom drawers of a filing cabinet? Do they hope and pray the floppy-disks that contain their more primitive novels have decayed with age so much so that they can never be published posthumously? Have these authors put a clause in their will to have all these unfinished floppy disks and computer hard-drives steam-rolled so they can never– ever– be published posthumously? If any friend or family member is reading this diary after I have passed, please, for the love of God, destroy everything that I have left *unfinished.*

What about novelists who have had careers? Does their first published novel pale in comparison to those that followed? Do they even look behind once a book has been published? Don't the successful novelists only look towards the future? The books they are writing now. The books they will want to write tomorrow.

I don't know. This is only my first attempt at a first novel. I have no other frame of reference.

O Muse,

Why did I choose to become a writer? Am I even a writer? Do I write for the fame? Do I write for the fortune? Do I just want someone, anyone, to read the words I write, the characters I create, the stories I want to tell? Am I eager for reviewers to immortalize their opinions of my novel in their newspapers? Do I really look forward to book signings, the long days sitting and meetings hundreds, or perhaps, thousands! of my fans, while dealing with hand cramps? Is my desire the deep-seated need to continue on the traditional began with the cave-painters, the Homeric poets, the bards, the playwrights, the novelists? Or do I *just* have stories that I want to tell– *need* to tell. If I don't find an agent, or an editor, will I always want to be a writer? Will the desire still be there to sit in front of my computer screen typing for hours upon hours a day for months on end? Will I be a writer, writing over a million words in a dozen or more books, that not even my closest friends will have a desire to even read? And if I do find that agent and that editor and my book doesn't sell, will I write a second? Or a third?

At this point, I can only hope so.

O! Muse,

In the beginning I created my protagonist and his world. And the world was without form, and void; and darkness was upon the face of the deep. And my creativity moved upon the face of the waters. And I said, Let there be light: and there wasn't any light. And I saw that it was freaking terrible. (I apologize for my heresy.)

I am trying to create an entirely new world for my characters to live in. I don't necessary have to create entirely new rules for physics, though I might need to at some point. What are the rules of the world I am creating? The world of my novel could have been exactly like the real-world, with the same sciences, religions, and countries. I could have set a police-procedural in modern day New York City or during the great fire of 1666 in London. Or the police-procedural could exist on the planet Vulcan in the year 2743. Then I would probably have to create new rules for physics or at least physiologies.

What if my world is entirely alien? What kind of evolution brought life from the primordial ooze to civilization and eventually the stars? What is the history of my world? Am I writing about the First Age, the Middle-Earth, or the Final Days? A world with history is a world that feels lived in, then it will feel real to the reader.

What are the biographies of my protagonist, antagonist, and every other character? I need to know the life story of my characters, even if that knowledge doesn't even make it to the page.

And, Muse, make a note, I can never forget this proverb of science-fiction, that applies to fantasy and even literary fiction: "If it looks like a rabbit and acts like a rabbit, calling it a *shmeerp* doesn't make it alien." Thanks be to James Blish for coining needlessly coined words– "shmeerps".

I know I want my world to be magical like Harry Potter, but set in real-world 21st Century New York City. Oh, and the gods of the Egyptians, Greeks, and Norse are still worshiped by people all over the world, including the "New" World.

That's it!

That's the length of my world building as of this very moment. I have so much farther to go if I am going to build a realistic world, particularly with magic being a "real" thing. Is technology magic? Or is magic technology? I don't know. And *that* is the problem.

Who knew there even needed to be rules for magic? Science-fiction by its very nature needs to follow, or at least acknowledge, the laws of science in its fictional universe. But magic needs rules?

Very. Clear. Rules. Apparently.

If anything is possible, then why should the reader care about the consequences. If resurrection is possible, even commonplace, then death become meaningless and utterly lacking in suspense. If I create a solution to one problem in one novel, then that solution has to be at the very least possible in *every* other situation for the rest of the entire freaking series! The stricter the limitations that I put on magic will eventually open up the sheer number of possibilities from which my fantasy novel can go.

O! Muse,

As I read and reread and reread my *attempt* at a novel and wept, I experienced the strangest thing that has every happened to me. Alistair Strange talked to me today. As strange and impossible as that may sound, I *heard* his voice speaking to me. Of course, I had read that characters sometimes took a life of their own, but I thought this was an exaggeration on the part of writers and their egos. How could a creation of your own mind have a mind of their own? How could a fictional character possess any sort of sentience? Until that very moment when Alistair spoke, I did not know what it truly felt like to be a writer. Had I written words? Yes. But that alone does not a writer make.

Alistair Strange spoke to me. He was just a minor character, a character for whom I had given a name for some reason, but didn't bother to describe his appearance or to even give a substantial part in the story to. He whispered over my left shoulder, "This is my story now. I know what happened. Let me tell you the story. It is the story of *my* life and adventures."

I turned around wondering if someone in the apartment through the wall behind me had said something. I heard nothing. I looked at the television set. It was dark. Who could have possibly spoken? Was there somebody outside the window? Was I going crazy? Had the deep depression I suffered from for the past week caused some kind of psychosis? Was I having a nervous breakdown?

Then the voice spoke again, "Get out of the way and let me tell the story my way. And hold on for the ride."

And I did.

But for some reason, I feel like a secretary taking dictation.

Am. I. A. Writer. Now?

"Rock bottom became the solid foundation on which I rebuilt my life."
    –J.K. Rowling

Chapter Two

ABIGAIL K.C. STERLING
PLAYB🐰Y Interview

Abigail K.C. Sterling types in the air as she speaks. It's not as flamboyant as your Italian grandmother's dramatic flourishes of gestures. Her hands float just above the table top as we sit in the coffee shop where she gave birth to Alistair Strange, the titular hero destined to save his not only his own fictional universe from an ultimate evil, but save Casey's life as well. Her pianist fingers dance above the tabletop typing out the words as she says them. I was momentarily distracted by the thought that she was imputing dictation of our conversation into her invisible keyboard. Was this visionary author actually a time-traveler from the future? She seemed to be– no correct that– she was typing her words as she spoke them, and correctly. Did she recite her novels as she typed them into a computer? And

14

this eccentricity has been ingrained ever so deeply in her muscle-memory!

The laptop, her most constant companion at all times, was the one modern extravagance she afforded herself. While she had bought an impressively modern and powerful (for the time) Apple PowerBook, she had found it as a functional display model in an electronics store. She was able to haggle down the price into a range befitting a young women living in newfound freedom and poverty, because the computer was missing several of its keys. She didn't need the missing right command and shift buttons, the caps-lock button, any of the missing operational keys above the numerical line, nor the down arrow key. But how was she able to type, let alone edit, a manuscript with three of the twenty-six letters of alphabet and the number 7 missing? And according to Scrabble, those were very important letters. Once I was able to pull my attention away from her pantomimed typing, I was struck by her elfish beauty.

She is a natural, platinum blonde, with an strikingly unnatural streak of raven black hair coming from above her left temple, like the stress of her young life, instead of making her hair turn white from fright, streaked her hair midnight black. Her eyes are the color of the bluest waters off the coast of Hawaii, her lips thin, her nose sharp, and her ears, not pointed like an elf's, but more like a leaf– no– the petal of a rose. Her clothes are wisp-like, like a cruel word would cause them to blow away. Her smile is instantly disarming. I felt like I would have quite some difficulty asking the hard questions about her youth, her obsessively strict Puritan preacher father, but while she looked fragile, she was as hard, unbreakable, and unflinching as a golem.

Her first novel THE XII LABORS OF ALISTAIR STRANGE was initially dismissed by critics as yet another Harry Potter clone. But they failed to see the deep philosophical and spiritual questions being asked. These types of questions would be esoteric and heady in an adult literary novel, let alone in a so-called Young Adult novel. She sought answers that her Christian upbringing simply could not answer. The mythologies of other cultures, the

Egyptians, the Greeks, the Norse, were not mere fairy tales, but were actual religions, worshiped by actual cultures. These ancient people believed in and were as devoted followers of their gods, more so than even modern followers of the Christ. She rankled the ire of the conservative evangelical communities by posing such questions to our children! How dare she! The alternative parallel reality she populated with her characters with was a 21st century where Christ and His followers were not victorious over the pantheons of pagan gods, and instead the religions of the Egyptians, the Greeks, and the Norse, not only thrived, but their gods took an active role in the lives of men and in the governance of the world. Truly heady stuff.

Perhaps the vocal, fervent, and down-right hostile attacks on Ms. Sterling and her novels by the political and religious Right drove her into reclusivity. She hasn't published the anticipated fifth novel in her series, despite repeated deadlines, self-imposed or otherwise, and Twitter announcements of its being "almost done". She hasn't done a book signing in years. She has been radio-silent for nearly a full decade, until yours truly, decided to seek her out for an interview, despite my editor's assertion, and her's as well, that this was a fool's errand. If I fool I need be, a fool I shall be.

PLAYBOY: *You were once on top of the entire world, and to a certain extent you still are. Your four previous novels are still on* **The New York Times** *Bestseller lists. I'm sure that if I don't ask this question first, all of the Strangers, your devoted and obsessive fan base, will crucify me. How is the fifth novel progressing. The fans are chomping at the bit to read the next chapter in the Alistair Strange saga.* **ABIGAIL K.C. STERLING:** It's coming along quite beautifully. I know it has taken much longer than the previous books to get to my editor. *Alistair Strange and Those Whom the Gods Detest Shall Not Be Unearthed* took a bit longer than I had wanted, and I missed my first deadline on that novel, but I did deliver it to my editor and it was published in time to be a "Casey For Christmas". This is one traditional I have no intention of upending. *But you have missed five or six Christmases without de-*

livering a Casey for your Strangers. I have. I have. I've never promised a Casey for *every* Christmas. I know I'm mincing words, but there will be another "Casey For Christmas", of that I have no doubt. I know I missed some deadlines, both self-imposed and by my publisher, on the fifth, still yet untitled novel. *You went on Twitter and announced that the fifth book was "almost" done. You went on Twitter again saying the book was going to be in your editor's hands "in a couple of months".* I know I know, but sometimes the Muse is a little quiet. Shockingly so. Frightfully so. Deathly so. I'm trying my hardest to get the book finished. It's just taking... time. *This is the first interview you've given and it's going on nearly a decade. You didn't do any press for the release of the fourth book. Are you becoming something of a recluse? Why are you sitting down for an interview now of all times?* To be perfectly honest, my editor insisted I get myself out into the public eye. Fame has not sat well on my shoulders, I'm afraid. I love my readers so much it hurts. But sometimes their love and their adulation is a little smothering. I have never desired sycophants. I never wanted to be worshiped like my Father kind of did. *What is your feeling about your Strangers fervently held belief that you are not producing material fast enough to satiate their insatiable appetites.* I love my Strangers, I really do. But there is a misconception that we writers can just produce a new book at the drop of a hat. *Let me play Devil's Advocate for the Strangers. You wrote the first novel despite not being paid to write it. You wrote the second and third books in rapid-fire succession, the fourth book had a three year lull in publication and now the fifth novel is taking far, far longer. You have missed self-imposed deadlines. The question is coming I can assure you. You have gone on Twitter to announce the novel is almost done. Your publisher has imposed deadline after deadline and yet you have not delivered any novel. Here's the question: why do writers devote years to writing their first novel without being paid and now that a publisher has no doubt paid a mighty advance, not produce a novel. What are you doing with your time? Why the delays?* It is a fair question, but at the same time it isn't fair at all. Yes,

I have been paid– paid well– to write my novels, but sometimes the Muse is a fickle lover. You want to write, you desperately do. I know I am being paid to write. But sometimes the words are just not there. I know my Strangers don't want to hear these words, but wouldn't they rather have a novel worthy of Alistair Strange instead of a novel that is a pale shade of an Alistair Strange novel. If my Strangers are so desperate for a new Alistair Strange novel, why don't they petition my publisher to hire a new writer to take over the Alistair Strange series? *That is an interesting question. I don't know if I have an answer.* It's because they don't want another Alistair Strange novel, they want another novel by Abigail K.C. Sterling. They want another "Casey For Christmas". *Let's shift a bit, shall we? No need to get heated. Your name is Abigail Kathleen Carol Sterling, but your prefer to go by your middle initials K.C. or as you prefer the phonetic name "Casey"? It makes for an alliterative marketing campaign, but you prefer to be called by your initials. Why?* Abigail is my great-grandmother's name, and Kathleen and Carol are my grandmothers' names, and I don't know why I also thought of those names as being old lady names. I always thought that boys at school who went by their initials: J.R., A.J., J.D., J.T., P.J., or P.T. were so cool. I wanted to go my initials, but my initials are already a name: "Casey". *When did it occur to you to begin dreaming of being a writer? Is being a writer what you were born to be?* Oh, Heavens, no, I came from a really old fashioned, evangelical family. My father was a minister as was his father, back into time immemorial. We were Puritans of the hardiest of Mayflower stock. My auntie Emily has our entire genealogy down to a science. She knows our family tree like she is an orchardist. *Orchardist? That's an interesting word. Is it old?* Most likely, it's a person who tends an orchard. And she has tended our family tree, branch by branch, generation after generation all by way back to the earliest days of our family's escape from British persecution. Oh, your question. Women in my family, despite being raised in the late 20th century were expected to be school-teachers, nurses, or mothers. And I wasn't interested in being any of those things, I would like to be a mother, at some point, but not barefoot-and-pregnant at eighteen like my sisters and cousins. Like I said, a really old-fashioned family. *And this extended to books as well? I've read, preparing for our interview, that your father didn't really care for modern fiction.* Oh, mercy! Yes. There was only one Book that mattered in my father's eyes. The Good Book. My mother on the other hand was a much more cultured woman, she came from a far more intellectual family with professors in the place of ministers. She always made sure I was well-read, even if it entailed sneaking books into our house, making sure Father wasn't aware of our subterfuge. As for the affairs of the world, they never really interested me. Those were the concerns of men. I cared not who the President of the United States was. I did not care what sports were or who won what championship or what movies were showing or what music people listened to. I was much too devout and proper a woman to seek such answers. But books... oh, books... these precious things I couldn't get enough of. The worlds that authors were able to create with just their own minds excited me to no end. *How long did it take you to begin to dream of being a writer?* Oh, the dream began early, but it took years to grow into maturity, almost as long to physically grew into maturity. Some children are blessed to know their chosen profession at a young age, but I never dreamed that being a writer would ever, ever be *real.* And yet, I still have the notebooks that I kept as early as the second grade that I filled with stories. I didn't date them. I wasn't that far-reaching. But based on my penmanship, I'd say the second grade. They were of course mostly plagiarized– that's not the correct term– I wrote stories in the worlds of Winnie the Pooh, Peter Rabbit, Dr. Seuss. I continued the adventures of the Boxcar Children. I followed Laura Ingalls Wilder well into adulthood in my own books. I wrote my own Nancy Drew mysteries. I was really just testing the waters. As I grew into my teens, more and more original stories started to creep into my creativity. But sometimes you have to put away childish things. By high-school, I had turned my attention to boys. Writing for a living wasn't something that I thought could ever be a reality. My father was grooming me to marry at eighteen, while my mother was insisting that I go to university and earn a degree, before even thinking of marriage. *But you didn't pursue the university life? Why did you move you Greenwich Village?* I needed to live my life on my own terms. Those are the only terms a man can live according to Orson Welles and his *Citizen Kane*. I wanted to give New York a shot for a least a year or two, before acquiescing to either my mother or– God forbid– my father. I came from a large family, ten brothers and sisters. I was the youngest and therefore the spoiled brat, the one that didn't have to become a school-teacher, nurse, or mother. I relished being on my own. My father didn't necessarily disown me, but I left with nary a possession except my clothes and a small selection from my library. I cooked alone. I bathed alone. I slept alone. I lived my live for the first time alone. And I loved every moment of it. I got a job as a waitress. My tips and wages were spent on rent, food, and books. And not necessarily in that order. *Even now your computer is your constant companion. How did you, despite your immense poverty, acquire it?* Yes, I go nowhere and do nothing without my MacBook. It is like my child. No. That's not right. My characters are my children. The computer is more a like security blanket. I had learned how to use a computer at school in spite of my father's old fashioned ways. I used the computer at the library. And within walking distance of my apartment there was an electronics store. I knew that it would probably take me months–if not years– to save up enough for a computer, any computer. PCs were, and still are, much, much, so very much cheaper than Macs, which would have been advantageous because of my situation, but I was drawn to the Apple PowerBook. *That is a caviar dream on a Ramon budget.* *[Laughs]* Most definitely. But a line had been drawn in the sand that I was unwilling to cross. *What line in what sand?* The older gentlemen who ran the store and I had spirited debates about that strange rivalry between Bill Gates and Steve Jobs. This "war" struck me as strange, yet strangely exciting. I was drawn towards an discipleship with Steve Jobs due to no particular reason. Maybe it was because Bill Gates seemed to be the stereotypical nerd every girl in school looked down upon. Maybe it was Steve Jobs' devil-may-care swagger. He certainly had the confidence of a jock, but was less at home in a locker-room and more comfortable in the A.V. room. He was also the underdog. Who doesn't love an underdog? Everybody knew Microsoft were the real conglomerate. They owned the entire business. Practically every computer in the entire freaking world ran on DOS, then Windows. But the prodigal son had finally returned to Apple. If Steve Jobs were a fashion designer, his dresses were the ones you saw on the Oscar's red carpet, not on sale at J.C. Pennys. Only Steve could take cast off technologies like MP3 players, smartphones, and tablets and turn them into staples of modern life. *True. True, but at that point in your life, you'd think that you'd accept any old computer, even a PC. A starving man doesn't turn his nose up at Micky D's.* Oh, I knew I couldn't afford a new Apple. Like ever. Ever. Never in a million years "ever". Heck, I probably couldn't even afford the broken display model. Old Joe had chuckled when I told him that, and said you never know, maybe if the price was right, he'd let it go. And before either one of us realized, I was the proud owner of a state-of-the art, down-on-its-luck Apple Powerbook. What it lacked in beauty and a few missing keys, it more than made up for in fueling my creativity like nothing else possibly could. I would do Steve Jobs and Old Joe proud. *And Alistair Strange was born in the very coffee shop we are enjoying this interview.* He was born of desperation. I knew nothing of the publishing industry. I bought books on writing. Every book I could find. By Stephen King. By Julie Cameron. By Ray Bradbury. A dozen or more by the Writer's Digest. I even bought a stupid book on how to write a novel in thirty days, because I was stupid enough to believe that was possible. *You don't believe it's possible to write a novel in a month? A know for a fact Anthony Burgess wrote* **A Clockwork Orange** *in around a month's time. As did Jack Kerouac with* **On the Road,** **Casino Royale** *by Ian Fleming,* **As I Lay Dying** *by William Faulkner,* *Fyodor Dostoevsky's* **The Gambler,** *Mickey Spillane's* **I the Jury.** It is certainly possible, but from an entirely different perspective. A novelist with several books, and dozens, if not hundreds, of short stories written and/or published has put in the 10,000 hours required to be really proficient at a skill to be able to write a book in thirty days. But for the novice, nascent novelist, this is an impossible task. Now, I know that in thirty days, you can certainly *start* a novel. Just that. And nothing more. ***What happened when you reached the end of the thirty days? Did you have a finished novel?*** Oh, no. Certainly not. ***How did you feel when you couldn't get your novel done in the requisite thirty days.*** I was dejected because I was nowhere near being finished with my novel. I didn't have a finished draft like the book said I would. There was nothing to send an agent. Let alone an editor. I didn't even have a first draft. I entered into a deep depression because the book wasn't any near to be finished. I printed what I had written in that single, solitary month. I read it through as if I was just a reader discovering a novel for the first time. Only then did I realize that I had the *beginnings* of a novel. Not the beginning, just a beginning. There was a spark. There were hints at a bigger picture. A much larger literary universe. There was Alistair Strange, then a minor character, whispering in my ear, from over my left shoulder, "This is my story now. Get out of the way and let me tell it my way. And hold on for the ride." ***You audibly heard Alistair talking to you, like a schizophrenic hallucination?*** This was the first moment in my entire life where I felt like an honest-to-God writer. My character had stopped me in my tracks and say, "No! No! No!" I was trying to write, to be in charge, to be the God in my little, third-person omniscient world. But Alistair needed to tell *me his* story. I had to throw practically every word I had written into the virtual trashcan on the desktop of my computer. ***Wasn't it painful to throw away a month's worth of work?*** It was excruciating. But sometimes the editor's pen is more like a scalpel and you need to debride the wound by cutting away the dead and dying flesh. It was painful, but it was necessary. Now, that I was *listening* and not *writing*, the story took off like a rocket. ***And Alistair Strange was born. Figuratively, of course.*** On the contrary. Literally. Alistair Strange was born. Literally. If a Christian can be born-again as the Lord instructs us, I have no doubt that a character can be born. It is a living, conscious, sentient personality. ***Are you saying writers have*** *multiple-personality disorder?* You are twisting my words into a gross distortion of the reality. Alistair Strange and all of the other characters live. They breathe. They laugh. They cry. They die. But they exist only in the mind. Of the writer. Of the reader. You laugh when they laugh. You cry when they die. There is a certain suspension of disbelief, as the thespian calls it, where you have to allow the characters to live their lives with their own free will. Sometimes they say something or do something, and they most certainly will, that goes against the plot that you have carefully constructed. It may be arrogant or even blasphemous to say, but I feel quite close to God when I write. Like I am experiencing the experiences of God. I don't pretend to be a minister or a theologian. To me, God is the Author of Life and as the literal Author in the story of our lives, He has a story to tell for each of us, but there is no predestination (that *is* blasphemy), our Author has given each of us the free-will to make our decisions. Just as nearly every writer has moment of clarity where they first realize their creative child is sentient. The character is alive. **Until you decide to kill them all off (looking at you George R.R. Martin).** That is a painful experience. It is excruciating. It is heart wrenching. These characters have lived through you, breathed through you, and now you know that they need to die. *[Chuckles]* Can you imagine the stage-mother of a young actress had had the audacity to walk up to William Shakespeare and say to him, "I'll let my daughter play Juliet, but only if you let her character live"? Who would do or say such a thing? Sometimes the character just has to die. The reader doesn't always agree. They are often very invested in the characters you have given birth to and don't want to see them die. The Author of Life doesn't want to see His creations die, but by the end we all do. There are seven billion stories being told by the Author of Life at this very moment. They all have a beginning and they all must have an ending. But until The End, life is truly a never-ending story. Novels unfortunately, or fortunately for the author, must have an ending. I don't think any publisher living is willing to pay the paper costs on a million page novel. **I certainly hope not. You say that the first novel in the series wrote itself.** Yes, but more accurately,

Alistair wrote it himself. ***And it happened quite quickly.*** I didn't even get close to being finished in the thirty days I still dreamed of fulfilling, but the novel writing was relatively painless process. It was a pleasure and a joy to write. The rewriting on the other hand, that was painful. I sent my mother my manuscript along with a red Bic pen. I wanted her to savage my novel. Make it bleed. I wanted my manuscript sent off looking like Julia Roberts, and hoping it came back looking more like Mary Kelley. There is a Zen to editing by making the writing the best it could possibly be by blooding it. Only hacks think their first draft is their final draft. Any writer worth his salt wants his manuscripts bloodied with the red ink of true and honest editor. It would be sacrilegious to your faith in your novel to demand of your beta-reader, "Only correct the spelling and grammar errors, make no mention of any problems with the story, the characters, anything other than spelling and grammar errors!" These are the words of a hack. Despite my youth as an author, I had come to that Zen of writing, the knowing that your editor only has your best interests at heart. The true art and joy of writing is in the rewriting. But it is a masochistic joy that is experienced only through submissive pain. ***That is quite a metaphor, Casey. Do you really have a dominant and submissive roleplay between editor and author?*** I didn't have an editor, yet. But I had learned from reading every book on writing I could find that your novel is never finished until it is published. At first you think your novel is finished with that first draft. Then others read it, give you their honest, but amateur critique it. Then you rewrite your novel until it is perfect. Next, if you're lucky, you find an agent to represent you and they make their "suggestions" and again you rewrite it until it is again perfect. Your agent finds an editor and the editor pulls out their wire-brush and excruciatingly debrides you of all of dead and dying flesh, so that your novel can be published healthy. ***I stand corrected. THAT is quite the metaphor. Is it true that you were rejected by twenty-nine different editors?*** Thirty-nine. And this doesn't take into account the dozens of rejection letters I wall-papered my apartment with from agents who couldn't be bothered with another young adult novel. They were all looking for the next J.K. Rowling or Stephenie Meyer to fill the already over-saturated market, but they weren't really looking. They don't want new authors. The industry isn't designed around discovering new authors. I was rejected. I was dismissed. I was ignored. That is until my manuscript somehow, through a friend of a friend of a friend, made it into the right hands, an agent who believed in another man-child who fulfills an ancient prophecy and ultimately his destiny by confronting an equally ancient evil. *They accepted you because you wrote a novel that had already been published a dozen times already?* There are only so many different plots. I read somewhere, I don't remember quite where– in one of the countless books on writing I've read– that there are only like seven different plots. Rudyard Kipling believed there were sixty-nine. Then these were whittled down to a few dozen and then seven and then perhaps fewer by now? I don't know. All of the stories that have ever been told: the myths, the legends, the comedies, the tragedies, the books, the movies, the television shows, all fit into a mere seven plots. Isn't that a kick in the pants? To answer your question, yes. The publishing world isn't really interested in the truly new. It just wants the newest variation on the tried-and-true. And my first novel fit that too a tee with just enough creativity and variation to hopefully stand out from the pack. *Weren't you afraid of being labeled a copy-cat? A literary tag-along?* To get my first novel published I didn't give two squirts of sour owl droppings what they actually thought of my novel as long at they published it and promoted it to the best of their marketing ability. *"Sour owl droppings"? THAT is quite the metaphor. Even in conversation, your dialogue is literary.* [Blushes] I would have my chance to stretch my wings and really fly on the second, third, fourth, and even fifth novels, if I was lucky enough to get that far. But the first novel had to get out of the slush-pile and onto the bookstore shelves. *I* believed in it. *I* believed it was creative despite being yet another hero fulfills an ancient prophecy and ultimately his destiny by confronting an equally ancient evil. This plot wasn't even original when King Arthur pulled the sword from the stone. Heck– despite my soul's protestations– the plot wasn't original with Jesus of Nazareth. *Touché* And my book made it through my agent, through my editor, past the publishing executives, and onto the shelves of bookstores and libraries. My book had been optioned for a movie before the ink was dry on the first print-run. And for some reason, the young readers who I had always dreamed of reading my book actually read my book. First by the thousands. Then by the millions. *Your book has been translated in 48 languages in over a hundred countries. What is the one moment from your fans that truly stands out.* There are so many. Just one? Okay... The midnight releases. The first book was released with surprisingly little fanfare. Despite my agent and editor loving the book, the marketing executives at my publisher didn't put their full weight behind the book. Yes, it was on bookshelves. Yes, Hollywood was already auditioning potential screenwriters. But the children didn't know when my book was released that a book had actually been released. But by the time the second book was preparing to be released there was so much anticipation. There where day-calendars printed that counted down the days to the book's release. There were midnight parties planned in bookstores around the world. Children dressed up as my characters as if it were Halloween. And the excitement for these midnight releases were not diminished by the time the third book is released. *What made you rent Madison Square Garden for the midnight release of the third book?* It was Madison Square-freaking-Garden. My grandfather, despite his academia, loved professional wrestling. He took the bus to New York to see Bruno Sammartino headline W.W.W.F. events at the Garden a dozen or more times. And to his dying day, he believed– despite the critics– he *believed* it was *real*. Granddaddy really, *really*– I can't overstate this enough– he really loved Bruno Sammartino and really hated the once protégé, Larry Zbyszho, for stabbing his mentor in the back. I know Granddaddy snuck a knife into Shea Stadium just so he could stab Zbyszko if he had gotten the chance, like the Living Legend stabbed Bruno Sammartino in the back. Then his fandom shifted to the Immortal Hulk Hogan. He even dragged a seven year-old girl, kicking and screaming, to some those 'Rasling shows. But now, as an adult, I wanted to honor my grandfather by headlining my own event at the Garden. *Midnight releases are the best part of being a writer. What is the worst aspect of their fandom?* Fan-fiction. *You answered that question without a moment's hesitation.* I can't stand it. I loathe the very existence of fan-fiction. I have spent years building this world. I have given birth to these characters. They are mine. My fans will hate reading that, but this is a *Playboy* interview and I doubt any of my newer fans are old enough to read your magazine. The older fans, yes, they've aged with my characters, but hopefully they aren't into such pornography. *And speaking of pornography?* Why is there such fascination in my adult fans with reading erotica featuring my beloved characters? Alistair Strange is a young man, a teenage, heterosexual boy. By the third book, he has fallen in love and had his heart broken by a young girl. Why eroticize him as a homosexual? Why eroticize him at all? Why do these so-called writers choose to write explicit sex scenes with characters that are teenagers? Where do these writers and their readers find the pleasure in that? And even the "regular" fan-fiction delights in painting my characters in colors that they shouldn't be seen in. Alistair Strange as the villain? Alistair Strange as a girl? Alistair Strange and Luke Skywalker in adventures in a galaxy far, far away? Batman and Alistair Strange, the new dynamic duo? Why explore plot-lines that even I haven't had a chance to fully explore? Why feature a minor character as the protagonist? Why write sequels to the first book that ignore where I took the second and third books? Why the prequels? Distant sequels when they're all adults? Why is there such a thing as a side-quel? Why can't my readers wait until I have finished the fifth book to discover where I take my own characters? Why so much needless speculation? Why so such theorizing? Can't they just enjoy the books for the sake of enjoyment? Can you give me any answers to any of these questions? *I?... I?...* I don't see why there is so much interest in reading these– I don't honestly know what to call them that is polite– non-canonical stories, maybe? *Arrgh.* Fan-fiction. This is where I must draw the line. Alistair Strange is my child. I gave birth to him and I'll murder him if I have to.

> *"Writing a novel is like driving a car
> at night. You can see only as far as your
> headlights, but you can make the whole
> trip that way."*
>   –E.L. Doctorow

Chapter Three

Of Characters &
Schizophrenic
Hallucinations

O! Muse,

    Alistair, all the other characters I created, and I have had the strangest, most schizophrenic of relationships. Every time I tried to pull the story in a direction that I thought it should go in, he invariably piped up and said, "No! No! No!"

    "That isn't in my character."

    "I'm not doing that."

    "I'm going to do this instead."

    "I'm not going to go there."

    "I'm going to go here."

    "I am not saying that."

    "This is what I'd say in this situation."

    "DO YOU NOT HAVE ANY IDEA WHO I AM?"

    "Or what actually happened?"

    "DO YOU?"

And it was almost always been for the best. There have been a time or two that I had to play the "author" card and insist. When this was successful, I was proud that I WAS THE WRITER. But many times (more than I'd like to admit), I just had to stop, back up, delete hours worth of work, and go where Alistair Strange wanted to go in the first place.

It. Was. Humiliating.

"WHY WON'T YOU SIMPLY LISTEN?"

"Are you DENSE?"

"Are you MENTAL?"

Okay, I admit I am exaggerating... just a wee little bit.

Oh, Muse, there is nothing worse then going down a road, devoting hundreds, if not thousands of words, to a scene or a plot-line, and discover it was all the naught. I'm thankful that my computer still possessed a "delete" button, because that scalpel came in mighty handy over the course of my writing the novel.

—Correction—

Receiving dictation from the many characters who decided to "speak up" and correct me.

Writing is so very, very strange. :P

O! Muse,

What is my authentic voice? Am I still that scared girl sneaking and reading books in the middle of the night? What was it about those books that awakened the dream to be able to write books myself one day? What is it about the worlds J.K. Rowling, C.S. Lewis, J.R.R. Tolkein, George R. R. Martin, H.P. Lovecraft (that's a lot of initials), and Philip Pullman created that I am repeatedly drawn to reread? When I first read them, I didn't know that Narnia was a fantasy world populated with pagan creatures created by a devout Christian or that Philip Pullman was a fundamentalist Atheist and his *His Dark Materials* series was strongly, vehemently anti-Christian.

What is it about my religious upbringing that feels like the Wizarding World of Harry Potter, Narnia, and Middle-Earth are pagan conspiracies to lure Christians away from Christ? Is their lack of Christ (except notably for Narnia) the reason I am repeatedly drawn to them? Is that why Christ never rose to ascendance in the modern world I want to create? Digging deeper, is that why the gods of the Egyptians, Greeks, and Norse, are still worshiped in my literary world? I felt that God was present in my life cause my father and his congregation were such a constant part of my childhood. And now? I don't feel God as a real, physical presence in my new life. Is that why the gods walk among men in my literary universe, answering prayers, healing the sick, helping men govern, and influencing them to make war?

What is it about writers that we are able to take our own unique situations and paint an entire new world that readers want to live in? Why am I compelled to tell this story? Why do I want to share this world with the rest of the really, real world? I hope they find it as interesting and as compelling as I do. This is the reason I love the Wizarding World, Narnia, and Middle-Earth. This is one of the reasons that I want to be a writer.

I certainly hope my friends will hear my actual voice when they read my words, except in those moments when I want to sound like somebody completely different.

O! Muse,

I had a friend up until just the other day– if I could have ever considered him a friend– when I told him I was writing a novel, he scoffed. As if I need to go to university to be a writer! He tried to sell me on the benefits of an MFA program as if he was a university recruiter. Of which he couldn't be further from. But I digress.

How could I trust amateur readers when I could be part of an MFA workshop? he asked belittling me. The amateur's opinions are based on what a reader expects of a novel, not what a professional expects of a novel. There is a vetting process in the application to and the acceptance into a program. Only the best are chosen. You need fellow writers to critique you and be critiqued by you. To go around the table and comment on what works in the piece, then go around the table commenting on what doesn't work in the piece. Then the instructor gives his two cents. (If he in fact has any sense, huh, Muse?). How can you trust you own instincts when the instincts of a dozen others tell you those instincts are wrong? You may have all the story up in that pretty-little head of yours, but if you don't get the right words onto the page itself, the reader won't give two licks about what you meant to write. If you can't please the writers in the workshop, how do you expect to get a good review from a reputable critic in a major publication?

O! Muse, his pooh-pooh-ment was so infuriating. I could just kick him.

But– but– I countered, if these writers are in the program to learn about how to write, how can I trust people just as inexperienced as myself? If they were outside the program wouldn't they just be amateur writers critiquing my work. Because they are in the program, I should inherently trust them more? Now that doesn't make a lick of sense. I don't want my writing produced with factory efficiency, with each product exactly the same as the previous product? Do I want my writing to sound like their writing? Isn't that inherently incestuous?

Oh, he continued, how could I expect to get through the editor's "slush-pile" when there are creative writers who trudged through these tutorial workshops where every aspect of their piece was scrutinized, the choice of every word analyzed, the plausibility of the plot considered, why characters have their names, and what is the symbolism of the symbolism (?). These sessions are as honest as they are brutal. How could I possibly publish a single word without the instruction, tutorship, and professional connections forged in these programs.

A journalist functions under a deadline. A factory worker works on a production quota. How could I expect to finish, let alone, write a novel without a deadline, a strict deadline, that has to be met, one that cannot possibly be ignored.

You learn just as much from criticizing other's work as you do from their criticism of yours. Only the best of the best get into a program, let alone, through the program.

A tempered sword does not break in combat, he scolded me.

But– but– if I am able to write a novel without the structure of the program, then I would always be able to write a novel without the structure of the program, I said.

And– and– what about Stephen King, George R.R. Martin, J.K. Rowling, Elizabeth Gilbert, Jonathan Franzen, Susan Orlean, Kurt Vonnegut, Jr. and every novelist of the 17th, 18th, 19th early 20th centuries who couldn't have participated in an MFA program, because they didn't exist, I asked.

And the conversation (and our friendship) ended and was never ever again reignited.

O! Muse,

Tonight is the night of my second thirtieth day. I've stopped writing– taking dictation– and printed out all of the pages I have written since I deleted that impotent and discarded first draft. I don't think I am a third of the way through the novel. Heck, I'm probably not even a fifth done. Sixth? Seventh? Who really knows at this point?

There really aren't as many pages I thought there would have been. Or should have been. Sure, the word processor keeps a running page and word count, but I didn't realize until the pages were printed, that thousands of words doesn't necessarily add up to a substantial novel. This was a lot of work for seemingly so little results. But I printed the entire manuscript as I had written it, cozied up in bed, and read—

—I have finished reading my novel. I don't want to sound arrogant I really don't, Muse, but it was... not bad. I quite enjoyed it. Is it narcissism to read your own writing and truly enjoy the experience? To experience the novel exactly as your readers will. To believe that your novel can earn its place on the shelves alongside the Harry Potter and *Twilight* novels. There was a part of me that felt like I was experiencing it for the first time. I know I had written the words. I remember the process of typing. I remember the frustrations of trying to find the right words or the perfect synonym. But at the same time there is a partial amnesia to my writing process. I don't really have a conscious recollection of really having written it at all.

While I wasn't staring at my own reflection in a calm, crystal-clear pool of water, I feel almost like I am drowning in the enjoyment of my own work. I am having the same visceral and emotional reaction to my own writing as I had been to secretly reading my contraband C.S. Lewis and J.R.R. Tolkien for the first time. There has to be something sinful in the– I am loath to use the word– masturbatory enjoyment of my own novel.

There were moments when I felt kind of like how Shakespeare must have felt when he was writing his sacred plays. Now, Muse, I'm not saying my book was worthy to be spoken in the same breath as the greatest wordsmith in the English language, but there were times when I was reading my novel that I felt what Shakespeare must have felt when he wrote, "A rose by any other name would smell as sweet" or "To be to not to be". You know the Bard leaned back, set down his quill, and thought, "Damn, I'm good." There were actually times while reading my own turns-of-phrase when I leaned back against my pillow and thought, "Damn, that's good." Really good. Really, really good.

It wasn't all gold, that for sure. There were sentences that weren't really sentences and there were words misspelled so badly that even that technological marvel spell-check couldn't assist me in deciphering what I had intended on saying.

Oh! and parts of the story made no sense outside of my own head. I came to the stark realization that while I have a lot of, if not all of, the story in my own head, I did not translate that to the novel itself all that well. Of course, I *knew* what the story was, but the novel itself wasn't fully telling the story. There were holes in the story, in the plot, in the characterization that I could easily fill in since I have knowledge the story not actually yet present in the novel. But for the reader without this inside, secret knowledge, they would have been totally and irretrievably lost. So miserably lost. I had to get better at telling the story better.

And I couldn't help but pull out the red ink (scalpel) pen and make corrections– and there were so many– so, so many– but now that I've had a chance to read it, really read it, and have put the manuscript aside for the night, I realize that I have *begun* a novel.

And this is the greatest accomplishment in my entire life.

O! Muse,

I believe that I am a pantser.

What is that if I may ask, Casey? Sounds a little kinky.

No. No. No. It's nothing like it sounds.

I write by the seat of my pants. During the course of my second thirty days and my third sixty days, I have found the source of my characters vocalizations: pantsing. I have allowed my narrative to grow organically. I have allowed intuition to be a governing force in my writing. I have chosen not to outline my novel in great detail, nor plot very far ahead. I read a inspirational quote where I'm driving at night with only the headlights on. I can't see very far ahead, but I can get to my destination. How exciting is that!

As a pantser, I am allowing my characters to live, to make their own decisions, to sometimes arrive at the plot-party completely unannounced. I have given my characters the power, the free-will if you will, to take my story in any direction, particularly if I couldn't have imagined it even moments before.

And what about the plot, Casey? Isn't it important to adhere to a strict and rigid plot?

I have planted the seed and I allow it to grow organically through the decisions made by my characters. Sometimes the decisions they make aren't always in the best interest of my "novel", but other times I am surprised by them. Who wouldn't enjoy that?

Casey, I think a plotter would detest that you write by "feel". Why wouldn't you choose to create an outline, making notes about the introduction of characters, their backstories and goals, their development, where to foreshadow, what the symbols mean, what kind of mood are you trying to create.

Why don't you choose to pace yourself? Joseph Campbell proved that throughout history the "Hero's Journey" was made step-by-step with a seventeen point structure that crossed, not only across the world, but throughout the millenia, intact. There is a reason the three-act structure works so perfectly in modern novels and in film.

In Act One, the first quarter of your novel, you have the beginning of the novel, your perfectly worded first sentence, you reveal to the reader the world in which your protagonist lives, what kind of genre you novel resides, what life was like before the Inciting Event. Then there is the call to action, the first turning point in the novel, where a problem occurs that changes the lives of your characters for the rest of the novel. In the Second Act, the next 50%, your protagonist must make a choice, that links the first and second acts and sets up the third. The action is rising and the main confrontation with the antagonist begins. Then the protagonist is met with failure, through reversal of fortunes, things have gone awry, the conflict escalates, sacrifices may have to be made. At the three-quarter mark, there is a disaster that is the defining moment in his life, he is stripped-bear and he must face the harsh truths. The antagonist is no longer a mystery to either the reader or the protagonist. There is a final crisis, a second turning point. In the Third Act, your protagonist must find the courage to continue against the staggering odds, but with renewed courage, to device a plan to defeat his antagonist in the climax of the novel and then live happily ever after in the denouement. And what were the word-counts for each of these moments?

Arrgh! That would be awful, Muse.

Who wants that kind of control? Where are the surprises? Where are the characters' free-will? I have no intention of being the god of my third-person omniscient little universe, plotting and planning every single moment of every single character's lives. If a critic looks at my novel and sees a three-action structure, then it would have been entirely by happenstance.

O! Muse,

Do the great ones doubt themselves? Is that the hallmark of greatness. I would like to think that by doubting the quality of my book, I can make it great. If I think my novel is perfect from the first word till the last sentence and that nary a word in between needs to be changed, aren't I already an awful writer? I could choose each and every word as I go, constructing each sentence until they are structurally perfect, each paragraph pristine, each chapter rapturous. But to me that would be impossibly difficult. Yes, each facet of a diamond has to be created precisely in order to produce the finished jewel. But novels can be rewritten. If that is your lot in life, all the more power to you. Don't I want my first draft to experiment? To go where I least expect it? Don't I want a flawed, but functional first draft? Sometimes I will have to go down the wrong path only to discover it is a dead-end, then backtrack until I find the right path. Sometimes I have to write thousands of words only to discover not a blessed one will end up in the final draft. That is a level of sacrifice few are willing to accept. And what if I have to discard the entire manuscript and start an entirely new story? Is all that time wasted? Are all those words for naught? Or did I learn what stories to tell because of the stories I couldn't tell?

O! Muse,

I am so torn and conflicted. I've read that you should begin your novel in the middle of the story. But what if there is a definitive beginning, shouldn't you start there? How much history does there have to be in a story? Does the past really need to have an effect on the present and the future? I don't know. Do I worry about my plot or do I tell my story first? I'm not sure what the difference between plot and story is.

I don't really understand Edward Forster when he writes in his *Aspects of a Novel* that a story "can only have one merit: that of making the audience want to know what happens next. 'The king died and then the queen died' is a story. A plot is also a narrative of events, the emphasis falling on causality – 'The king died and then the queen died' is a story. But 'the king died and then the queen died of grief' is a plot. The time-sequence is preserved, but the sense of causality overshadows it."

So which is more important? I'm still confused. There is, according to Aristotle apparently, a difference between the events that happen in the real world, the "incidents", and the elements that a writer choses to arrange in what is called the mythos, or "plot". I've heard horror stories of writers who included something that really happened to themselves in real life in their novel, only to be criticized because it sounded too fictitious. If truth is stranger than fiction, how can the truth sound fictitious and the fiction sound like the truth? This doesn't sound right, but apparently it is true.

O! Muse,

I know I am writing a fantasy novel about a modern world with the Internet and cellphones, albeit one where the old mythological gods are still worshiped and very proactive in both personal and worldly concerns. But I want, I need, the world to be authentic. I don't know why capturing all the five senses is proving to be so difficult.

Music only uses the sense of hearing to evocate our emotions. The cinema and television use only sight and hearing to evoke. But with books, the author needs to use every single one of five senses in order to create a world that lives, breathes, and feels lived in. If a writer only wanted to communicate what the reader sees or hears, we are depriving them of fullness of the wondrous world we are creating.

If I am writing about New York City, but have never set foot in the city, how can I convey the sheer magnitude of the size of skyscrapers or the neon lights of Times Square, the sounds of traffic, construction, and sirens that keep outsiders awake at night, but lull New Yorkers to sleep, the smell of seven million people and the exhaust from their cars, the taste of a Jewish Deli, New York pizza, or Italian food from a neighborhood place, or the touch from every pedestrian I brush past on the sidewalks or the rattled shake of the subways? I can't. Sometimes I actually have to walk in the very footprints of my characters.

And my dialogue needs to sound real. If I am lucky enough to get an audio-book as part of my publishing contract, will the voice-actor have difficulty reading my dialogue. Will it sound... off? Listen closely to real dialogue between people. It doesn't sound like dialogue from a book, movie or especially a stage-play. That's because people talking is boring, its glacial, it wanders, it often conveys nothing of substance for minutes on end, if ever. The dialogue in a book needs to sound like its written for the stage. My characters need to sound like themselves and not me, their age needs to be apparent, their vocabulary and dialect needs to be appropriate to every aspect of their surroundings: their setting, their time-period, and their culture.

One problem time-travelers would have is human language, particularly the English language, changes, it evolves surprisingly quickly. New words are coined constantly or new meanings of older words change, slang mutates words and means different things to different people in different eras. Am I using words and turns of phrases that are far too modern? I also don't want characters in a 1970's exploitation novel to sound like they've been plucked from the 1590's Shakespearian stage.

The reader has to believe that my weird modern world is real. They have to see the Egyptian, Greek, and Norse gods as real entities, their temples as physical places, and the prayers, hopes, dreams, and relationships the characters in this new world have with their gods.

One of the problems I have with the Wizarding World of Harry Potter that I didn't want replicated in my world, was the disconnect between the magical folk and the so-called "muggles". The world Harry Potter enters is kept secret from the rest of the world and the threats posed by "He Who Must Not Be Named" only really affect this Wizarding World. In my world, Alistair Strange, his companions, and adversaries would not be kept a secret from the general population. Their interests would be in line with or in conflict with the populous. To most people, just as our own political systems pigeon-hole people based on ideologies, Alistair is a hero, to others he is a vigilante, and still to others he is the villain of the story.

This is all part of creating a living, breathing world. A three-dimensional, five-sensational world. A descriptive world. A living, breathing world.

"What really knocks me out is a book that, when you're all done reading it, you wish the author that wrote it was a terrific friend of yours and you could call him up on the phone whenever you felt like it. That doesn't happen much, though."

—J.D. Salinger, *The Catcher in the Rye*

Chapter Four

Where-oh-where R our Caseys 4 Christmas?

by alistairstrange#1fan

Casey, as she is affectionately called by her "Strangers", has disappeared from the face of the earth. There was a time when she was everywhere. She was the belle-of-the-ball for television hosts: Jay Leno, Regis Philbin and Kelley, Ellen DeGeneres, and Rosie O'Donnell. Her book signing tours seemed to be never ending (how she managed to write so prolifically on the road was an unfathomable mystery). Magazines fought in expensive bidding wars for every one of her dozens of Alistair Strange short-stories, magazine-racks were stripped bare of any issue with a Casey in it.

At one point in time, not so long ago, Casey was so wonderfully prolific. I don't know how long it took her to write the first book, *The XII Labors of Alistair Strange. Alistair Strange and the Clash of the Olympians*, her second book, was published within a year of the first, despite being twice as long. And again a year later, *Alistair Strange and the Dark Seas Sleeper,* the third book, was published and it was a massive tome. Her publisher's marketing campaign for her second and third books was delightfully alliterative, "A Casey For Christmas". How wonderful is that?!?

And what Christmas it was! For all of us in the Tri-State area, we were to receive the greatest gift of all for Christmas season! Casey had rented Madison Square Garden for the midnight release party to end all midnight release parties.

Thousands– nay– tens of thousands of Strangers descended on the Garden. There were cosplayers everywhere, as far as the eye could see. It was like the San Diego Comic-Con, yet populated exclusively from the Alistair Strange universe. Not a single cosplayer dared to be Harley Quinn, or any other non-Casey character. Her literary universe had come to life!

Around 9 p.m. Casey took to the stage to do a Q&A session. It was wonderful to hear from her the insight she had into aspects of her characters that we knew nothing about. She is their creator, so, of course, she knew more about them than we did.

At 10 o'clock, Casey began reading from the new book. I have never heard over 10,000 people be to utterly, eerily silent. There were no whispers. There were no coughs or murmurs We were completely enraptured by her voice, her passion, her new adventures. Not a single person out of ten-thousand in attendance wanted the evening to end.

At 11 o'clock, several lines began forming so that we could get our copy of the new book. By buying a ticket to the event, the new book was included in the ticket price. And she didn't upcharge us or anything. The ticket price was the same as the cover price of the book. All we needed to do was get the book into our hands and we were free to go. While many did rush home to read the book, it seemed like thousands just sat in the stands and read. It was like they couldn't tolerate the long subway ride home, we all just had to know what had happened to Alistair Strange and his companions at that very moment.

Many of us when we finished the third book, immediately started reading the first and second books over as well. Her ability to foreshadow books in advance made rereading a delight. We could see how far in advance she set up elements of her story. OMG! HOW COULD WE HAVE BEEN SO BLIND NOT TO SEE IT!

Then we missed a Christmas or two. IDK. No, Casey for Christmas to usher in the New Year. No Casey to force us to reread the previous books, though we always reread the previous books. Then as the next Christmas approached, the posters and card-board cut-outs began appearing before Halloween, "A Casey For Christmas"!

She was back! *Alistair Strange and Those Whom the Gods Detest Should Not Be Unearthed* (Whew!). We had our Casey for Christmas!

Although she did no interviews for the fourth book's promotion.... although her activity on the Internet was eerily silent... although there was no midnight Garden release party, we still devoured her book. Heck, she could have rented a football stadium and the Strangers would have filled it. But we didn't care a lick about a party. We had a new book in our hands. A new adventure to experience. At least, she was back! Maybe not in the public eye, but we had an Alistair Strange novel in our greedy little hands. She was back!

All the Strangers around the world devoured the fourth book. And it ended on the most wonderful cliff-hanger. How could she leave us, literally, hanging like that?

The tension and anticipation of how the ending would be resolved was killing us. But we knew that the fifth book just had to be around the corner. There would be another Casey that Christmas. Of that, we had no doubt.

Then a Christmas came and went with no Casey. WTF! When the second Christmas came and went with no Casey, the Strangers began to grow genuinely concerned. She broke her silence by tweeting that Christmas morning that she had a deadline from her publisher and the book would be in the editor's hands before long. She tweeted that there would indeed be another "Casey For Christmas".

When the next Christmas passed without a Casey, she woke us up that Christmas morning with a new tweet. The Strangers were delighted to learn that the book would, in fact be published that next year.

Only it hadn't been. It probably won't be.

At one time, not so long ago, Casey seemed delighted by our passion for Alistair Strange and the world she has created. Casey showed up at a random midnight release party for the second book, shocking and delighting the hundreds in attendance. She walked the red carpet for the Hollywood premiere of the first movie to the screams and adulation of her Strangers. Her book tours looked and sounded like Beatlemania. And tours went on for what seemed like years, they were supposed to be endless. She seemed to be a true roaddog. Do I need to mention the Garden again? OMG, it was GLORIOUS!

After the fourth book was published, by and far the best book in the series, Casey has decided to take her ball and go home. IDK why. There has been complete radio silence on her Twitter account after that Christmas day tweet. She no longer converses with her fans. The short-stories magazines that had once been financially fought over dried up. The Alistair Strange website is no longer updated. Her last interview was in *Playboy*. Why she chose that medium is beyond even a devoted Stranger like myself. It seemed like she was placating us. Tiding her Strangers by until the fifth book is... finally... eventually... published.

And now, there is no fifth book. Halloween passed into the ether with no posters and no card-board cut-outs announcing a "Casey For Christmas". Her tweets must still haunt her to this day, and they should! She tweeted that we would have a fifth Casey for Christmas and the Grinch has stolen our Casey every year since then.

IDK if I can go another Christmas without a Casey.

IDK if I even care anymore.

> *"Who is more to be pitied, a writer bound and gagged by policemen or one living in perfect freedom who has nothing more to say?"*
> –Kurt Vonnegut

Chapter Five
Writer's Block
& Writer's Amnesia

O! Muse,

My characters have become eerily silent. I don't know what to do. I don't know where to go. I think I am experiencing Writer's Block for the first time. And oh, it is so debilitating.

It isn't exactly a block, now is it, Muse? A block sounds too much like a brick. And it isn't a Writer's Brick, is it? It is more like an entire freaking wall. A wall that is so infinitely long that you can't see around it and so impossibly tall that you can't see over it. A wall built on a foundation so solid and unshakable, there is no burrowing beneath it. It is nothing less than a freaking Writer's Wall!

Before I started writing my novel, I read about Writer's Block in my library of books on how to a write book that will end up on the shelves of a library, but I couldn't truly comprehend the experience of having the inability to write. Now, I appreciate the debilitating disease that is Writer's Block. I don't know how to continue. I don't know where the story goes next. My novel has come to a screeching halt. The fire I felt over the last several weeks has been utterly extinguished.

I. Do. Not. Know. What. To. Do.

I thought staring at that first blank page was not only intimidating, but incomprehensibly oppressive. How could I possibly fill, not only that first virtual blank page in my word processor on my computer screen, but all the nearly insurmountable subsequent blank pages? Once, I had that first sentence, that first paragraph, that first page written, I thought the writing process would steam-roll after that. But no matter how many pages I filled, there was seemingly infinite blank pages to follow. Each sentence, each paragraph, each page, each chapter was always followed by yet another blank page. What was this perplexing paradox? No matter how many pages I filled, no matter how many words I wrote, there was always another blank page awaiting me. What would the next sentence be? What would the next paragraph say? What would compel the reader to turn to the next page? What story would the next chapters tell?

I. Do. Not. Know.

And now I don't where the story goes now. I don't know what my characters are supposed to say or do. Their lives have come to a shockingly sudden halt. I am so unfathomably lost. I don't know if I will ever find out what happens to Alistair Strange next. —

— I didn't know that not being able to write would be so depressing, so crippling. Writer's Block is strangely bi-polar. I have experienced the mania, the exhilaration, the ecstasy of writing.

I've watched with glee as others plunked their quarters into arcade cabinets trying to achieve that game's highest score. There was a competition that came from getting one's initials on the high-score screen. There was the strangest sense of accomplishment to achieve this virtual– and virtually meaningless– goal.

Who really cared how many dots and ghosts Pac-Man ate? Or how many centipedes you were able to blast into mushrooms. But as I wrote, as the words became sentences, sentences became paragraphs, paragraphs became chapters, there was this number that continued to grow in the lower-left hand corner of the word-possessor: my word-count. I wanted– nay– needed this number to continue to grow. The faster it grew, the greater my own sense of accomplishment. The desire to maintain a certain– a certainly arbitrary– number of words written each and every day was addictive. And because of the Writer's Block, my word count no longer increases. In fact, because of my doubts, I am rewriting the words that I have already written and the number is shrinking!

And now- AND NOW– I know the depression, the debilitation, the withdrawal of Writer's Block. This is a strange self-inflicted emotional abuse. You blame yourself for not being able to give your characters further life, not being able to write that next page, next paragraph, next sentence, even next word. You don't want to get out of bed in the morning. You can't get to sleep at night. The depression is overwhelmingly debilitating.

I feel uncomfortable using these words to describe Writer's Block, because there are too many people whom have experienced pain and loss that caused irreparable depression and debilitation. The fact that creativity, the greatest gift that the human mind is capable of, can also be spoken of in the same breath as the mind's greatest weakness. How could the depression caused by Writer's Block be the very same depression caused by the worst of the human experience. It can't, of course. It simply can't.

But– there is always a but– Writer's Block is real. It may not be recognized by the psychiatric community as a mental disorder worthy of psychotherapy, nor should it be. But– but– the depression it causes is real. Oh, so very real. The debilitation is crippling. Your entire life is disabled so completely as to render life essentially functionless. To everyone who is not a writer, the experience of Writer's Block cannot be fully comprehended. And because they cannot comprehend it, there is no empathy. In fact, to the non-writer, the writer's cries of Writer's Block only bring feelings of shame and pity.

When you work as a cashier at a grocery store, there is always another customer. When you are a medical biller at a doctor's office, there is always another claim to be processed. But for the writer there isn't always another chapter... until there finally is.

The reader doesn't know the pain of Writer's Block. The reader only has to turn the page to receive the next page, another chapter. For the reader, the only applicable sensation to Writer's Block is when you finish a novel and you must wait years to discover the conclusion to the cliff-hanger and where the story leads to next. To the reader, waiting for the further adventures can create an isolation, a longing that only the midnight release of the next book can satiate. You may wonder what happens to your beloved characters after the ending of a cliff-hanger and perhaps the writer does as well.

I was once a reader who pined for the next installment of a beloved series of novels. How dare the writer not produce the next novel in a timely fashion? They have successfully been published. They have made it successfully through the labyrinth constructed by the publishing industry to weed out the talentless hacks. Only the truly gifted can survive the slush pile to get an agent, then an editor, and then the Holy Grail: your book on the shelves of the Barnes & Noble bookstores. These rarefied few have made their advances and royalties from thousands, if not millions, of sales. Their novels have been optioned by the film industry as a feature-film or as a television series. Writing is no longer as dream, but is now their job. If they are lucky, it is their *only* job. They have, more likely than not, made millions in advances toward the publication of a novel that they are seemingly *not* writing. How dare they take years between novels? How dare they? How dare they!

I understand that the Reader's Anticipation is just as tangible as Writer's Block is. But the reader can have their "fix" by reading another book. The publishing industry is always publishing new books, whether from a new writer or from an established writer continuing a beloved series. While the reader can get their fix from other books, the writer is, more often than not, lashed to their own series. They cannot simply begin writing a completely new or different novel. The published novelist has signed contracts with certain, often specific commitments. They are under these contractual obligations to deliver on those agreements in a timely fashion. Imagine for a moment, these kind of pressures. I am in the midst of my first novel, the first book in a hopeful series of beloved novels. I have set and missed my own personal deadlines for the writing of my own novel. I cannot imagine the pressure, not only from the publisher and their bottom-line, but from the fans because of their own Reader's Anticipation. These pressures can only worsen their author's own Writer's Block.

The writer wants nothing more than to fulfill their contractual obligations to their publisher; they want nothing more than to relieve the Reader's Anticipation, but her Writer's Block can only be alleviated when she pulls that first, intimidating, painful next sentence from out of the abyss—

—And I've finally pulled that exquisite sentence from out of the abyss. I don't know where it came from. The words were so strange how they came to me. The words were like a lightning bolt. The words came without any warning. The words were just there. I don't think I actually wrote the words. One moment the words weren't there, and the next moment the words *were*.

I had been *trying* to create that one line repeatedly as the days turned into weeks. But then it was there like it was there the entire time. Why hadn't I seen it before? Had it always been there waving its arms at me, saying "Here I am! Here I am!" and I didn't see it. Just like a snake that would have bitten me? Now that the sentence is typed into my computer, I don't really know where this one sentence is going to lead me. And I don't really care. That one sentence has became a paragraph and led me to page after page after page. I was finally back in the saddle.

This. Is Glorious.

Is this the benefit of having experienced the depression and debilitation of Writer's Block? That this one cryptic sentence leads to enigmatic paragraphs that lead to mystifying pages that you had not anticipated nor outlined. Muse, I have already talked about how characters sometimes tell you what they will or will not say or do or where they will go.

Sometimes Writer's Block can be so very precious.

O! Muse,

Aaaaaaaand it's back.

I wish I was writing right now in the dead of winter, so I could use my novel as kindling. Yes, I'm writing on a laptop and not real paper, so there is nothing to actually burn, and no, I'm not going to put my computer into the fire, but I hate everything about my book. Alistair Strange has become a sniveling little sh– calm yourself, Casey. I am so bored. Nothing seems to be happening. There has been no real progress. I am not enjoying myself at this point. I seem to be writing for the sake typing words onto the screen. Why did I decide to do this in the first place?

My mind hurts. My mind is sluggish. I don't know where to go. The characters who I loved telling me what to do either won't cooperate with the story or are outright defiant to the point of being bull-headed. Very few scenes click anymore. The scenes I used to see so clearly have gone out of focus.

I need counseling, like I'm in a marriage that is failing. I need to rekindle whatever it was that made me love being in love with it in the first place. What was it about the story that drew me to it? Why aren't we really communicating anymore? Why hasn't this all turned out like we expected it to? Do we need a break? Do we need to be honest with ourselves that this just isn't working and a divorce may be final? Or maybe we need a vacation?

Maybe I just need to get into the car and drive. It's the darkest of nights where I can only see as far as my headlights shine (like in the E.L. Doctorow quotation), I know I can make the entire trip not seeing anything beyond. I just have to write and keep writing. I can and will revise at some point. But first I have to complete the journey.

O! Muse,

    The first draft is FINISHED!

    There is an overwhelming sense of relief when I typed "THE END". But there is also a devastating sense of grief. I do not know what to do now. The life that I have been living for the past year and some odd months and more is suddenly over. Has it really been that long? That year positively flew by. :)

    This has been my life: I woke up a few hours before I was to be at work and I wrote. I went to work. I thought about writing while I worked. I wrote on my lunch-break. I thought some more about writing while I worked. I came home. I wrote. I ate dinner. I wrote. I wrote. I wrote. And I went to bed a few hours later than I should have. I slept far too little. That is the life. Was my life. :(

    I read somewhere where Dorothy Parker mused, "I hate writing. I love having written."

    I can't say that I disagree more. I. Loved. Every. Moment.

O! Muse,

    • "The first draft of anything is shit." – Ernest Hemingway

    Now, I need to find a beta-reader. I don't know how to find one or how to ask. My social circle feels really small at the moment. I don't really have that core group of friends that I can share the wonder of my little world with. The loneliness is rather oppressive.

    Maybe I can find a writer's group at the local library. Find like minded individuals whom desire to cultivate the growth of my novel. If I find a writer's group what should I look for. Do they have a mission to promote writing? Do the writers in the group have any desire to read the genre or type of writing I am writing? Do the others offer constructive criticism, meaning the criticism is objective, specific, relevant, useful, and has the goal of improving the quality final work and not mean-spirited and demeaning.

    Also, are there clearly defined rules on how the writer is expected to react to criticism? I have to recognize the importance of constructive criticism to improve the value of my work. Am I willing to play role reversal and assume the perspective of the critic? Am I willing to listen, instead of becoming defensive, welcoming the criticism? In the end, do the other writers in the group recognize my inalienable right to make my own decisions about my novel, particularly if it is counter to their criticisms?

- "There are three rules for writing a novel. Unfortunately, no one knows what they are." –W. Somerset Maugham

Maybe I should have tried to find a beta-reader when I had a partial draft of maybe the first five or six chapters. Maybe I wouldn't have spent 80,000 words going in directions that don't appeal to a wide-range of readers. Maybe my readers were expecting something else and I've wasted all this time and all these words for nothing. I could have discovered at 20,000 words that the entire blasted thing should have been scrapped. The prose may not be as beautiful, as graceful, as poetic as I think it is.

Now that I have my first draft, I will find that it is a very rough draft, filled to the brim with typos, despite not having any red-squiggly-underlined words (strange how words can be spelled "correctly" yet be grossly misspelled). Do I want my beta-reader to be my copy-editor? Spending all of their time and energy correcting the grammar, the spelling. I don't believe I need a copy-editor at this point. I can hire one of those at some point in this extremely long and demanding process.

I'm afraid that my beta-readers will be afraid to be honest, brutally honest. Once my book is in front of the review desk at *The New York Times*, they aren't going to pull any punches, so I need my beta-reader to be honest, brutally honest. I'll need to reassure them that I'd rather hear the brutally honest criticism now, when I can easily fix it, then present a flawed novel to an agent or an editor or reviewers or actual readers (*shudder!*) and receive rejections that I could have easily avoided early in the process.

Writers spend a lot of time (perhaps too much time) on that opening line, the opening paragraph, the first chapter, crafting an interesting hook. Did the story grab your attention from the very beginning? When you got to the end of the novel, did I fulfill the promises I made in the opening chapters? Would you have bought the novel if you were reading the book in the aisle of the bookstore? To say it matter-of-factly: did you freaking enjoy reading my mother-loving novel?

I've spent a lot of time world-building. Did you understand the world that I was putting you in? Was the time-period clear? Did you understand the book was fantasy, science-fiction, a police-procedural, or a romance from the very beginning? Did you know who the protagonist was? What city you were in, without me explicitly saying anything?

Do you even like the protagonist? Was he relatable? Does he (*shudder!*) come across as a complete asshole (which wasn't at all my intention, but could be another author's intention)? Are you eager to go on his journey with him? Does his story or problem appeal to you? Do you feel something, anything about this character. Do you care about him?

This extends to the supporting, minor, and antagonistic characters, too. Are the protagonist, minor characters, and the antagonists all fully-realized, three-dimensional, five-sensational characters and not stereotypes, archetypes, cookie-cutter, paper-thin characters? Were my characters believable even if they were aliens in a science-fiction novel or a dragon-race in fantasy? Did you find them compelling? Are you sympathetic to their causes, their plights, their motivations? Were the likable characters likable enough? Are you eager to root for success of their story-lines or their failure, as the case may be with the antagonists? Are the motivations of the protagonist and the antagonist believable even in genres that are fantastical? Did you hate the antagonists? But on the flip-side, did you, at least, understand their motivations? Do any of the characters, even the main protagonist, feel worthless, like they contribute nothing really to the story and should end up on the cutting-room floor?

Were you able to keep track of all the characters without a *dramatis personae*, a veritable who's who? Did I write too many characters to easily follow, as if I as trying to hard too be Leo Tolstoy writing *War and Peace*?

I have the entire story in my little head and I may not have communicated things as well as I could have. Was anything in the novel, a scene, a plot-line, an exchange of dialogue that confused you? Something that made you backtrack to see if you had missed something important that you didn't catch on the first pass? Did you want to throw the book down in frustration? Were you ever annoyed?

Was I inconsistent or have discrepancies in my descriptions of characters or places? Was the sequence of events consistent, even if I jumped around in time like I was a young Orson Welles on *Citizen Kane*?

One of the hallmarks of a well-written novel is the writer's ability to show rather than tell. Did I use all of the five senses: not only sight, but also sound, smell, taste, and touch? Did I *show* the reader the story, instead of merely *telling* my reader the story to further the plot? Did the characters use their own voice to develop their three-dimensional characterizations? Do my sentences use a passive voice (i.e. use the word "was") instead of using action verbs and picture nouns to describe the events in the story? Did my scenes serve the purpose of advancing the plot, showing conflict between characters, creating suspense?

- "Don't tell me the moon is shining; show me the glint of light on broken glass."– Anton Chekhov

Does the novel take too long to really get going? Are the stakes high enough to create the tension necessary to create a compelling novel? Is anything in the book cliché: the descriptions, the characters, the dialogue, the settings, the plot? Or have I successfully taken a well-worn trope and put a fresh spin on it. Are any of the plot twists telegraphed chapters in advance? Were you able to foresee the ending of the novel before you actually got to the end of the novel? Do you wish more of the plot was unforeseen and unexpected? And on the flip-side, what surprised you? Were they pleasant surprises? Or were they so completely unexpected that they were utterly unbelievable and drew you out of the story?

In all genres, particularly those like science-fiction and fantasy, are the actions or reactions of characters plausible? A novel can't rely on that crutch of conspiracy-theorists: plausible deniability.

Was my dialogue natural or too wooden and stiff. Did some characters sound natural, but others sound artificial? Even artificial androids need to have dialogue that sounds natural. Was the dialogue consistent? Did characters not sound like themselves from scene to scene, without some apparent change in their character or motivation? Does the dialogue read well? Does it sound like it was written for the stage? Does the dialogue advance the story or did my characters seem like they were speaking just to hear themselves talk? Was there too much or too little dialogue and/or narration? Was there a balanced mix of the too? Did you feel like you were reading a play-script and not a novel?

- "Dialogue concentrates meaning; conversation dilutes it." – Robert McKee, *Dialogue: The Art of Verbal Action for Page, Stage, and Screen*

Are there parts when I get wordier than a gossiping hen. Are there descriptions that are too detailed? Is the exposition too exhaustive? Did my dialogue ramble on and on, like the aforementioned gossiping hens, instead of succinctly telling necessary information? Or does it all feel like I've only given you the Cliffs Notes of a scene or novel instead of an entire scene or novel? If so, then I am really in desperate need of adding more description or exposition.

- "So the writer who breeds more words than he needs, is making a chore for the reader who reads."– Dr. Seuss.

Who doesn't need a Dr. Seuss screed to cheer up their year? (Rhyming is really, really hard. Stick to what you know, Casey.)

What was your opinion of the ending? Would you have regretted buying my novel when you finished reading it? Or would you be looking forward to the next book in the series, if it will be a series, or the next book that I write, if it wasn't part of a series?

Please know that I know you aren't copy-editors, and I didn't hire you for that purpose. BUT were their any obvious errors in spelling, grammar, jargon, punctuation, terminology, semantics, and formatting? Were there? Hint. Hint. Hint.

But I also need to know what works. Not every type of criticism needs to be negative. This kind of positive critique will help me avoid changing things that actually work, things that actually move the reader, or cutting things that shouldn't be cut. Sometimes a little praise will go a long way in keeping my spirits high during these stressful times.

O! Muse,

I read somewhere that a movie is made in the editing room. That the director has shot every scene, every line from a variety of different camera angles and lengths of takes. He has shot innumerable takes capturing ever possible inflection of speech. He has shot scenes that wouldn't be worthy of the deleted scenes section of the DVD. He has shot figuratively everything. It is now the job of the editor to turn his masturbatory (that word again) excess into a film. While he, who related this aspect of Hollywood film-making, was far more pornographic in his description than I will ever dare to be, this is true of my chosen professional as well.

A rewriter, as I prefer to call myself now, has to take everything that we have written in our first draft and figure out which words, plot-lines, scenes, and characters will survive the arduous journey towards the "Final Draft". Not everyone or everything will complete the quest. There will be pitfalls and travails along the road. The fates of all those who began their journey in the "First Draft" is uncertain. What will your Fellowship look like when you finally reach the fiery foot of Mt. Doom? Up until this point in our adventure, every single word has been precious to me– yes, my Precious– *my Precious!*

Rewriters must to be to our novels as the LORD will be with man when His winnowing fork is in His hand, He will thoroughly purge his threshing floor and will gather His wheat into the garner, and He will burn up the chaff with unquenchable fire.

Rewriting reminds me of the psychotherapy. I never wanted to speak to my psychotherapist. She wanted me to talk about my experiences so could work myself through any traumas I had suffered during my youth, which I didn't believe were necessarily traumas at all. I read their Freud. I read their Jung. I needed to understand why the counselors believed the way they did. Who were these men they revered as prophets? Why did they think I needed to react in the ways they expected? As I would learn there something cathartic about being truthful and honest with yourself. This is nothing new, of course, people have been confessing to their priest-confessor for millennia.

O! Muse,

I received my first critique. It came from a lady I met at the library, who is a veracious reader, one whose taste in books is similar to my mine. She wasn't a friend. Barely even an acquaintance, which I felt was best for this little experiment of mine. She had never read an unpublished novel in her entire 50-plus years of life. She was so excited. And I was terrified. She sat across from me in a favorite bookstore/coffee shop with all of the great literature and pulp fiction surrounding us. It was the best of places to receive criticism from the best person at the best time. It was the worse of places to receive criticism from the worst person at the worst time. I hoped for the former, because my book would only be improved by her criticism. I dreaded the later, because Oh! The Unpleasantness! The Pain. The Humiliation! The Suicidal Tendencies!

When she made her first criticism of the book my first reaction was, Murder! Mayhem! Death! No. No! Not towards woman I barely knew. But towards my novel. Even the littlest criticism made me quick to slash anything and burn everything from the book. If the judge didn't like it, it had to be stricken from the record! But I had to reign in my own murderous appetites. I desperately want the novel to be the best thing it can be and if someone, anyone didn't like something, Murder! Mayhem! Death! But the next beta-reader could absolutely love the very things the first one didn't and you would have already razed the ancient temples from your novel, like a heathen horde, depriving all future generations of your genius.

Take a breath, Casey.

My beta-reader is a reader, not a writer. She only gave me her insight based on how she reacted to what she read. If she were a writer, she may have given me insight into how she would have written my novel. Neither is better or worse than the other. And all writers do view the world through the prism of how they would have written it.

When we sit with our beloved and watch television, don't they hate it when we finish a line of dialogue exactly right because that is how we would have written that line, or when we criticize the movie or T.V. program based on how we would have written it? Non-writers hate this. Hate it. Hate us.

I sat patiently as she went over each and every criticism. With each point she made I wanted to challenge her. It was only natural to defend your child from any and all criticism. But I tried to keep on my composure, but it was so difficult. When she gave a negative criticism, Murder! Mayhem! Death! was still a common reaction, but with each criticism both negative and positive, I learned a little more about her likes and dislikes, her taste in books in general. I was successful in reigning in that murderous tendency, and I started to gain an almost euphoric appreciation of my novel. While each negative criticism felt like I was being water-boarded, but each positive criticism felt like a hit on a joint during your rebellious college years. It felt so good to hear good things about my novel. Really good. I only had my extremely biased opinion of every aspect of my book and now I was able to see my book through the eyes of my beta-reader. It was a glorious out-of-body experience.

But as the minutes have turned into hours, and I've had time to reflect on her opinions, I realized they were just that... opinions. At the end of the day, I am the writer of this story and no one else is.

This book is my child, a child to whom I've given my name, and in the end, all the people in the grocery store may want to parent my screaming, willful, disobedient child for me, but I must parent my child as I see fit. It was a painful realization, that this almost complete stranger in whom I gave my trust, she gave me her honest, sometimes brutal "parenting advice", from a place of true friendship, is not my child's parent. In the quiet of my home, only I can make the decisions that are right for my child.

I respect her. I asked her to put my novel on trial. To investigate it. To interrogate it. And to bring charges against my novel for the crimes of being boring, poorly written, cliché, having wooden dialogue, nonsensical or predictable plots, two-dimensional characters, or the worst crime of all– passive sentences. These are all great crimes with long sentences in the Prison of Editorial Hell. But I must defend my own novel to the best of my own ability. No one else will. But I must also be the jury and the judge and ultimately executioner if needs be. I must be prepared to convict my novel on certain counts and exonerate her on others. But the best part of this metaphorical trial, I can go in time back and rewrite the crime scenes so that no crime had ever been committed. Case dismissed!

Just as every reader, every critic, every agent, every editor is different, so is every beta-reader. They will bring their own preferences, dislikes, and biases with them. Every critique will be unique (Hey!). I will learn something different about my very same novel from each different beta-reader. And my reactions to and edits inspired by their criticisms will change, as well.

With each phase of my novel writing process, whether the novel is still in progress, or finished first draft, or fifth draft, or this-is-the-one-that-gets-send-to-an-agent draft, will require different things from the beta-reader. If I know something doesn't work or a scene I'm planning on rewriting, I'll let her know, so she doesn't have to devote energy to give me as full a critique as to not waste anyone's time. If I know something does need work, I'll have her focus her attention on these scenes, characters, or plot-lines. She needs to know if this story is deeply personal, my emotions are still raw, and criticisms of "this" and "that" may be difficult for me to accept at this time, or perhaps the story is just good old-fashioned pulpy goodness that can be ravaged like good and proper.

I need to let the beta-reader know that I have a thick skin (if I have a thick skin that is and if I don't, well this isn't going to go well). That brutal, though honest, criticism would be appreciated. I know you don't want to hurt my brittle writer's ego, but also I know you only want what is best for my book just as I only want what is best for my book. We are on the same side! This is not an adversarial relationship, thought I may get defensive– I'm sorry, in advance. I really, truly am.

O! Muse,

There was a piece of advice that I received concerning the rewriting process. I needed to let go of that first draft for a couple of weeks. Print it out and put it in a drawer. When I come back to the manuscript, I will see it with new eyes. In the separation, while I went for walks, enjoyed evenings with my girlfriends, attended the theater, both stage and cinema, read books by someone other than myself, that my novel would stew in the back of my mind. When I next gaze upon the printed pages with red (scalpel) pen in hand, I will see it completely anew. Plot points that I thought were obvious would present themselves practically imperceivable and the veiled plots that I thought were brilliantly fore-shadowing would be glaringly evident. Sentences which aren't really sentences would stand out. I would notice misspelled words easier.

Why is it that you can't see your own misspelled words when you read your own stupid novel? Muse, I would really like an answer to this question. I know that the word processor brilliantly underlines a misspelled word with that red-squiggly-underline, but sometimes words are misspelled, but are spelled correctly (?!?). Wrap that paradox around your little head, Muse. And other times when you click on a red-squiggly-underlined misspelled word, the suggested words are in no way any kind of help in deciphering what you actually meant to say.

But I am pleased to say that distance from my novel really did work. My own weird amnesia concerning my own writing really was also a benefit to the rewriting process. And my amnesia was only intensified by those few weeks. There was a particular scene that I was suddenly inspired to add to second draft, only to discover several chapters later, that I had already written that scene in the first draft.

My Writer's Amnesia is a blessing and a curse.

"I love deadlines. I love the whooshing noise they make as they go by."
    –Douglas Adams, *The Salmon of Doubt*

Chapter Six

Ambiguous Legal Remedies

—Internal Memo—

To: Christopher Hanson, Publisher
From: Brett Walton, Esq.

Due to a lack of commitment to delivering her fifth contractually obligated novel in a timely manner, our legal team has reviewed the publishing contract with Abigail K.C. Sterling for any and all legal remedies. Due to her failing to meet an initial personally chosen deadline to submit the manuscript of the fifth novel to her editor to begin the editorial and publishing processes, and her subsequent failures to meet nine publisher mandated deadlines which

has forced the repeated postponements of publication and the loss of any and all marketing expenditures, we must find a legal means of publishing a
fifth novel in the Alistair Strange series.

There has been a ramp up in continued pressure from
the Hollywood studio which owns the film rights to
the Alistair Strange cinematic universe, to provide
them with the manuscript– any manuscript– so they
may begin pre-production on the film adaptation of
the fifth novel in the Alistair Strange series. The four
released films have to date earned a collective $2.3
billion worldwide and had become a cornerstone of
their release schedule for three consecutive Christmas releases and a fourth release after a two year hi-
atus, before the lack of delivery of a fifth manuscript
has forced them to produce other films to fill their
release schedule each of the last several years.

At the most recent stockholder meeting, our stockholders loudly expressed their concerns that any
further delays in the publication of the next Alistair
Strange novel could have an adverse effect on our
stock price and Wall Street confidence in our publishing company. The stockholders produced a
strongly worded letter to deliver to Ms. Sterling,
which has yet to receive an adequate response from
the author.

The wording of her contract specifies the publisher
has <u>unlimited</u> rights to publish any and all sequels,
prequels, and any derivative work set in the Alistair
Strange literary universe. The publishing company
has given Ms. Sterling great latitude when permitting the publication of short-fiction stories within

the literary universe of Alistair Strange with various magazines around the world in exchange for a percentage, despite our complete legal rights to said material. The wording of her publishing contract with our house is <u>ambiguous</u>. But ever-so slightly in our favor. From a legal point-of-view, we, as the publishing house on record, have the complete freedom and discretion to publish a fifth and any subsequent novels in the series <u>whether or not</u> said work has been written by Abigail K.C. Sterling.

What does this gain us?

In the underground "fan-fiction" community, there is a novel, *Alistair Strange and the Weight of a Feather*, that purports to be a fifth novel in the Alistair Strange series, picking up where Abigail K.C. Sterling left off story-wise after the publication of the fourth novel, *Alistair Strange and Those Whom the Gods Detest Should Not Be Unearthed*. According to our research, it has been universally well-received and is an apparently a very well-written addition to the Alistair Strange universe, written by the pseudonymous Alex Kennedy Corey (K.C.) Silver, While "fan-fiction" is traditionally considered by the publishing industry to be a violation of author copyrights and trademarks and the publisher's rights to said materials and verboten in general, we would be well-within our rights as the owner of the publishing rights to publish this "fan-fiction" as the fifth book in the Alistair Strange literary series <u>with or without</u> the permission of or a contractual relationship with the author of said "fan-fiction".

As the author of the work of "fan-fiction" dare not

and cannot legally claim copyright to her own work because of its inherent violation of Abigial K.C. Sterling's own copyrights, howbeit our publishing house would be within its rights to legally claim the copyright as a "work-for-hire" and publish independently of <u>either</u> authors' wishes.

It is the legal opinion of our department that the publishing house should prioritize the signing of a contract with the author behind the Alex K.C. Silver pseudonym as soon as humanely possible, so that we can publish of this "fan-fiction" novel as an official release. If contracts can be signed within a timely manner, this will permit the necessary editing, graphic design, and marketing promotions be completed prior to a Christmas release of the fifth novel in the Alistair Strange series, *Alistair Strange and the Weight of a Feather* by Alex K.C. Silver.

Chapter Seven

R Strangers Reduced to This? Fan-fiction?!?

by alistairstrange#1fan

It has been so long– so so very long– since Abigail K.C. Sterling has graced us with a "Casey For Christmas", that many Strangers have turned the seedier side of our fandom: fan-fiction. IDK why Strangers would waste their time on such poorly written, often self-aggrandizing, stories that simply pale in comparison with the beautiful, graceful, poetic prose of Abigail K.C. Sterling!

I know, my fellow devoted and obsessive Strangers, the wait has been insufferable. It has been far too long since we were able to cosplay and attend a midnight release party with all of the other Strangers. I haven't had to use any of my sick days, so I can stay up all release night and the next several days binge-reading the new book.

But we don't need to turn away from the shining light of Ms. Sterling to the dark, sordid, and disreputable bullsh*t of fan-fiction.

I don't care that some readers turned "writers", devoted Strangers themselves, believe that this character and that character deserve a love story that is out of both of their characters. I don't want to read homosexual or even heterosexual erotic fan-fiction.

Why is this even a thing? This a series of children's books, even particularly well-written and sometimes mature-themed children's books. I don't care that some Strangers want to retcon that big change made in the third book— you know the storyline I'm talking about— so that decision that Casey made for <u>her</u> characters and <u>her</u> story, could be utterly erased from history.

This is not the mark of a true fan. A true Stranger. The only stories we should be interested in have come from the pen of Abigail K.C. Sterling.

Most of these stories are barely stories. I've been to the fan-fiction sites. I've seen their word-counts. I've seen how many people "fav" them, "follow" them, and "review" them. The numbers are not impressive to say the least. Casey has been increasing her own numbers for each of her books. *The XII Labors* was seventy-plus thousand words. Then eight-five-plus thousand for *The Clash of the Olympians*. A hundred-plus thousand for *The Dark Seas Sleeper!* And *For Those Whom the Gods Detest Should Not Be Unearthed* was damn near two hundred thousand words. These fan-fiction authors barely have the creativity and drive to write a few thousand words, if that.

And her sales have reflected her exponential growth as an author. And the ticket sales from the film adaptations of her novels as been in keeping with this growth. With each book and movie, the coffers of the publisher and studio just keep getting fatter at the same exponential rate. And the fan-fiction? For a series that has consistently sold in the tens of millions of legitimate books, the number of downloads are laughable.

Yes, I have heard the rumblings from Hollywood. The fourth movie is about to be released this Christmas much to the delight of the Stranger who want any kind of Casey fix. And the producers of the film series want to begin working on fifth movie. Like now. Right now. The trade papers from Tinstletown and the studio executives and stockholders want the producers of the films just to keep going. Continue making movies without Casey's input! Why would they do such a thing? I don't think such a thing should be legal. They don't have the rights? Or do they?

What don't we know? What doesn't Casey know? What schemes have the lawyers made with the Devil that even Casey is unaware of?

I'm not a lawyer, so I don't know what terms and conditions are in the contracts they signed with Casey Sterling to acquire the film rights to her series, but I am a Stranger and we don't want Hollywood to continue the story. We want the story to come from the beautiful, graceful, poetic mind of Casey Sterling. Any fan who would settle for an Alistair Strange movie that came from the computer of a screenwriter is no true Stranger. And even if Casey gave Hollywood an outline for a potential fifth film, this movie would be nothing more than Hollywood-sanctioned and financed fan-fiction.

Hollywood has already taken liberties with the novels by cutting out some of the most important sub-plots. They have proven time in and time out, movie after movie that they don't understand the world that Casey has created. I shudder at the very thought of a bastardized fifth film by the yes-men of Hollywood, those talentless hacks who don't understand this world in the slightest. I have no doubt they could pull something out of their backside that is no better yet infinitely worse than the fan-fiction that pollutes the Internet.

But that won't stop Hollywood from making this abomination of a movie. Casey has published dozens of short-stories in a whole bunch of magazines over the last decade. Surely, they have the rights to those stories. Those stories are at least canon. They were not only written by Casey Sterling, but their publication was <u>authorized</u> by Ms. Sterling. Pick the bones of those stories and don't you dare write your own continuation of the world of Alistair Strange.

And speaking of continuations of the series... yes, my fellow Strangers, I have heard of *Alistair Strange and the Weight of a Feather*. The comment sections of this blog as well as my twitter feed have been blown-the-F-up with passionate debates and flaming fights over whether or not a true Stranger would read this fan-fiction.

It is apparently well-written. Surprisingly so, I've heard. I have not read it, nor will I read it. I won't download the file to my Kindle nor will I read it on my computer screen. I will not sully my technology with this bullsh*t story. It is nothing more than a virus that infects the computers and Kindles of passionate Strangers. Sure, it isn't a traditional computer virus that causes blue-screens-of-death, but it is a computer virus none-the-less. One that has infected the imaginations of Strangers turning them against Casey herself. This is an plague that can only be inoculated with an authentic "Casey for Christmas"!!! I want to read an honest to God hard-bound book in my hands after I attend a communal midnight release party.

This Alex Kennedy Corey (K.C.) Silver has the audacity and arrogance to believe she has the talent and the right to publish the fifth novel in the Alistair Strange series. And her pen-name smacks of desperation to be recognized. The exact same initials as our beloved Casey Sterling. And Sterling... Silver. Really? OMG!

You've got to be freaking kidding me. Who is this chick and why do we really care?

I know I don't. But enough Strangers have downloaded and infected their Kindles, phones, and computers with this bullsh*t virus that she has become something of a phenomenon. I cannot escape the gravitational pull of this destructive black-hole. Eventually, I may have to give in and read this bullsh*t, just so I can strengthen my arguments with my fellow Strangers against this cancer in our community called: fan-fiction.

Chapter Eight

R Strangers Reduced to This? Fan-fiction?!?

by alistairstrange#1fan

COMMENTS SECTION

IHeartAlexSilver: Why is everyone so sensitive when it comes to "fan-fiction". I discovered Alex K.C. Silver's novel. I downloaded the MOBI file to my Kindle. And I was able to read the further adventures of our beloved Alistair Strange BE-CAUSE Casey isn't giving it to us! Alex's novel is really, really good. It wouldn't be a phenomenon in the fan-fiction community if it was dreck. If a fan has put the time and energy into its creation, then I think the original creator should be proud. Programmers make remakes of their favorite video games, yet companies like Nintendo sic their lawyers on them, serving "cease-and-de-sist" letters. The companies should be excited that their fans are putting the hours into remaking and rebooting long forgotten games. These programmers are devoting thousands of hours of their own lives to bring these old video games back to shining new modern graphics life. And so what if a fan wants to devote the thousands of hours to author a new novel, bringing new life to a stagnant or even abandoned literary universe? Casey surely isn't giving us, the fans, what we want. We are at the tipping point in fandom, when the creators must cede the power to us, the fans.

> **VampressFromMars:** Haven't you ever heard of "copyright"?!? The author, and in the case of the deceased, their estate, needs to be able to protect their intellectual property from theft and misappropriation. These creators have devoted too many years of their lives to have their creations appropriated by the general public.

> **IHeartAlexSilver:** Oh, don't get me started on copyrights. This is a disgusting modern construct. Shakespeare wasn't criticized by the theater-critics in his day or by scholars in the centuries since when he wantonly plagiarized nearly every single one of his plays. Nothing original came from his pen. I even wrote an essay in college about this very subject. Some of my research included Robert McCrum of *The Observer* (which I will quote here so I don't get charged with that unconscionable crime called plagiarism), "If all writers are pickpockets, then Shakespeare was an inveterate 'snapper-up of unconsidered trifles', like Autolycus in *The Winter's Tale*. He swiped the best bits of *Antony and Cleopatra* (notably "The barge she sat in, like a burnished throne/Burned on the water...") direct from Plutarch, and took 4,144 out of 6,033 lines in Parts I, II and III of *Henry VI* verbatim or in paraphrase from other authors. Apart from *A Midsummer Night's Dream* and *Twelfth Night*, the plots for all his plays were ruthlessly appropriated from other, often classical, sources." Had the Berne Convention been

a legal precedent in Elizabethan England, all but three of Shakespeare's plays would have been banned as having violated "copyright"! Instead, this author of "fan-fiction" is hailed as THE greatest wordsmith in the history of the English language. Hahahahaha.

VampressFromMars: If you hate copyright so much, just wait until the work is in the public-domain?

IHeartAlexSilver: Public-domain? That is just the government placating us. Why do we have to wait, not only until the author is dead, but seventy-five years after that, for the public to finally own a property. Sherlock Holmes is well into the public-domain, but that doesn't stop the Conan Doyle estate from suing anyone and everyone for publishing stories featuring the iconic detective, using the legal maneuvering that the later stories are still in copyright despite almost all of the stories being in the so-called public-domain? We wouldn't have had the recent, albeit short-lived, publishing phenomenon of super-natural retellings of classic novels birthed by Seth Grahame-Smith with his *Pride and Prejudice and Zombies*. These authors and their publishers had to tip-toe around copyright by selecting public-domain works just to further fuel the phenomenon.

VampressFromMars: If the author can't own their own creation, then who owns it? The publisher? The Hollywood studio? The government? Don't make me laugh.

IHeartAlexSilver: Of course, the author should own their own world. They created it. But at some point the ownership becomes transferred to the fans. I don't know when it happens or how it happens, or even why it happens, but it always happens. *Star Wars, Star Trek, The Game of Thrones, Harry Potter.* Their fans all claim ownership over those cinematic, television, and literary universes. Even J.K. Rowling, who lives in rarefied air, routinely publishes new tidbits about the Wizarding World on Pottermore.com. When she let it slip that Albus Dumbledore is gay, her more conservative fans lost their ever-loving minds. "If you believe that, you should have written that in the blasted books," they cried. "We didn't need to know a beloved character was a reviled homosexual!" The Internet trolls cry that Ms. Rowling should just let her novels exist without any further supplementary materials. Yet these same trolls were the ones that cried the loudest that she announced wasn't going to be an eighth or ninth or tenth novels in the series. And in ten years or twenty years, when she decides to publish that mythic eighth novel, I can hear the lament of the trolls.

VampressFromMars: Joanne has every right to continue to produce stories set in her own world. What I object to is soulless corporations continuing the stories above and beyond that of the source material.

IHeartAlexSilver: Then we wouldn't have any James Bond movies beyond the 1970's. Did Timothy Dalton, Pierce Brosnan, and Daniel Craig all star in fan-fiction? Even Sean Connery starred in a non-canonical James Bond movie due to conflicted beliefs on who owned James Bond or at least *Thunderball.* Two producers went to legal war over their rights to Ian Fleming's iconic creation. Michael Crichton wrote his very own fan-fiction with *Jurassic Park: The Lost World* when he retconned the death of Ian Malcolm. If a novel's author can be bent to the will of a Hollywood studio, then how sacrosanct can the source material be. Even the gratuitously over-bloated *Hobbit* trilogy, which edged dangerously close to "fan-fiction", was filmed within the rights sold to Peter Jackson by Christopher Tolkien and the Tolkien estate. The fans may have questioned Peter Jackson's sanity at turning an average-length children's novel into nine! hours of cinematic narcissism.

VampressFromMars: Why all this concern over what is and what isn't fan-fiction? Your very name, @IHeartAlexSilver, screams that you're already read and adored that fan-fiction novel. You must have gone to your seedy, unseemly websites and illegally downloaded the file to your computer or your Kindle, IDK. But what I do know is I've never seen the allure of reading stories by unpublishable authors not creative enough to write their own characters and worlds. I don't want to read a "fan-fiction" about Hermione Granger marrying Harry Potter, or Neville Longbottom actually being the hero of Sybill Trelawney's prophecy to Dumbledore. I happen to be one of vocal few who hates that J.K. Rowling keeps dropping new stories on her Pottermore website. Yes. Yes. I would have loved to have had an eight or ninth or tenth Harry Potter novel, if she had chosen to continue them THEN. But she didn't. That ship has sailed a long time ago. She wants to be Robert Galbraith instead. Fine. But now, every time she adds some back-story to this character or that character, I hate it. Her every comment about the Harry Potter world is nothing but "authorized" fan-fiction at this point.

IHeartAlexSilver: I for one enjoyed *The Weight of the Feather* even though you don't seem to believe it is or ever should be "canon". We fans love to cry when something is or isn't canon. Let me quote from a *Starlog* interview with the nerd-god himself, George Lucas, "I don't read [the authorized, yet ultimately non-canonical novels and comic books published by our licensees] . I haven't read any of the novels. I don't know anything about that world. That's a different world than my world. But I do try to keep it consistent. The way I do it now is they have a Star Wars Encyclopedia. So if I come up with a name or something else, I look it up and see if it has already been used. When I said [other people] could make their own Star Wars stories, we decided that, like *Star Trek*, we would have two universes: My universe and then this other one. They try to make their universe as consistent with mine as possible, but obviously they get enthusiastic and want to go off in other directions."

VampressFromMars: George Lucas is the creator of the *Star Wars* cinematic universe. Just as Gene Roddenberry is the creator of the *Star Trek* television universe. Of course, they would consider of the books and comic-books they licensed to be non-canonical. But Abigail K.C. Sterling is the creator of a literary universe. There can't be other non-canonical <u>books</u>.

IHeartAlexSilver: I for one am sick and tired of this what is canon and what isn't canon debate. D.C. comics decided their comic-book universe had grown unwieldy due to three decades of thousands of comics books created by hundreds of different creative teams. So they did a hard-reboot of their universe which itself was a hard-reboot of the Golden and Silver Age universes with, the so-called *New 52*. Anyone here old enough to remember the Crisis on Infinite Earths reboot of the D.C. universe?

VampressFromMars: I for one won't be reading *The Weight of a Feather* or any other fan-fiction until it has the publisher's logo emblazoned on its cover.

....

IHeartAlexSilver: Burn! I know I'm nerco-ing this thread by posting in it a year later, but... Burn! Alex's novel is now canon. Team Griffindico has won! Double-burn! Hahahahahaha!

"The only kind of writing is rewriting."
  —Ernest Henningway, *A Moveable Feast*

Chapter Nine

Never Meant to be a Writer, Meant to be a Rewriter

O! Muse,

Now, that I am finished with the first draft and received my first few critiques, I now seek to discover what Ernest Hemingway meant when he said, "The only kind of writing is rewriting." What did I just spend the last year or so and some odd months doing? Twiddling my thumbs? I had been living my life as a writer. I don't mean to be smug. I don't mean to be arrogant. But my first draft had to have been proof that I had been writing. That I was a writer. Our profession isn't called "rewriters". We are writers. I didn't sign up for being a "rewriter". Or did I?

I loved every word I wrote. I had painstakingly picked each word out of the ether and put into my novel, just where it needed to be. Sometimes I read the dictionary and the thesaurus for hours on end looking for just the right word.

Are you telling me that all that was for naught? That now I have to have debride my own novel of the dying and contaminated flesh? How could all that beauty actually be necrotic flesh?

Is there a poetic or esoteric reason why our novel at this point is called "The First Draft"? Is there some mystical truth that writers are passing down from generation to generation? Are the Muses trying to cull the hacks from the actual writers with that choice of words: "First Draft"? If the novice, the amateur knew that there was something even more insurmountable task after the first draft, then perhaps they wouldn't bother writing the first draft in the first place. Now that I had written my first draft, am I willing to spend the next several months working on the second draft? And what then? Will there be a third draft? A fourth? Dear God, a fifth draft? Is there no end to this Sisyphean task writers have been condemned to?

And what happens when I get that sacrosanct "Final Draft" finished. Will there truly be an end? I've read in my writer's books that the next step after the "Final Draft" is finding an agent. Will she accept my "Final Draft", or will she take her red (scalpel) pen and bloody my darling? When I finally get an editor at a major publishing house, I have no doubt in my mind that she will take her own red (scalpel) red and bloody my darling. In the name of all that is rational, what is this life that I have chosen? Will there every come a time when I am finished with a book? I'm not sure there ever will be. I can only hope when my book finally gets on the shelves of the bookstore that it will finally be finished. Or will I and my editor have simply abandoned it on the shelves truly and utterly unfinished?

Now I have come to the realization that I. Am. A. Rewriter.

I would now live the lives of every rewriter who has come before me. I would live the immortal words of Vladimir Nabokov, "I have rewritten– often several times– every word I have ever published. My pencils outlast their erasers." In the modern age, the word "delete" will, no doubt, become worn down by my repeated pressing of the key, instead of an eraser wearing down. But the worn-down key will still function and have meaning.

Now, I knew I would need to break out the red (scalpel) pen and "kill my darlings, kill my darlings, and when it breaks my egocentric little scribbler's heart, kill my darlings", with my sincerest apologies to Stephen King.

O! Muse,

The first thing we need to do Muse, is head down to our local office supply store to purchase the following shopping list: "Whiteboards, bulletin boards, index cards, markers, magnetic boards, chalkboards, sticky notes, pens, thumbtacks, tape, and scissors." Don't forget the following, Casey: "An atlas, maps, a calendar from the time-period in question (remember, Casey, there are only fourteen different calendars possible, so finding one with accurate days-of-the-week shouldn't be too difficult), travel books (if set in a city we're not completely familiar with)."

The second thing to do once I was ready to begin the Sisyphean task of rewriting, was print the bloody thing. I went whole-hog on the process. I wanted a crisp, clean print so I invested in a cheap (but not necessarily inexpensive) laser-printer. There was a part of me that desperately wanted it bound with brass fasteners and a card-stock cover, so that my manuscript would feel as close to a book a humanly possible. But I didn't need to compile my book, instead I needed deconstruct it.

The next thing I needed to do was approach my novel as if it were a crime-scene that I was investigating. I divided each chapter into its own stack and laid them out on the floor of my living-room (the room with the largest open floor). I took a sticky-note and wrote that chapter's POV character, narrative point in the story (i.e. setting, inciting incident, plot point one, first culmination, darkest moment, plot point two, climax, denouement, etc.).

I hung a white board on the wall, like I was a detective in a police procedural. I gleefully clipped photographs from Hollywood rags and assigned (cast?!?) a different actor or actress to each character and I began linking the characters with lines and sub-branches like I was trying to uncover a criminal conspiracy.

I marked notes on the lines detailing the events that linked the characters. I tried to make sure every scene, major event, story arc, had been traced and was traceable on this board. If I could see the entire novel in the relationships between characters, scenes, and plot-lines, then I could solve the mystery of the rewriting process.

Next I had torn apart my Rand McNally atlas to plot the geography of the story. I needed to make sure the people, places, and things in my novel could easily be located on a map. Did the action move between scenes in a physically realistic way? Was the drive or flight time feasible? Had I taken into account time-zones? Did scenes jump around the world? Going from day to night from morning to evening accurately? And I added a calendar above my physical map. I needed to know when this scene happened in relation to the next scene. Was I given proper amounts of time between events. Did time flow correctly? Even if my novel jumped around in time, did all of the flashbacks and flashforwards and the here's and now's come together logically and consistently. I couldn't let my readers find themselves Lost. Irretrievably lost.

Then I needed to storyboard the novel like I was a director of the film adaptation. I didn't necessary need to be an artist and create an actual story-board that resembled more of a comic strip. No. I took index cards and arranged each scene scene-by-scene with a simple one-sentence summary of the plot and *dramatis personae* of the signature characters in the scene. I needed to be able trace through colored cards the different POVs. Seeing the entire novel within a single gaze gave me great insight in my vision for the novel.

Once I solve this crime-scene, then I am ready for the interrogation!

O! Muse,

Now is my chance to pretend to be the audio-book reader of my book. Of course, Muse, I know that I will not be reading my own audio-book. The publisher will choose a voice-actor with experience and a voice like silk to read my words. But at this stage in the game, I have to read my own novel, for it's own sake.

With my novel reassembled, I begin reading my book: out-loud. I also recorded my reading the novel so I could go back and listen to it later for not only the pure enjoyment of it, but also to listen for errors again.

By reading the manuscript out-loud I got a more immediate sense of the sound of the English language. Sentences that aren't really sentences proclaim themselves as sentence fragments and run-on sentences, your verbs scream tense errors, subjects and verbs fight over not being in agreement, and nouns and pronouns proudly boast when they're in conflict. Spelling errors are surprisingly more noticeable (I hate that we cannot spot our own spelling errors. How my mind just read the word "correctly" and move on as if the spelling error had never taken place, when in fact, it was staring at us in the bloody face. But when I read the word, it smacks me upside the head). Dialogue comes across as either natural, or wooden, stilted, or unnatural in tone when read out-loud. I discovered characters either leap off the page or hide in the shadow, sometimes when I meant them to be the opposite. I got a better idea of the flow of my novel through the simple act of reading out-loud. How characters and scenes interact. My "audio-book" told me if I am wordier than a gossiping hen or if I barely have any flesh on my bones.

We writers like our sentences to look right on the page, but they also have to sound right. The reader is speaking the words she reads in her mind and although that doesn't utilize her sense of hearing, she *can* hear the structure of our sentences, the poetry of our prose, the dynamics of our dialogue. We have gone to great lengths to choose the correct words to create beautifully realized scenes in the mind's eye of our readers, but we must also make the words sing in their mind's ear.

O! Muse,

Rewriting is like the Japanese art of crafting bonsai trees. We have planted the best possible seed of the tallest of trees in the smallest, shallowest of pots. The seed we planted is that of the world tree, Yggdrasil. We must grow an entire world, sometimes an entire universe, in our six-inch deep flower pot. We must give our own little world the room to grow, but it will never be the realization of the true world tree, but instead something smaller, yet in no way less important. We must snip, trim, prune away every branch that is not necessary to create the perfect little bonsai, otherwise our bonsai will collapse under the weight of the unnecessary branches. Our bonsai novel is not a pale imitation of Yggdrasil, but the perfect reflection of the world tree in miniature.

Murder! Mayhem! Death!

I feel kind of like God did when condemned the world to be buried under the flood waters. My novel is corrupt and filled with unpoetic prose. I have, like the god of my third-person omniscient world, looked upon it, and, behold, it was corrupt; for all flesh had corrupted his way upon the world. And I say to my protagonist, "The end of all flesh is come before me; for the earth is filled with violence through them; and, behold, I will destroy them with the earth. And, behold, I, even I, do bring a flood of waters upon the earth, to destroy all flesh, wherein is the breath of life, from under heaven; and every thing that is in the earth shall die. But with thee will I establish my covenant; and thou shalt come into the ark."

I am, at this very time, the vengeful God of the Old Testament. I desperately want to Murder! Mayhem! Death! But I love this world. Can I be more like the God of the New Testament, whom was wounded for our transgressions, he was bruised for our iniquities: the chastisement of our peace was upon him; and with his stripes we are healed; all we like sheep have gone astray; we have turned every one to his own way; and the LORD hath laid on him the iniquity of us all? As God of my world, I have not sent My Son into the world to condemn the world; but that the world through Him might be saved.

My apologies, Muse, for my blasphemy, but this feels true.

O! Muse,

I find myself almost forced to hire a professional assassin, internationally acclaimed hit-man to murder my precious– *My! Pre-*

cious! Am I willing or even able to hire a professional editor? Can I subject my "prisoner" to that level of non-Geneva-accord-level interrogation? Cramped confinement, dietary manipulation, nudity, stress positions, sleep deprivation (my own apparently), and waterboarding. I know she alone can get the information out of my prisoner, but do I have the will to hand my prisoner over?

I know what working with a professional editor will certainly be a crash course in brain-surgery. How many patients will die under my uncertain hands before, I learn the strengths and weaknesses of my prose, my plotting, my characterizations through receiving feedback filtered through her professional experiences. She knows the professional writing world I want to enter better than I do, so there is no better guide. This is her industry. She knows the tips and tricks to survive in this inhospitable climate, she knows the back roads and oases that will get us safely through enemy territory, so that I can complete my mission: getting published!

You're mixing your metaphors, Casey.

But in the end, I believe that I am the only one who can complete journey, even without a proper guide. I will edit and reedit, I will cut and trim, I will grow and cultivate it until it is absolutely perfect county-fair prize worthy swine.

But, Casey, don't over-edit. Remember this piece of wisdom: "Some birds are not meant to be caged, that's all. Their feathers are too bright, their songs too sweet and wild. So you let them go, or when you open the cage to feed them they somehow fly out past you. And the part of you that knows it was wrong to imprison them in the first place rejoices, but still, the place where you live is that much more drab and empty for their departure." At some point, you need to let your manuscript go, let it fly.

Write your query letter!

Chapter Ten

RE: Legitimate publication of illegitimate fan-fiction

Hello, Ms. Alex K.C. Silver,

I am sending you this email regarding your writing and subsequent publication of a "supposed" fifth novel in the Alistair Strange literary universe on a popular, illegal fan-fiction website. You should be made aware that writing and publishing the "fan-fiction" *Alistair Strange and the Weight of a Feather* is a violation of Ms. Abigail K.C. Sterlings' copyrights and our publishing rights.

However, I am not contacting you today to chide or threaten you with legal action for having such passion for the world of Alistair Strange that you devoted your time and energy into the writing and self-editing of a novel-length work of "fan-fiction".

The world you have continued is as creative and popular as the world created by Abigail K.C. Sterling. The characters are as realized, the plot-lines as imaginative, and your prose is truly excellent for an amateur writer devoting herself to fan-fiction. You have written a truly worthy successor to *Alistair Strange and Those Whom the Gods Detest Should Not Be Unearthed.*

In the history of publishing, there have been many instances when other writers are chosen to author the continuation novels in beloved series posthumously after the authors untimely death.

- Van Lustbader has continued Robert Ludlum's *Jason Bourne* series.
- Mark Greaney, Grant Blackwood, and Peter Telep have continued various Tom Clancy espionage series.
- Brian Herbert continued his father's, Frank Herbert's, *Dune* series of science-fiction novels with co-writer Kevin J, Anderson.
- Brandon Sanderson completed Robert Jordan's long-running *The Wheel of Time* series of fantasy novels at the request of the widow.

Fortunately, Abigail K.C. Sterling is alive and well, but unfortunately, she has become somewhat reclusive. I need not go into the specifics or provide details because these should remain confidential between author and editor.

What I can say is the continuation of the Alistair Strange series is of the highest priority at our publishing house. The Hollywood studio which owns the film rights to the series also considers the publication of a fifth novel and subsequent pre-production on a fifth movie in the film series as of the utmost importance. Ms. Sterling's editor has exhausted all possible options available to her. Our lawyers have exercised all due diligence to providing a legal remedy for this situation.

It is an unfortunate situation we have found ourselves.

Our legal remedies are few and far between. As of this writing, Ms. Sterling has chosen not to submit a publishable manuscript during the given time-frame. Therefore, it is in the best interest of our publishing house and the Hollywood studio to publish a fifth novel in the series.

And since, you have already illegally written and self-published on a popular fan-fiction website said novel (which according to Ms. Sterling's own editor is beautifully written and fantastically plotted), we would like to offer you the opportunity to be the continuation writer for the Alistair Strange series of young adult novels.

Please respond with all due diligence so that we may move forward with the publication of your "fifth" novel in the Alistair Strange literary universe, *Alistair Strange and the Weight of a Feather.*

Regards,

Christopher Hanson,
Publisher

_____

Dear Mr. Hanson,

I am genuinely confused. I have read and reread your email several times and I don't quite understand what you are offering. There is the obvious, of course. But the obvious does not make a lick of sense. You are seemingly implying that you would like publish my fan-fiction novel, but that, in and of itself, is beyond my comprehension. This is an unimaginable proposition to be entering into.

I don't know how to respond. And with what words? Color me paranoid, but simply acknowledging your email could possibly be considered an admission of guilt in copyright infringement.

Best,

Alex K.C. (Kennedy Corey) Silver

———————————————————————

Hello, Ms. Silver,

I understand your reluctance and hesitation given the history publishing houses have with these fan-forums, fan-fiction websites, piracy websites, and reddits that distribute these illegal continuations of legally protected literary universes.

However, we find ourselves living in interesting times, Ms. Silver. The Internet has created a fascinating paradox. In the past, publishing houses have had to power and influence to provide readers with a wealth of reading material from their favorite "fandoms" (I believe I am using this term correctly). Fans of *Star Trek, Star Wars, Dungeons & Dragons, Warhammer, Doctor Who* and an entire litany of various "fandoms" have an insatiable appetite for further stories of their beloved series, far beyond what the literary, film and television industries can provide them. In the past and present, publishing houses have entered into legal contracts with the film producers to solicit the writing of and the publication of a series of novels set in a literary offshoot of the cinematic universes. In the present, fan-fiction has supplanted the traditional publishing house as the source of these stories. The fans themselves have chosen to write the continuation of literary, television, and film series of their own accord.

Other popular culture novel series have featured any number of different authors writing in a universe often shared with the television or film series. *Star Trek* and *Star Wars* novels have remained a staple of the publishing industry for decades and none were written by Gene Roddenberry or George Lucas. When Disney purchased LucasFilm, they relegated decades of these non-canonical literary works into the realm of "Legend".

The difficulty we find ourselves in concerning Ms. Sterling and her Alistair Strange literary universe is the medium in her she writes. If she were the creator of a television series, like Mr. Roddenberry, or a film series, like George Lucas, the "work-for-hiring" of prose authors for the series of novels would be far more cut and dry.

If she were the author of a novel that has been adapted for television, the television writers often go to great lengths to expand and continue the story told far beyond what the novel had entailed. It would not be unheard of for a television series to continue at a faster pace than the literary author could keep up with his or her novels and eventually eclipse the story in the novel series, forcing the television writers to venture into territories with the story that the original author of the novels had not yet provided source materials.

The Hollywood studio which possesses the film rights to Alistair Strange would like to be within their rights to hire a screenwriter to write a fifth film in the series, but the wording of her contract with the studios providing them the film rights have certain <u>unambiguous</u> restrictions in place that limit the stories the studio can tell concerning characters and story-lines that have appeared in her series of novels and short-stories.

Without going into specifics, the contract we have in place with Ms. Sterling is... <u>ambiguous</u>. Here, we find ourselves in an undiscovered country. We have the rights to publish any and all se-quels, prequels, and derivative work in the Alistair Strange literary universe. But whom the author must be is, again, <u>ambiguous</u>.

We are within our rights to hire an author, under a standard "work-for-hire" contract, to write this fifth novel. We are within our rights to have the novel ghost written using the Abigail K.C. Sterling name. And we are within our rights as a publish-ing house to publish your *Alistair Strange and the Weight of a Feather* as the "official" fifth novel in the Alistair Strange literary universe.

We have chosen the later option.

Since you have already written *The Weight of a Feather,* a fifth novel that continues from the ending of the fourth novel, the editor on the series has chosen to work with you. She believes that your novel is the best continuation in the series available to us at the time of this writing. She believes in your story and your own voice as an author. She had taken the liberty of editing your novel with her suggestions to be more in line with our overall vision of the series.

A PDF of *The Weight of a Feather,* with her complete notes, has been included as an attachment. Please review her notes and suggestions and respond at your earliest convenience.

Regards,

Christopher Hanson

Dear Mr. Hanson,

I am genuinely shocked and pleasantly surprised at this turn of events. I have never, even in the wildest of fantasies believed that my devotion to Alistair Strange and my own desire to create stories in the wonderful, wondrous world created my Abigail K.C. Sterling would lead me towards receiving the kind of offer you just made me.

I thought you would have preferred that I write stories in my own worlds that were of my own creation. Isn't that the goal of the publishing industry? Finding new and exciting worlds? Or has fandom's insatiable and passionate appetites for the already established worlds of their favorite authors ever so subtly changed the course of the entire publishing industry? Up until your email, there has been a stigma in the genre of fan-fiction. And there probably always will be, I doubt your email will change that.

Ms. E.L. James, is by far and away, the most notable and infamous member of our community. While her *Twilight* fan-fiction, *Master of the Universe,* was not only popular, but incredibly concerning due to its graphic sexual content. Our community led her towards rewriting the stories, not as fan-fiction, but as an original story. Now, Ms. James sits in the best-selling sanctified air reserved for likes of Stephenie Meyer and the esteemed J.K. Rowling.

I thought my own path to fame and fortune would be to rewrite my Alistair Strange novel according to the practice of what we in the community call "pulling-to-publish". This is exactly what I had intended to do all along. You have to believe me. If fact, I have already gone to great lengths to already completely rewrite *Alistair Strange and the Weight of a Feather*, changing character names and descriptions, settings, and plot-lines from Alistair Strange into something a little more original.

But *The Weight of a Feather* went viral. Quickly. Far more quickly than even I thought possible. You're lucky if you get a thousand "favs". You're lucky if you get a hundred "follows" and even fewer "reviews". My novel exceeded all these any an order of magnitude. I wanted desperately to pull-and-publish, but the fame and celebrity even in our tight knit community was far too overpowering. Their adulation. Their recognition was intoxicating.

If you allow me to be honest with you, pulling-to-publish has proven to be extremely difficult. I am married to *The Weight of a Feather*. I have written in the wondrous world of K.C. Sterling. My novel picked up beautifully where she left off. Her characters fit the story I wanted to tell, or to be honest you with, my story fit her characters too well. I couldn't separate where she began and I ended. I had woven the two threads, hers and mine, so completely in that beautiful tapestry, that when I pulled on my string to separate them, the entire thing started to unravel. It was impossible to tell my story without using the source material. The "pulling-to-publish" draft was lifeless without that spark of life created by Abigail K.C. Sterling. The one couldn't exist without the other. "Pulling-to-publish" became an impossibly.

And now, I don't know what to think. This doesn't seem real, it really doesn't. There is no way that Stephenie Meyer or Little, Brown would have allowed E.L James or any other writer of *Twilight* fan-fiction, erotic or otherwise, to be published in anyway other than surreptitiously in PDF, EPUB, and MOBI formats found only in the darkest, shadiest parts of the worldwide-web. *Fifty Shades of Grey* had proven there were 125 million reasons why "pulling-to-publish" was the wildly successful alternative to fan-fiction purgatory. There would be no way, could be no conceivable way, that *Master of the Universe* would ever have dared be found on the bookshelves of Barnes & Noble.

And now? You seem to me to be daring to put my novel on these very same sacred bookshelves. I don't see how my book can sit alongside *The Twelve Labors, The Clash of the Olympians, The Dark Seas Sleeper,* and *Those Whom the Gods Detest Should Not Be Unearthed.* How can *The Weight of a Feather* be counted as the fifth? Officially, that is.

Even when I began to write my novel, it had been years since K.C. Sterling that published her last novel. This is exactly why I felt compelled to write the continuation of the story. She had gone on Twitter and said that the novel would be coming. We would have a "Casey For Christmas". But we didn't. Not that year. And again, she said the novel would be published. And it wasn't. Do you know how frustrating that is for a devoted Stranger, like myself? So I took it upon myself to write THAT book, *The Weight of a Feather.* To tell the story that she couldn't tell or perhaps didn't want to tell. Or perhaps more accurately, couldn't find it within herself to tell. Did she have writer's block? Did she simply not know where the story was going?

Was she so unsure that her current prose couldn't live up to her past poetic prose? Has she been crushed under the weight of fame, fortune, and celebrity. I don't have these answers. Perhaps, you of all people in the entire world possesses these answers. I don't know.

Is that why you have contacted me?

I don't know.

Best,

Alex

_____

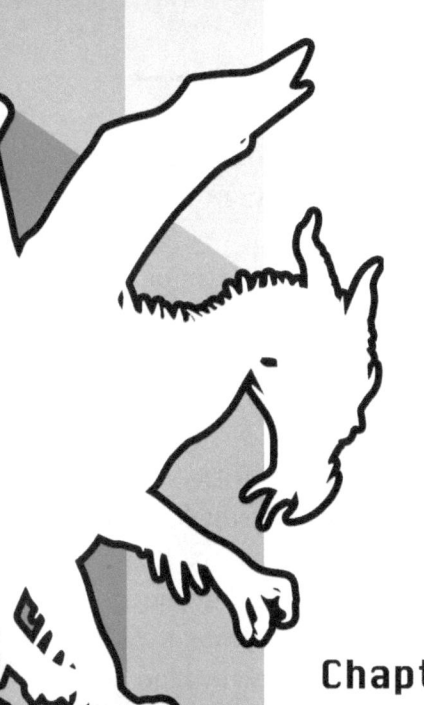

> *"Rejections slips, or form letters, however tactfully phrased, are lacerations of the soul, if not quite inventions of the devil—but there is no way around them."*
>   —Isaac Asimov

> *"I love my rejection slips. They show me I try."*
>   —Sylvia Plath

Chapter Eleven

Oh! The Pain!
It Hurts So Bad!

O! Muse,

I got my first rejection letter. Oh, how it stings. It hurts. It really, truly does. I just want to crawl into bed and die. How do you steel yourself for this kind of rejection?

Is this what men experience when they ask a woman out on a date and she says "No"? How have men done this for the past several thousand years. I cannot imagine the courage it takes for a man to walk up to a complete stranger and ask them out on a date. To be rejected time and time again all the while looking for a little companionship.

And what about the agent is this metaphor? I have had men ask me out in the most inopportune situations. Some of them are beyond relentless and refuse to take "no" for an answer. Is this the pain the agent feels for having listed themselves as open for unsolicited submissions in the *Writer's Market*? They must be confronted with writers whom refuse to take no for an answer. These writers are so convinced of their own genius that any form of rejection is met, not with pain and depression, but shock and anger and a deep-seated need to convince the agent just how wrong they are.

That first rejection letter was just a form letter. There wasn't any thought put into the letter other than absentmindedly folding it and inserting it into the self-addressed stamped envelope that I had already provided her. I don't know why she rejected my query letter. And that is all that she rejected. She never asked to read sample chapters, let alone the entire novel. If there was any kind of explanation on why she rejected me, then I would have details to improve upon. Does the agent think they are being kind by only sending a form letter? Does the agent feel bothered by receiving my query letter in the first place? That she has to take time out of her busy day to read a few hundred words, take a copy of the rejection letter from a pile of form letters, fold, and return it in my own SASE? I'm surprised she took the time to mail the damn thing.

Casey, you are being too hard her. Can you imagine all of the query letters she receives on a daily basis from writers just as eager as you to get their novels read? All the sample chapters she gets mailed to her when she explicitly says on her website or in the *Writer's Market* she doesn't accept sample chapters until she requests them. Only a query letter. And I'm sure, there are many writers arrogant enough to send the entire freaking manuscript, because it is the most brilliant crap in the universe and she simply must have the entire freaking thing right now. She has other clients for whom she is trying to sell their novels. She isn't getting paid to read query letters. She isn't getting paid to read sample chapters. Heck, she isn't being paid to get novels from the authors she does represent in front of carefully groomed editors. At least not up front. She'll get paid when the publishing contracts are signed. She is doing you a courtesy by opening herself to a veritable flood of unsolicited query letters.

Unsolicited? I hate this term. How in the blue blazes am I supposed to get a solicitation? I don't know anyone. I don't have a friend who has a cousin who is dating the brother of an agent to get my precious manuscript into her bloody little hands.

The query letter has to be one of the most frustrating things I have ever attempted to write. You need to sell your novel, yourself, in as few words as possible. The query letters only purpose is to get a request for three sample chapters or perhaps the entire manuscript if we're lucky. That's it. All of those hours spent honing and whittling my synopsis into a few choice sentences. Hoping beyond all hope that you will get as acceptance letter in the mail.

I. Feel. Like. A. Prostitute.

Is there such a rare and elusive creature as an acceptance letter? I've read stories of that once J.K. Rowling, long before her Harry Potter fame, had finally gotten through the agents' slush-piles due to a rather enthusiastic response from the first three sample chapters. Who was this person who no doubt was part of a ancient magical prophecy to fulfill *The Philosopher's Stone*'s publication? But even with an agent, Ms. Rowling was rejected by twelve different publishers. I know these publishing houses are not clairvoyant enough (at all!) to see into the future and know that this was the J.K-freaking-Rowling, an author who dared to cross the billionaire threshold. And what about that mythic thirteenth editor who decided to part with a £1500 advance? While Barry Cunningham's career at Bloomsbury would, no doubt, eventually have been set for life, he bafflingly advised Ms. Rowling to get a day job, because there is no money to be made in writing children's books.

–Cough–One billion pounds–Cough–

And what ever happened to the Dick Rowe of Decca Records who would go down in history as "the man who turned down The Beatles" because he advised his boss that "guitar groups are on the way out, Mr. Epstein."

I know hindsight is twenty-twenty. And nobody knows what the future holds. For every J.K. Rowling and the Beatles, there are thousands of publishli– well, there are only one J.K. Rowling and the Beatles, once in a lifetime freak accidents. Everyone else is just a book on the bookshelf, hoping beyond hope that a reader plucks your book down with no other prompting than the title on the spine seemed "interesting", reads the brilliantly worded dust jacket if you're one of the lucky few to get a trade-cloth edition, and decides to purchase the damn thing.

I don't know how I go on sending out my query letters. It is hard enough finding the addresses of agents willing to receive unsolicited query letters. And what if I get that request for sample chapters, or– hope-beyond-hope– the entire manuscript? Won't that rejection letter hurt even worse? Can I go from being a man asking many women on dates, to a man asking that one once-in-a-lifetime woman to marry him and then being rejected?

I don't know if I have the constitution to deal with this process.

O! Muse,

What is the most important thing to my success as an author? I am asking this question truthfully and honestly, because I don't know. At this point in my career, I'm looking for an agent, who will in turn help me get an editor and sign that big, big, deal. Or am I at the mercy of publishing trends, or God forbid, luck.

What makes a successful author? There are those who churn out pot-boiler after pot-boiler, never seeming to slow down from their rapid-fire pace and plotting. And there are others who patiently and poetically craft exquisite prose that is so good it aches.

I'm afraid that publishing a novel, even a young adult novel, is more like publishing pornography. Now, Muse, don't flinch. The courts have defined pornography not on a legal standard, although they claim otherwise, they define pornography as "I'll know it when I see it." Do agents and editor simply know when they have a bestseller because "They'll know it when they see it"? Or are they blind to the possibilities?

Do publishers want originality? Then why do they follow the

trends if they want originality. Nobody wanted Harry Potter, now everybody is tripping over themselves for the next Harry Potter, unless you are a little too close to Harry Potter, they reject you for not being original enough. Do I ignore what books are on the shelves? Or the rules of storytelling? How do I write a satisfying novel by being original, yet follow the rules they expect me to inherently know, and heel the trends, and gambling over the roll of dice just to get a shot at that Holy Grail of publishing: the contract.

Why do we creative types always choose careers where rejection is the norm? Stock-brokers play their game because they tend to pick the winners and those who fail in their chosen field fail based on calculable factors. The writer gets rejected by agents and editors. Actors get rejected by casting agents, first at cattle calls, then if they get a call back, they get rejected again and again and again. Musicians get rejected by first by small venues, potential managers, then by record labels, and eventually by the bigger venues.

Why do we play a game that is rigged against us?

And why do agents and editors want something "safe" if the reader doesn't? I'm sure there's some allure to picking up a novel that is marketed as the next Harry Potter, but the reader really just wants another Harry Potter by J.K. Rowling. They also delight in discovering something new and exciting, being the first to have jumped on the bandwagon, the new trend that is going to inspire a legion of copy-cats. The reader is smart. They know if the book being crammed down their throats by the marketing departments of publishing houses and bookstores is a knock-off, a pale-imitation of a beloved book.

And if you're writing genre fiction how do you give the fans of the genre what they want without falling into traps like two-dimensional character stereotypes, predictable plots, and typical genre tropes. Yes, the reader of romances wants a love story. The literary reader wants polished poetic prose that sings about the realities of life itself. The readers of mysteries want to play a game with the mystery writer to see if they can discover the who-did-

it, why-did-it, how-did-it before the author chooses to reveal the
mysteries. The reader of horror wants to have the crap sacred out
of themselves by the written word and the inverse is also true, the
readers of inspirational or religious books want to be Inspired–
with a capital "I".

O! Muse,

The second rejection letter came. And then the third. And then
the fourth and fifth and twentieth and twenty-first, and so on *ad
nauseum*. I started wall-papering one wall of my apartment with
the rejection letters. They became a badge-of-honor, a testament
to my bullheadedness. I was not going to stop until someone, any-
freaking-one asked for my entire manuscript.

And the acceptance letter finally arrived. No, no. It wasn't a
contract to represent me. No, an agent was requesting the en-
tire-blessed-manuscript. Not three sample chapters. Not a synopsis. The entire-freaking-thing.

And I sent my manuscript off. It was expensive. Far more expensive to mail than I thought it would, because several hundred
pages of a traditionally formated manuscript weighs a lot. But I
felt it was money well spent, because now that I have passed that
initial first-date query-letter stage of my relationship with this particular agent, that we were going to have a passionate and fruitful
agent-author relationship. I was going to get that agent representation contract. I was going to get that advance from an editor. Then
I would be one step closer to crossing the billionaire threshold
myself. Okay, Muse, millionaire threshold. Better?

As the weeks turned into months and I hadn't heard back from
my agent– no, not yet, don't ahead of yourself, Casey– the agent,
fear began to creep into my consciousness. I couldn't help but daydream about that acceptance letter I would receive any day now. I
was distracted at work. I was distracted at home. I couldn't function like a productive member of society. All of thought of was the
acceptance letter that just happened to be in the mail and would
arrive tomorrow.

But in the immortal word of the White Queen, "jam to-morrow and jam yesterday – but never jam today". The letter never came today, it would always come to-morrow.

Until it did arrive today! And I feel like crawling into my bed and dying. It was a rejection letter. But it wasn't a form rejection letter. She was ever so kind to brutally thrash me within an inch of my life.

Casey, once again, you are being too hard on her. She was kind enough to give you brutally honest criticism.

—Brutally honest– my backside.

Casey, she gave you the greatest gift possible in this situation. She gave you her honest critique of your novel and the reasons why she chose not to accept you as a client.

—The greatest gift possible would have been a contract to represent me– Bitch!

Casey! I know that you're hurting. But this can only make your novel a better novel. You need to take her criticism and give rewriting your novel one more pass Her criticisms were– are– valid.

—She can shove her criticisms of my book up her wazoo!—

Chapter Twelve

OMG! OMG! A New Casey 4 Christmas!

by alistairstrange#1fan

UPDATE 2: WTF! WTF! WTF! HOW IN THE FLYING BLUE F*CK CAN THE "OFFICIAL" TWITTER ACCOUNT ANNOUNCE THE AU-THOR OF THE NEXT ALISTAIR STRANGE NOVEL AS ALEX K.C. SILVER!

WTF! WTF! WTF! WTF! WTF! WTF! WTF! WTF! WTF!

I'M GOING TO DIE! I CAN'T F*CKING BELIEVE THIS IS REALLY HAPPENING! WTF! IDK! I CAN'T BREATHE. I'M F*CKING DYING! I'M F*CKING CRYING!

HAS THE WORLD GONE F*CKING MAD? HAVE I SLIPPED INTO AN ALTERNATE REALI-TY WHERE ALISTAIR STRANGE HAS ALWAYS

BEEN PUBLISHED BY ALEX K.C. SILVER? THIS IS THE ONLY THING THAT MAKES ANY GOD-DAMN SENSE.

WHY WOULD THE PUBLISHER THINK THEY COULD GET AWAY WITH THIS BLASPHEMY? THERE WILL BE A REVOLT! THE STRANGERS WON'T STAND FOR A COUP. WE WON'T ALLOW THE USURPER ANY MEASURE!

WHY WOULD ALEX SILVER PUBLISH FAN-FICTION IF SHE WAS THE CHOSEN HEIR-APPARENT TO CASEY? WHY IS THIS ALEX SILVER CHOSEN TO REPLACE OUR BELOVED CASEY?

OMG! OMG! OMG! YOU DON'T THINK CASEY DIED, DO YOU? IS THAT WHY THERE WAS BEEN SUCH SILENCE ABOUT HER NEXT BOOK? WHY WOULD THEY KEEP THAT A SECRET?

SHE CAN'T HAVE F*CKING DIED! SHE JUST CAN'T HAVE DIED!

HAD CASEY BECOME SUCH A RECLUSE THAT NOBODY KNEW SHE DIED! MY MIND IS SPINNING OUT OF CONTROL? DID A HOUSEKEEPER OR FAMILY MEMBER FIND HER LONG DEAD AND MUMMIFIED CORPSE AT HER COMPUTER? THIS IS THE ONLY THING THAT MAKES ANY SENSE!

SHE CAN'T HAVE F*CKING DIED! SHE JUST CAN'T HAVE DIED!

NONE OF THIS MAKES ANY SENSE!

IDK! IDK! IDK! IDK! WTF!

UPDATE: WTF! WTF! WTF! You've got to be f*cking sh*tting me. I don't understand how this could have possibly happened.

The "official" Twitter account for Ms. Sterling's publisher has released the title of the fifth Alistair Strange novel. ALISTAIR STRANGE AND THE WEIGHT OF A FEATHER.

WTF! WTF! WTF! WTF! WTF! WTF! WTF! WTF! WTF!

IDK WHAT TO SAY! I really don't. There was no mention of Abigail K.C. Sterling in the announcement. I know she wouldn't have chosen the same exact title as a f*cking fan-fiction novel. Would she? Was this fan-fiction author so clairvoyant that she knew what Casey was planning on naming her own novel.

The only thing that makes sense, is this Alex K.C. Silver is a f*cking hacker. She has somehow hacked into Casey's beloved MacBook Air and stolen her manuscript and published it on those god-forsaken fan-fiction sites. This is the only thing that makes f*cking sense.

Was this why the fan-fiction novel was so well received? Because it was actually written by the beautiful, graceful, poetic mind of Abigail K.C. Sterling!

ORIGINAL: OMG! OMG! The twitter account for the publisher of Alistair Strange has posted a release date for the next Alistair Strange novel! Come this December, we will have a new "Casey for Christmas"! OMG! OMG!

I know what many of you are thinking. I thought the same for a moment, a very brief moment. This tweet did not come from the Twitter account of Abigial K.C. Sterling. It came from the Twitter account of her publisher! She has been radio-silent on Twitter since her last promise to publish the book and we have had several Christmases come and go without an actual "Casey for Christmas"!

No book title. No plot synopsis has been released yet, but this. But we have a date and that is all that matters to me. No more vague "next Christmas" or "next year" bullsh*t. Casey Sterling has finally delivered her manuscript to her publisher and the book is already, as we speak, being edited and designed, a marketing campaign being readied, no doubt posters and day-calendars and cardboard stands are being designed and manufactured this very moment. The bookstores around the world will be wall-papered in Alistair Strange promotional materials. And I wouldn't have it any other way. We find ourselves again filled with eager and breathless anticipation.

I don' know how long the publisher has had Casey's still-untitled fifth novel. Yes, fellow Strangers, have I no doubt that Casey's manuscript has the title emblazoned on it, and it has already been accepted by her editor and publisher and the graphic design team is already working on a title logo and cover for the book. Yes! OMG! OMG! OMG!

I CAN'T WAIT TO KNOW THE TITLE! TO SEE THE COVER!

I'M OVER THE FLIPPING MOON!

Chapter Thirteen

Hollywood Adaptations: Authorized Fan-Fiction

by alistairstrange#1fan

COMMENTS SECTION

IHeartAlexSilver: I am so sick of Internet trolls crying "It's fan-fiction" ever single time there is any deviation from the sacred, sacrosanct source-material. I have been a fan of *Game of Thrones* from the moment I first read the first book, but every time HBO changed a plot-line or killed off a character whom George R.R. Martin didn't kill first, there are a chorus of cries, "This is just fan-fiction. This isn't in *A Song of Fire and Ice*". Oh boo-hoo! And now, that the HBO series has announced they are continuing on with a sixth, seventh, and even eighth seasons, in spite of the fact that George R.R. Martin hasn't even finished the sixth novel, I can hear the lament of the Internet trolls at <u>every single</u> decision the show-runners will make. The Internet is nothing if not predictable. "BUT IT'S FAN-FICTION"! When does it all stop? Is Brandon Sanderson finishing *The Wheel of Time* "fan-fiction"? Are the new Dune novels "fan-fiction"? Even the video-game industry is ceding more and more power to the so-called "modders" who continue to breathe life into games, long after their creators have moved onto bigger, brighter, and shinier games. We have entered an age of "authorized" fan-fiction and I can't be more excited.

VampressFromMars: I agree that in the case of the death of a creator, the estate has the copyright to assign new authors to continue the literary universe. It is their right. Their copyright. And I also agree that George R.R. Martin signed over certain rights to HBO and that HBO is within their rights, their film-adaptation-rights. But I don't see the case with Alex's novel being an "authorized" fifth novel in the Alistair Strange series, just because it is printed with a hard-back cover, a shiny dust-jacket, and emblazoned with the logo of the publisher on the back.

IHeartAlexSilver: When Disney bought the rights, THE COPYRIGHTS, to the *Star Wars* universe for four-freaking-billion dollars, they unilaterally removed hundreds of novels and thousands of comic-books from the *Star Wars* canon. *The Heir to the Empire* trilogy, which was a brilliant continuation of the universe five years after the destruction of the second Death Star was brilliantly written by Timothy Zahn. Now, all of those novels that we bought and devoted years of lives reading are now regulated to "Legend". Disney with a wave of their hand turned canonical books to nothing more than "fan-fiction". All so that they would have a blank slate to further their movies, their books, their comic-books, without any hindrances to the future plots. If the creators have this kind of unilateral power over their universes, then

I don't see why we, the fans, can't have the same power.

AlistairStrange#1Fan: Since this is a comment string on my article about a supposedly "authorized" fan-fiction, I thought I'd chime in and say, even "authorized" fan-fiction is still fan-fiction in the end. Alex Silver can't own the copyright to her own novel because it violates the copyright law: "It has to be original. You cannot claim copyright protection to work that was created by someone else or copy someone else's work and claim you are the author or artist." Abigail K.C. Sterling's publisher violated not only the letter of the copyright law by publishing "fan-fiction" based on Casey's own copyright protected universe, but the spirit of the publisher-author relationship. Why would any author trust this publisher in the future if they can't trust the very words written in their contracts? The publisher, in the quest for the almighty dollar, has damned themselves to a hell devoid of any future authors. No agent in their right mind will ever send another manuscript to any editor at that publishing house. So no matter how loud the Strangers cries for another novel had become, *The Weight of a Feather* wasn't written by our Casey, so it should never have been considered for publication.

IHeartAlexSilver: Nobody, not even her editor, has had the luxury of reading the so-called "authorized" canonical fifth novel in the Alistair Strange series. We, the normal fans, do not have this luxury. Not until it is finally published. IF EVER! Doesn't the publisher have any rights? You go to great lengths to condemn them. But they weren't making any more money on the series they have invested millions into marketing. The series had stagnated because Casey missed deadline after deadline after deadline.

AlistairStrange#1Fan: NO. The publisher DID NOT have any right to do what they did. They may have found some mumbo-jumbo legalese that allowed them to publish that abomination of a novel without any input or authorization with Casey.

VampressFromMars: Preach, Sister, preach!

IHeartAlexSilver: Don't the fans have any rights?

AlistairStrange#1Fan: NO!

IHeartAlexSilver: Wow! That was just– Wow!

AlistairStrange#1Fan: No. The fans don't have any rights. Whether the universe is one created by George Lucas– now owned by Disney, or created by Stan Lee and Jack Kirby– now owned by Disney, the fans don't have any rights over these universes. Yes, we have devoted ourselves, and in some cases like my own blog, devoted our very lives to these entertainment universes, BUT in the end, we don't have ANY rights. We are beholden to the mercy of their creators. HBO have every right to continue the *Game of Thrones* series because George R.R. Martin <u>sold</u> them the rights. Did Casey sell her publisher these rights? They believe she did through their legal mumbo-jumbo, but in the end, the owner, whether it is human creator or "soulless corporation", is afforded all of these rights.

VampressFromMars: The RIGHT to COPYRIGHT!

IHeartAlexSilver: But these "human creators" or "soulless corporations" would have all of the rights to worthless properties if it weren't for their fans. Nobody would care about the novels, television shows, or movies, if the fans didn't care about them in the first place. *Star Wars* would have been a cinematic sci-fi flop if it wasn't for the fans. We kept the universe alive while George Lucas completely ignored it, then restored it with those God-awful "special editions", continuing to tinker and toy with the films until he chose to grace us fans with the prequels. And you know, what, maybe it's a good thing that Disney owns *Star Wars* now, because George Lucas' vision for *Star Wars* certainly doesn't mesh with his fans' visions. Almost every decision Lucas made from a far-too-young Anakin Skywalker to *cough-Jar-Jar-cough* to all the political claptrap, has been rightly criticized. It'll take a *Star Wars* "Superfan" in J.J. Abrams finally holding the reigns to deliver a movie worthy of continuing the *Star Wars* story. THE FANS OWN THESE WORLDS! NOT THEIR CREATORS!

VampressFromMars: I don't want to own anything. I just want to live in their worlds.

AlistairStrange#1Fan: Believe what you will, @IHeartAlexSilver. But nobody will create anything if there isn't some kind of ownership included inherently. Why should Disney invest hundreds of millions of dollars in the next *Star Wars* or Marvel movie if there isn't some ownership there. If any Hollywood studio from the big-boys to the little indie shops, could make a Marvel movie, why would Disney invest in them? I know, I know there are fan-films out there that are submitted to no-account local film festivals, but they are just fan-fiction that cost more to film. Marvel Comics has, no doubt, regretted many of their earlier forays in Hollywood, because they no longer own the film rights to their own creations: Spider-Man, the Fantastic Four, the Incredible Hulk, the X-Men, including Deadpool and the Wolverine! And no matter how many of these movies flop, the Hollywood studios only have to keep making movies to retain these film rights. Would J.K Rowling or George R.R. Martin spend years creating and writing their novels if they could not own and therefore protect their own intricately and passionately created literary worlds? Copyright protects not only the original work itself, but the right to make copies of the work and sell them, import or export the work, make derivatives or revisions, distribute or publish the work, perform the work, display the work, or record the work. Now most authors can't do all of these things on their own, so they have the right to <u>sell</u> or cede any or all of these rights to their publisher, a Hollywood studio, or anyone else they so choose. These are the rights that are recognized and protected by our government and the governments that agree to the Berne Convention. J.K. Rowling can say what she whatever wants about Harry Potter. George R.R. Martin can take as long as he wants to finish *The Winds of Winter*, if ever! As much as we might want to believe otherwise. WE DON'T OWN DO-DIDDLY-SQUAT! We are at the creative mercies of those we idolize. End of story.

VampressFromMars: Burn!

> *"Remember: when people tell you something's wrong or doesn't work for them, they are almost always right. When they tell you exactly what they think is wrong and how to fix it, they are almost always wrong."*
> –Neil Gaiman

Chapter Fourteen

Pregnant SASE's

O! Muse,

One of my self-addressed stamped envelopments came in the mail today. I am still shaking even though it has been hours since the postman delivered it. The envelope looked pregnant. It wasn't thin and anemic with only a simple rejection form letter, it was thick, practically overflowing with folded paper.

I wanted to tear open the envelope like it was the shirt of a lover, ripping buttons off, desperate for his flesh to be again my own. But cooler, less passionate thoughts prevailed. I ran to the silver-ware drawer in the kitchen and used a butter-knife to open ever-so-carefully open the envelope. (I know, Muse, I should have invested in a letter opener, but butter-knives do the job just as well.)

Dear Ms. Sterling,

Let me first apologize for taking so very long to get back with you. Our small agency is simply overflowing with submissions. Your query letter was beautifully written and compelling– enough. I wanted to prioritize the reading of the manuscript you promptly submitted at my request, but unfortunately life and work often conspire against us. Your manuscript sat on the slush-pile for far too long.

After finally giving the time necessary to read THE XII LABORS OF ALISTAIR STRANGE, I have also given copies to each of my colleagues to read and an offer me their own opinions of your work.

Your writing has beautiful, graceful, poetic prose. It was a pleasure to read. Your main protagonist, however, appears to be a cookie-cutter variation of Harry Potter. These types of protagonists are a dime-a-dozen these days, due to the wild success of J.K. Rowling's series. But I believe there are qualities to the character that are truly unique and fascinating enough to appeal to the large audience of readers. With the correct rewrites and guiding hand, Alistair Strange can be transformed into a unique hero who would stand out on the book shelves. But this is job of the editor. My job, however, is finding the right editor and publisher for your book.

The selling of fiction in this day and age, particularly young adult fiction staring a young, male protagonist, who is in your own words, is "the fulfillment of an ancient prophecy to defeat an equally ancient evil," is particularly difficult these days. And your plot skews towards a more mature audience due to the supernatural terror-tinged H.P.

Lovecraft influences and the nostalgic call-backs to 1980's Stephen King horror.

But– and this is the <u>but</u> I know you've been waiting for during the difficult task in locating an agent to represent you– I am convinced that the complexity, depth, and consistency of the world you have created, your minor characters, and antagonists truly stand out against the competition. Your prose has the perfect amount of narrative drive to make it a pleasure to read. And the more mature-audience aspects of your plot may be unique enough to attract much older audiences to a novel, a novel which may appear at first glance to be yet another young adult novel in the already saturated young adult market.

And am pleased into include a copy of our standard author representation contract. Please read it thoroughly, sign it, and return it to me at your earliest possible convenience.

Please know in advance, that I will be adding you to an already full plate of authors whom I am trying to get published. I am devoted to you all, but there are only so many hours in the day. This may take time. Time to talk to editors. Time for editors to read your manuscript. Time to analyze rejections (this part of the process isn't over just yet, I'm afraid).

I look forward to beginning our author/agent relationship.

Sincerely,

Elizabeth Krupa

O! Muse,
   I am dancing on the ceiling!

The first thing I did was frame the letter and hang it on my rejection wall. While there is a part of me that wants to tear down all the rejection letters and hang *just* the acceptance letter in their place, I can't yet part with the reminder of what has inspired my life for the past eighteen months. Now that I have that acceptance letter I know that all of the decisions I have made, from working in as a waitress in order to put a roof over my head and food on my table *while* I devoting the ever-so-long hours writing. I have made the right decisions and for that I am proud.

Even before the rejection cycle began, I read books about the process to steel myself for this very moment. I know what my rights are and how the agent do with respect to my literary work:

- Review an author's work.
- Provide an assessment of its quality and potential market-ability.
- Offer editorial guidance.
- Suggest possible strategies for securing its publication or production.
- Advise about trends, market conditions, practices, and contractual terms.
- Establish contacts with firms and persons acquiring rights to appropriate types of literary or dramatic material.
- Market the work and rights therein, including negotiation and review of licensing agreements.
- If a work is licensed, monitor licensees' marketing activity.
- Review royalty statements and keep the author informed in financial matters

I want to sign that contract *now*, but I know that I need to give myself a little time and space from this exhilaration that I am feeling at the moment. I am going to take the contract down to the coffee shop, buy myself a latte, and carefully read the contract. Tomorrow, I will need to consult a lawyer, *just in case*. You never know when the wording of a contract would be– what is the right word– ambiguous and I could get myself in trouble.—

—I signed the contract and put it in the mail. I know, I know,

Muse, I should have waited until tomorrow and had a lawyer look over the contract. That I shouldn't have gone to the now-closed post office and put that contract in the slot, but I didn't find anything in that contract that seemed... untoward. I believe it is your standard representation contract. There were no red-flags or warnings like my writing books warned: She didn't ask for an upfront payment, charge for editing suggestions, guarantee my success, and her cut is the industry standard 15%.

Yes, yes, Muse, I should have asked more questions. I should I done my due diligence. I have read the suggestions in the many books on writing I've bought and read. There are recommendations from various associations like the Association of Authors' Representatives, Inc.. I should have. I know. I know. I should have asked the following questions:

- How long has the agent been in business?
- Is the agent a member of the Association of Authors' Representatives?
- Are there agency specialists for movie and television rights?
- Sub- or corresponding agents in Hollywood?
- Are there agency specialists for foreign rights?
- Sub- or corresponding agents overseas?
- Will the agent handle the work personally?
- Will fellow staff members be familiar with the work, the agreements and ongoing status?
- How closely will the agent keep the author apprised of the work being done?
- Is there a standard agent-author agreement?
- Will the agent consult with the author on any and all offers?
- What is the language of the agency clause in contracts?
- With 1099 tax forms at the end of each year, does the agency include a detailed account, including gross and net income, commissions and other deductions?
- In the event of an author's death or disability, what provisions exist for continued representation?
- If agent and author should part company, what is the pol-

icy for handling any unsold subsidiary rights?

But the contract is in the mail. I can't turn around now.

O! Muse,

I was able to ask these questions today over the phone. In my elation for having received a contract and a night's worth of paranoia for having signed and mailed it, I didn't tell her either of these. I doubted that even the United States Postal Service could have delivered the contract to her in that short amount of time. There was a part of me that was terrified that I wouldn't like the answers she gave, or that she wouldn't give me the answers I requested. I was afraid that I signed a legally binding contract that would have caused me nothing but grief. A contract that would have haunted me for the rest of my life. Or worse. Stolen my children from me.

Thankfully, I am satisfied with the answers she gave to these and even more questions that I had. This really feels much more like a personal relationship than a strictly professional one. I was able to get an assessment of Ms. Krupa's policies and practices. We discussed those questions I should have asked before signing that contract and more. So much more:

- The particular works of the author, and the specific rights in those works, subject to the relationship.
- Any timeline or benchmarks that may govern its duration.
- The compensation or method of computing the compensation due the agent in relation to potential outcomes.
- The extent to which up-front expenses, undertaken by the agent, are to be reimbursed by the author, and the schedule for any such repayment.
- Since the relationship is, by its nature, both ongoing and fiduciary, arrangements must detail the agent's fiscal responsibility for funds collected on the client's behalf.

This is the start of a beautiful relationship.

O! Muse,

I don't know if I can handle any more rejection. Why did I

delude myself into believing that once I got that acceptance letter from a agent, this would be all smooth sailing towards the promised land of finding an editor and getting a publishing contract. I don't understand how an editor could reject me at this point. Isn't that the point of getting an agent? I could have gotten rejection letter after rejection letter from editors on my own. I didn't need an agent for this. Hasn't the agent already spent her career cultivating relationships with editors to avoid this situation entirely?

Casey, you are being to hard on her, again. Every editor is different. Has different tastes. Has different goals. Their only desire is to find and publish books that they think will make their publishing house money. Just as an agent only wants books that she thinks she sell to a publishing house, so in the end she can make money. Do they feel passion for the books they represent? Of course. In the end, they are looking for the next big thing.

And if they aren't feeling it. If there is some aspect of the novel they do not absolutely believe it, they aren't going to invest their time and reputation on something. This is a subjective business. There is no crystal ball that sees into the future to tell them that this or that novel is going to be the next big thing. This is only one opinion. There will be other opinions, Casey. There are many other editors in this business you are trying to break into. You only need to find one.

Twelve rejection letters, Muse! I don't know how much more my heart can take.

Casey, your agent believes in you, and chosen your novel to present to all of these editors whom she has cultivated relationships. She is trying to find the right editor. THE one that will believe in you.

It is worth being patient.

But what if no editor believes in me, Muse? What do I do then?

Then you self-publish your novel, Casey.

O! Muse,
I don't want to be one of those authors. There is an unshakable

stain when an author choses to self-publish her novel. Why do they not have the patience to find an agent, to find an editor, to find a publisher willing to publish their novel?

Casey, you did your research into the history of publishing. You know that self-publishing has a far older and richer than either the public or book industry realizes. *The Joy of Cooking*'s first edition was self-published. As was *A Christmas Carol*, the novel that saved Charles Dickens from debtor's prison. After fielding rejection letters, one of the most cherished of all children's books, *The Tale of Peter Rabbit,* was self-published by Beartix Potter. Mark Twain not only self-published, he became a publisher himself. Don't you want to follow in the more modern footsteps of James Redfield, who self-published *The Celestine Prophecy* to both fame and great popularity just few years ago?

I don't have the money to self-publish, Muse. First, I would have to self-edit the book thinking more like an editor than a writer; to be ultra-critical of every aspect of the book: every word, scene, plot-line, and character must be put on chopping block. I'd need to pay a copy-editor to remove all the spelling and grammatical errors from by book, because as you well know, a writer as difficulty seeing her own misspelled words. There are grammar Nazis out there who delight in finding each and every little mistake in even the professionally published books. I can't imagine how euphoric their delight is in finding misstakes in a self-published novel would be. Then I would need to hire a graphic designer to design a professional looking book cover and layout the interior. I've seen the self-published books in the bookstores. They scream to high-heaven that they are self-published. They simply don't look like the other books. And what about the cost to print a 1,000 copies of a book? Or what about 2,000 or 5,000 copies? The more copies you print through off-set printing the cheaper each book is. What am I supposed to do with that many copies of my book? I live in a one-bedroom apartment? Do I rent a warehouse? How do I pay for something like that? Or a self-storage locker might be more economical, I don't know. Then I have to convince Ingram or Baker and Taylor to distribute my novel. And what if they choose to reject my book? They don't *have* to distribute your book. I've heard the horror stories. Authors with boxes of books filling their garages, because they couldn't get past the distributors. How do I get the book into book stores without a distributor? Or what if I do get a distributor, but the bookstores don't want to carry my book. The system is rigged against the self-published author. Bookstores don't want to carry such books, unless the demand from the public demands that they stock the books. What am I supposed to do? Sell books out of the truck of my car?

The stigma of self-publishing is only washed away when your sell enough books to get a publisher to print the second printing. You self-publish as a means to the end of getting a publisher! How do the ends justify the means?

There are no easy roads, Muse. If there were, everybody and their dog would be doing things that way. Whether you choose to self-publish and be the editor, copy-editor, designer, marketing manager, sales representative and publicist yourself or whether you choose attempt to get an agent, editor, and publisher, there are just different equally difficult roads.

I am staying the course. Until I choose to alter it.

Chapter Fifteen

ALEX K.C. SILVER
PLAYBUY Interview

After playing a playful game of phone-tag, the newest, most controversial literary sensation and I finally we able to sit down for a messenger interview. It seemed only fitting that a publishing phenomenon that could only be born in the 21st century, would chose messaging over something as archaic as the telephone or as old-fashioned as a sit-down, in-person interview. How blessedly Millennial Alex was proving to be. I would like to describe her as a cute little Millennial with bubble-gum pink hair, antique horned-rim glasses, a cute little dress that looked more like a knight's shining armor, with a Horde tattoo on her wrist (a *World of Warcraft* reference), but I can't, because even I don't know what she looks like. The only image I have of Alex K.C. Sterling is based on our messenger conversation. But I don't think I'm too far off from my description of her. She is truly the 21st century nerd. A no-doubt adorable, cosplaying, *World of Warcraft* obsessed, *Magic: The Gathering* tournament contending, *Star Wars* nerd-girl. Too cute.

PLAYBOY: *How has being a nerd influenced your ascension to being an instant, literally overnight* **New York Times** *bestselling author?*

ALEX K.C. SILVER: My first taste of writing professionally was the "Blizzard Global Writing Contest". They were asking the fans, the actual subscribers to *World of Warcraft* to write a short-story set in the Warcraft, StarCraft, or Diablo universes. I couldn't believe we were being asked to write fan-fiction, but "authorized" fan-fiction. I can't tell you how import it was for me to take my little Troll Druid (oooh bat-flight-form!) and create a role-playing story based around my character's embrace of the Emerald Dream during the Cataclysm caused by Deathwing. My story didn't become a finalist or even get an honorable mention, but fact that I was allowed to, invited to write the story in the first place, lit a fire under my butt. I wanted to create more stories in these worlds that I loved so much.

And you have become the defacto queen of fan-fiction. How do you choose which worlds to write in?

I have been writing myself into stories since I was a child. I couldn't watch my favorite shows without imagining myself as a character in that world. When read the Harry Potter or *Twilight* books, I imagined that I was not only a character in the books or an actor in the screen adaptation, but also J.K. Rowling or Stephenie Meyer themselves. I thought myself as a character in practically every television series I watched: *Battlestar Galactica*, *Doctor Who*, *Farcape*, *Supernatural*, *Lost*, and even the animated *Futurama*. I would fantasize that I was in the unique position to not only write the stories for the television show, but also bring my own character to life as an actor on the set. At school, working the concession counter at the movie theater, when I walked around my neighborhood, I brought these stories to life in my head. I just never thought about writing my little fantasies down on paper.

Until that writing contest?

Exactly. I once I had pulled my finger out of the dike and the ocean broke through the embankment and flooded my entire world. I wrote short-stories and teleplays and screenplays and with *The Weight of a Feather*, an entire novel. I never had the courage to send my teleplays or screenplays to Hollywood agents, though.

Why didn't you want to get your episodes actually on the air?

Some shows were open to submission, but most shows were explicitly against receiving teleplays that weren't from their own writing staffs. that weren't from agented writers with previous screen-credits. *Star Trek* had once said they were more open to receiving submissions from the fans, but by the time I starting writing down my stories, there wasn't a *Star Trek* series on the air anymore. I was able to gleam the insider knowledge that you didn't send a *Supernatural* script to *Supernatural*, but instead sent it to the producers of *True Blood*. Strangely you would be more likely to get onto the staff of *True Blood* with a *Supernatural* script than you would with a *True Blood* script. Maybe they would see the flaws in your characters more, since they were "their" characters. IDK? But I didn't have the courage to be rejected. Even today, now that I am a published author, I'm still petrified about rejection. And because of the controversy surrounding the publication of my Alistair Strange novel, I'm even more gun-shy than ever

Is that why you're conducting this interview over messenger?

In part. While the response at midnight release parties and the millions of sales have been a confirmation that I did the right thing writing my Alistair Strange novel, I have encountered the more destructive side of the Internet and social media: death threats.

Your life is being threatened? By Team Dracarys? Book nerds

are capable of issuing death threats?

Haven't you been on social media for the last decade or so? People on the Internet can't wait to any kind of offense, no matter how slight, just so they can attack. They not only look for reason to be offended themselves, they will be offended for other people, other groups. I can't tell you how many of my friends, friends that I know in real life, and get along with great, that I've had to unfollow on Facebook, because, while they are great, true, and honest friends in real-life, on Facebook they are insufferable.

Yes. I am continually surprised in my own news-feed how trollish my dearest friends get over the simplest, most innocuous posts.

And don't get me started on online multiplayer games. *League of Legends, Call of Duty, Eve Online,* even *World of Warcraft!* The spirit of competition has been transformed with a level of toxicity that is practically impossible to conceptualize as being a part of the human psyche. The Internet is home to the most worrisome trolls imaginable. The Internet Troll is egocentric, *only* their religion, political party, belief system, video-game ability is of any consequence, and everyone else is the enemy whom must be utterly destroyed. The Internet Troll is racist, anti-Semitic, and homophobic, misogynistic, spewing hatred and slurs like vomit. The Internet Troll has serious anger issues, I mean the kind that requires psychiatrist assistance and medication to be a functional member of society. The Internet Troll has a complete and utter lack of maturity and respect for other members of our society and our world-wide online community. The Internet Troll simply cannot admit when they are wrong, *only* their opinion matters, even when confronted with a litany of facts, they shut down, lash out, become even more trollish. The Internet Troll has learned the art of distilling all of their negativity into 140 characters.

The older generations look at Millennials and consider them to be the most self-centered, egotistic, slothful generation yet. How does that make you feel?

I'm not one to cry about this generation being the worst generation of all time. In 1952, Billy Graham thought the post-World-War-II generation was the worst generation imaginable, yet now Tom Brokaw believes they are the "Greatest Generation". Every older generation looks at the young generation as being incapable of inheriting the world, but we all grow up to be just like our parents. Every generation comes into their own by middle-age. So I don't fear for the Millennials, just as Baby Boomers no longer really fear Generation-X. We all mature.

Is trollish behavior a modern phenomenon or has this been simmering under the human psyche since ancient times?

I'm sure if the Egyptians or the Roman Empire had the Internet they'd be just as trollish. If they had cell phones, they'd be taking "dick-pics". Internet pornography would have horrified the young Apostolic Church as much as it offends modern Evangelical Christianity. Trollishness has been part of human psyche since we crawled out of the trees, but the Internet makes trollishness all the more accessible.

But this trollish behavior has not only caused your reclusivity, but Casey's was well.

Yes. Yes, it has. It is only a matter of time until an Internet Troll leaves the protection of humanity's newfound anonymity on the Internet, and actually acts on their words. Once they leave the world-wide-web and enter the real world, then they will promote themselves from being an Internet Troll to being a domestic terrorist. My editor has been submitting the emails and tweets from the so-called Team Dracarys that have been threatening my life to the FBI. Can you believe that? The Federal Bureau of Investigation has taken the case, my case. There is a case file open about me as a possible victim in a crime. I'm afraid to let anybody know what I look like, or where I live, because of the anger and resentment caused by the publication of my novel. I just wrote a book, for Christ's sake.

But you have taken over somebody else's book series? A series beloved by literally millions of people. They have poured their passions into the world of Alistair Strange. Surely, you didn't

*think there wouldn't be blow-back. The publisher chose to de-
throne Abigail K.C. Sterling as the author of Alistair Strange,
in favor of, I don't mean to offend you, but you're a usurper.*

I didn't expect the reaction to be so murderous. I kind of
feel that had I tried to write a sequel to the Holy Bible, instead of an "unauthorized" Alistair Strange book, I don't even
know. When writing my fan-fiction, I didn't think people held
Alistair Strange and his adventures so sacrosanct.

And what about books that are literally sacrosanct?

Exactly my point! Can you imagine the reaction from Christians and Christianity itself if I had had the arrogance to write
a sequel to the Bible, called–I don't know– The Next Testament. What if such a book existed? A book purporting to be
the Word of God given to a modern author in the early decades of the 21st century! The Old Testament tells the tales of
the Jewish Patriarchs and Prophets, beginning with Creation
itself and ending with a curse from Malachi, the last of the
Prophets of God. Furthermore, the Old Testament is the sin-
gular story of God's relationship with His Chosen People and
His promise of the coming of the Messiah, His Only Begotten Son, Jesus the Christ. Its Messianic prophecies could only
be fulfilled in the books of the New Testament, the second
Testament of the Holy Bible Trilogy. The New Testament tells
the Good News of the birth, ministry, crucifixion, and resurrection of Jesus of Nazareth and the infancy of the Apostolic
Christian Church. Moreover, the New Testament is the fulfillment of the Messianic prophecies of the Old Testament that
could only be fulfilled with the coming of the Messiah, God's
Only Begotten Son, Jesus the Christ. But it is more than this.
Its own Apocalyptic prophecies, by John of Patmos and Jesus
of Nazareth Himself, could only be fulfilled in the books of the
Next Testament, the third Testament of the Holy Bible Trilogy.
The Next Testament, on the surface, would tell the stories of
the infancy of the Apostolic Christian Church through to the
destruction of Jerusalem by the Romans. The Next Testament,
in reality, would be the fulfillment of the Apocalyptic prophe-

cies of the New Testament, which are believed by the majority of Christians to be events to be fulfilled in our own time, but were, in fact, fulfilled through the destruction of Jerusalem by the Romans in AD 70. Only in The Next Testament would you be able find the prophetic story Mysteriously left untold by the young Apostolic Church. The Word of God would have been silent for two thousand years, but now, the Holy Spirit would break this silence through the books of The Next Testament, being the third Testament of the Holy Bible Trilogy. Holy sh*t! The audacity!

That really would be the ultimate "fan-fiction".

It would. It truly world. To a devout Jew, the New Testament is probably seen as nothing more than Biblical "fan-fiction".

I wouldn't go there, if I were you.

No. No. I really shouldn't should I? The Internet Troll is a modern phenomenon, but religious persecution dates back to time immemorial. As a Roman Catholic, I was always struck by the fact that the Holy Bible just "stopped" after the beginning of the second century of the common era. Why didn't religious people keep writing "Biblical" books. Why didn't the inspirational writings just continue to be added to the Holy Bible? Weren't the Crusades worthy of having their own Crusadic (is that even a word?) Testament? Wasn't Joan of Arc worthy of having a book in yet another Testament? But then again, when you look at fan-bases today, that would have been a sh*t-show if there ever was one. I can't imagine how *Star Wars* fans are going to react to new films made by Disney. There is a reason by *Star Wars* movies and books are considered "canon". It is a very specific, and entirely accurate word. *Star Wars* fan-boys are elevated their reverence for these movies to the point of religious obsession. No story that Disney releases is going to be "worthy" of the title *Star Wars*. No writer or director will be distinguished enough. No new story will be canonical enough. Every sub-plot or character's action will be analyzed to see if it is "canonical". God forbid if there is any creativity or surprises. No actor or actress is going to be accepted playing a character set in the *Star Wars* universe. The casting of Jesus in a motion-picture will be met with less bitterness and resentment than the casting of a young Han Solo, or *-shudder-* the recasting of a beloved fan-favorite. And if an entirely new character doesn't seem to fit their vision of the *Star Wars* universe, the racist and misogynistic vitriol is going to be damn-near nuclear. This is exactly a reason why there haven't been new books written in the Holy Bible for two thousand years. *Star Wars* fans aren't likely to burn people at the stake. *Figuratively*, yes. *Literally*, no.

I'd be careful where you tread, Alex.

I don't mean to conflate new *Star Wars* movies and New Testaments to the Holy Bible. I offer my sincerest apologies to anyone reading this interview who may have taken offense at my stream of contentiousness.

Stream of "contentiousness"?

Stupid auto-correct. Stream of consciousness. LOL

But this is Playboy magazine, after all, we have a slightly more liberal readership. I really don't think fundamentalist Christians are reading this kind of "smut" for an Alex K.C. Silver interview.

True. True. That's a relief. Who really "reads" Playboy for the articles?

LOL. You have a pretty good concept. Maybe you should write The Next Testament of the Holy Bible Trilogy.

Oh, dear God, no. I don't even have that kind of audacity. All I've ever wanted was to write *Star Trek* or *Doctor Who* episodes, a *Star Wars* movie. This is where my passions lie. Pop-culture. I just wanted to tell a Alistair Strange story. And Casey wasn't writing them. I don't see what I did as all that terrible.

On the bright side. Team Griffindico has your back. Despite the near-riot at the Manhattan bookstore, the midnight release parties were a confirmation that many of the fans were eager to make your book an instant New York Times bestseller. I can't remember a time when a first time author sold millions of books within the first few hours of publication.

It was so much fun. I happened to sneak into my local book-store. It was a good thing nobody knows what I looked like. I looked like any other Stranger, who cosplayed as their favorite Alistair Strange character. The Strangers seemed genuinely ex-cited to read my novel. The bookstore employees hosted trivia contents. There was, of course, a costume contest, which is always so exciting to see the level of detail Strangers are willing to put into their cosplay. At the stroke of midnight, the lines started to move and Strangers clutched their new Alex K.C. Silver novels to their chests as they hurried through the doors, to the cars, so they could get home as quickly as possible to begin reading the latest adventures of Alistair Strange. Teenage girls were crying.

You got no hint of the riots, the tensions that were escalating in New York City.

There were passionate debates between Teams Griffindico and Dracarys about the legitimacy of new novel, but thankfully we were all oblivious to everything that was unfortunately occur-ring in Manhattan.

When did you learn about the violence confrontations between Teams Griffindico and Dracarys?

I got a text-messages from my editor, warning me that tensions had boiled over in New York. That Strangers had been arrest-ed and the midnight release party canceled. I couldn't believe things had escalated so quickly in the real-world. I had hoped the war between Teams Griffindico and Dracarys would be relegated to Twitter, Facebook, and the comments sections of blogs. I didn't want the trollishness of the Internet to turn into real-world arrests. That hurts my heart to think that Strangers, whether they were Team Griffindico or Team Dracarys were spending the night in a Manhattan jail-cell. That is no place for a passionate fan to find themselves for the crime of attend-ing a midnight release party.

But their crimes were not limited to simply attending a mid-night release party. The protests of Team Dracarys escalated into violence. Punches were thrown. Mace was sprayed. The

Manhattan bookstore looked like a war-zone.

And it pains me even now. The emotions are still so raw. It only happened a few days ago. I don't know if the Strangers, our little community of devoted Alistair Strange fans will ever recover.

What do you think it will take to heal the wounds caused by this "civil war" between the two factions of fans?

IDK. It is certainly an unstable situation. I think the only person who can heal these wounds is the one person whose wounds many never ever heal: Abigail K.C. Sterling.

Are you saying you regret having wounded Abigail K.C. Sterling by usurping her literary creation?

Yes. Most certainly. I never wrote my novel to usurp her throne. This isn't a Game of Thrones were I plotted and planned to take her throne from her. There was no scheming or dreaming of her figurative assassination. But in the end, that is exactly what I ended up participating in. Hindsight being twenty-twenty, my editor– her editor– was as silver tongued as Tyrion Lannister, manipulating a young and foolish upstart into claiming a throne– THE throne– that doesn't belong to them. I had no right, no copyright to write my novel in the first place. And my editor had no right, no copyright to manipulate the situation as she did by relieving Casey of her rightful place as the queen of her literary world. This was assassination through legal maneuverings– nothing more and nothing less. I had no right to sit on Casey's throne. And yet, as I sit on the throne, the demands have begun.

I'm not sure what you mean by "demands"?

The sixth novel in the Alistair Strange series. As the usurper to the throne, I am being forced to fulfill the obligations of she who sits on the throne. The sixth novel is now my responsibility. I never thought beyond *The Weight of the Feather*, and now, I am alone being expected to continue the series. I don't know where to go with the series. I never thought beyond writing fan-fiction of a fictitious "fifth" novel in the Alistair Strange series. And now, I am the ruler of Casey's literary world. The fates of characters are in my hands alone. The direction this world takes is mine alone to determine. I have been crowned by the very act of publication as her legitimate heir and successor – heavy is the head that wears the crown.

Chapter Sixteen
Let's Start a Riot!
Dracarys vs. Griffindico

by alistairstrange#1fan

I spent last night in jail. I feel the same joy and ex-hilaration that my parent's felt going to jail for their civil rights, anti-war, hippy-dippy counter-culture beliefs. They knew the previous generation were wrong, just as I feel that the publication of that abomination of a novel is wrong (and no, I don't feel bad for comparing my parent's noble protests with my own).

Jail was as scary, if not more so, than I could have possibly imagined. Thankfully, the holding cell I was placed in for the shockingly long night was filled with fellow Team Dracarys members. But there were enough prostitutes, gang-members, and other violent female offenders that I never felt safe. And being unable to leave, being imprisoned, was claustrophobic and my paranoias began to spin out of control. I like feeling like I can leave. If I go to a party, I like to drive myself because I don't want to be beholden to anyone else's time-table. If I want to go home, I simply go home. Even being in a traffic jam creates that feeling of imprisonment that I detest. I don't think I can ever watch my beloved *The Shawshank Redemption* again, because my experience of prison is now so overwhelming.

But in the end, I feel that it was worth it. When the Team Dracarys Facebook page announced they were going to protest the midnight release party for *Alistiar Strange and the Weight of a Feather* in Manhattan, I drove into New York, parked my car in a parking garage, and took the subway to the station nearest the bookstore. What did the Manhattanites think when they saw a twenty-something young women dressed in her Alistair Strange cosplay holding four handmade poster-board signs?

There were dozens of protesters when I arrived at the midnight release party. But we were dwarfed by the ungodly number of Team Griffindico and other curious book readers standing in line. There was an outside line! The bookstore was filled to the point of violating fire codes! How is this possible? This was blasphemy! They were disregarding every core tenant of being a Stranger!

The protests were peaceful– until they weren't. The riot came completely out of the blue. It was a few minutes after the stroke of midnight, when that first cosplaying Team Griffindico came out holding a pristine first pressing of *Alistair Strange and the Weight of a Feather*. She shoved the book into <u>my</u> face. Of all the faces of Team Dracarys she could have shoved that non-canonical blasphemy, she chose to shove it in mine! And I shoved back. That's all it was was a shove. And all hell broke loose.

Punches were thrown. Kicks were landed. Pepper spray

was, well, sprayed. At first Team Dracarys had seemed to have the overwhelming numbers because the number of Team Griffindico outside the store, those who had already purchased their books were few because it was only a few minutes after midnight. And while the bookstore was filled to violating fire-codes, the blocks-long outside line was, well, outside. They must have been fed up by our protest, our calling them names, our cursing, our vulgarity, our general Internet trollishness, because when that first coplaying member of Team Griffindico went down, the line disintegrated and they rushed us. The once peaceful protest had become a full-on riot (of course, I know now that is how it always starts). The few security guards hired to keep the peace were far too few and far between and by the time police arrived, the riot had spilled into the bookstore. Books were knocked off shelves, shelves were pushed over. Some fools decided to use the excuse of the riot to steal from the cash-registers, and others began to loot the store. You see this kind of behavior on the news during an L.A. riot or in the aftermath of a natural disaster.

I don't know how civilized people attending a midnight release party for a young adult fantasy novel and a peaceful protest can turn into savages so quickly.

Who knew that the tinderbox that is our passion for a fictional literary universe was so explosive? I am proud that I went to protest. There is a strange joy and exhilaration that comes from being part of a mob and a riot, as strange as that sounds. Now, having spent my first night in jail, having for the first time punched someone in the face, having been kicked when I was knocked down, that is all foolishness. It is a stupid book.

That is why when I finally got home after being bailed out by my parents (how embarrassing is that) I went to my local bookstore and bought a copy of *The Weight of a Feather*. I wanted, no needed, to know what why we rioted. I wasn't going to let my passion and love for Abigail K.C. Sterling turn me into a uncivilized savage.

I am going to read this book and enjoy it. Freaking-aye.

[Update}: I've got one word for you: "horsesh*t". It doesn't even do fan-fiction proud. I've read the *Fifty Shades of Grey* and those novels are AWFUL, with a capital A and W and F and U and L. How they started out as *Twilight* fan-fiction shouldn't freaking surprise anyone. I've read <u>Bored of the Rings</u> by the National Lampoon, it was literally my father's favorite book. No, he never bothered to read the immortal <u>The Lord of the Rings</u> by J.R.R.-freaking-Tolkien, but he'd sit down and read that parody crap. And E.L. James novels aren't even laughable parodies of BDSM, and I DON'T KNOW ANYTHING ABOUT BDSM, but I know Mr. Grey is laughably tame and inconsistent with what the community is probably actually like. *The Weight of the Feather* is also laughable. The author attempts to write in Casey's voice, but fails on every account, there is no poetic prose. She tries so hard to be the master mimic, that she understands Casey's voice, but she doesn't understand her <u>soul</u>. I truly hope she has grown as a writer in the subsequent years, because her version of Alistair strange is horsesh*t.

If she is going to master "fan-fiction" I hope she attempts to write is other "voices" before returning to the Alistair Strange universe. I'm sure she could learn at the literary teat of someone like IDK Charles Dickens. If she could masterfully mimic that esteemed literary voice in such a way that the reader couldn't tell what was written by Mr. Dickens and what was written by her, then she could call herself a master of "fan-fiction". Well, write me a play in Shakespearean verse and I'll bow down before you and call you <u>Master</u>, instead of a talentless hack.

"I was on a train of lies. I couldn't jump off."
   –Clifford Irving

Chapter Seventeen
The Loud Silence of Recluses

—Internal Memo—

To: Christopher Hanson, Publisher
From: Iris Reilly, editor

You advised me– nay, ordered me– to begin preparing Alex K.C. Silver and her novel, *Alistair Strange and the Weight of a Feather*, for publication. You believed Abigail K.C. Sterling to be a latter-day Howard Hughes, far too eccentric and reclusive in her fame to contest the publication of this sham of a fifth novel in the Alistair Strange series.

The first tweet you authorized received overwhelming elation in his fans, whom call themselves Strangers. They couldn't believe after all these years and those two infamous tweets, that they would have another "Casey for Christmas". Only you weren't delivering to them a "Casey for Christmas", instead we are publishing an "AleX for Xmas". The second tweet of the title of the novel a few hours later caused much confusion and consternation. Many Strangers had already encountered a fan-fiction entitled *Alistair Strange and the Weight of a Feather*. And the third tweet announcing Alex K.C. Silver as the author who would continue the series was... the words absolutely fail me. Murderous? Nuclear? Apocalyptic?

You, like Clifford Irving before you, believed she like "Hughes would never to able to surface to deny it, or else [she] wouldn't bother." You believed there would be no repudiation, no protestations, no denouncements from her concerning our continuing her series, because of, not in spite of, her reclusiveness. Why, in the words of Jean le Malchanceux, did you believe, "You may look for motive in an act, but only after the act has been committed. An effect creates not only the search for a cause, but the reality of the cause itself. I must warn you, however, that the attempt to establish relationships between acts and motives, effects and causes, is one of the most time-wasting games ever invented by man. Do you know why you kicked the cat this morning? Or gave a sou to that beggar? Or set forth for Jerusalem rather than Gomorrah?"

Ms. Sterling had not communicated with me or anyone else at our house, nor been seen in public, and had been utterly silent for over eight years, save for two tweets that could be chalked up as an aberration. She was not nearly as eccentric and reclusive as Howard Hughes, but she certainly would give Harper Lee a run for her money.

And you were proven correct. Ms. Sterling sent no emails, no direct messages, nor any phone calls. Her lawyers sent no cease-and-desist letters. There were no challenges– legal, public, or otherwise– to our plans to publish *The Weight of a Feather* as the "official" fifth novel in the Alistair Strange series.

Promotional materials were sent out to bookstores. Midnight release parties scheduled. And pre-ordering opened. Your stern-in-the-face-of-adversity belief in the profitability and popularity of this continuation novel was confirmed by overwhelming pre-orders and a mind-boggling amount of media attention. Readers and critics divided themselves into two camps: Team Dracarys, whom remain to this day devoted to Abigail K.C. Sterling and Team Griffindico, whom were more open to receiving Alex K.C. Silver as the new heir-apparent. The Twitter wars between Teams and numerous Reddits threads were continuous from your first tweet to the publication of the novel only several days ago.

The midnight release parties were a cause for concern. The number of people that turned out to purchase Alex's novel were staggering. We knew that Team Griffindico would turn out in droves to read the continuation novel, but the number of fans who were did not count themselves on either Teams Dracarys or Griffindico and the curious readers who had never read an Alistair Strange novel turned out in droves. Yes, there were protests by Team Dracarys, but those, for the most part, were peaceful. Loud, often vulgar, words were exchanged, but the passions Team Dracarys reserved for Casey and Team Griffindico had for <u>any</u> new Alistair Strange novel, for the most part, never translated into violence. There were no riots to speak of–except the one in Manhattan. But that was an aberration. We won't speak of it.

And once the book was finally released, the critical response has been shockingly and overwhelmingly-positive. The book has been received as the "official" fifth novel, by most of the critics, and at least half of the Strangers. Even the rash of one-star Amazon reviews by Team Dracarys has not crushed our average due the sheer number of four and five starred reviews from Team Griffindico.

No doubt, our Hollywood partners are just as ecstatic as you are concerning the stunning response. Production on *Alistair Strange and the Weight of a Feather* has apparently already begun. A few of the actors have protested the exclusion of Abigail K.C. Sterling as author of the series, but these actors are already being recast with strikingly familiar doppelgängers.

The reason I had contacted you via this memo is not to rehash history. I only wanted to remind of the situation you have put us in, because—

—I have received my first communication from Abigail K.C. Sterling in over eight years. It is an email, from a verified email address she has used in communication before. There was no message. Just an attachment. A Word document for the fifth novel in the Alistair Strange series. <u>Her</u> fifth novel. In <u>her</u> series.

The gauntlet has been thrown down!

"Publishing a book is like stuffing a note into a bottle and hurling it into the sea. Some bottles drown, some come safe to land, where the notes are read and then possibly cherished, or else misinterpreted, or else understood all too well by those who hate the message. You never know who your readers might be."
—Margaret Atwood

Chapter Eighteen

Galleys and Proof I Am an Author

O! Muse,

Oh my God, I don't think I can survive. My heart is pounding. My mind is racing. I got the call, that call, from my agent. The call I have been awaiting for. The thirty-ninth time was the charm, Muse. I have an editor at a major publishing house wanting my book. My book! She has made her offer to my agent and my agent is going to begin the negotiations with my new editor. My editor. How glorious are those two words together?

My editor!

O! Muse,

The editing process is far more painful than I had anticipated. I wrote, then rewrote, rewrote, and rewrote my manuscript until positively sang. There were no extraneous words. The plots wove in and out of each other brilliantly. The characters, even the antagonist, were fully-fleshed out three-dimensional, five sensational people.

But I received my first red (scalpel) pen bloodiest manuscript. This time I was convinced I sent it off looking like Julia Roberts. The manuscript had been made up for a Hollywood premiere with all the glitz and glamour imaginable. The dress had been selected. The hair and make-up done. And then Joan Rivers and her daughter decided to go on their E! Oscar special as slash her repeatedly, her blood staining the equally red carpet.

And it hurt, Muse. It hurt so much! It was so painful to see the criticisms my editor had with the book. There didn't seem to be anything she liked about the entire manuscript. Why had she bought it in the first place if she thought it was this... damaged.

I sat and I cried.

I propped myself up in bed, with my laptop on my lap and the bloodied manuscript by my side. As I read her honest critiques and brutal criticisms, I began to get the strange, paradoxical feeling that she only had my best interests at heart. Page after page, I began to see my novel through her trained, seasoned, and professional eyes. I was the amateur. I was the one to whom this was the first novel.

I copied and then renamed the word processor file, so I could be sure to separate the original manuscript from the first edited one. I had steeled myself just let go. I don't know if there is a Zen to writing, but I decided that I wasn't going to fight. I wanted to see what this novel was that she envisioned. When I was done with the revision, I would print it out, go down to my favorite coffee shop, and read with new eyes her preferred version of my story. Then and only then would I fight her.

It was not easy to say the least. There were times when I saw her edits and her suggestions and I burst into tears. I couldn't imagine how she didn't like what I had done with my own story.

But, time and time again, I tried to center myself, be Zen, and trust the Sensei. There was a peace, a serenity to my absolute surrender to her will. We were in this fight together. She was preparing me, my manuscript, to enter the real world where the attacks would be very real and deadly. She was preparing us for the coming battle to win over the hearts and minds of the book buyers and defeat the harshness of critics through beautiful, graceful, poetic prose.—

—I took the revised manuscript to the coffeeshop and sat with my latte and read. I had my own red (scalpel) pen readied to correct any errant spelling and grammatical errors, but also use that very same keen editorial eye to critique the revision and if necessary defend to the very death the decisions I made in my final (first?) draft.

And I have to say, Muse, I was shocked and horrified by how much I enjoyed and respected the revision. My editor only wanted the best out of me. Her only desire was for this novel to be the best book not only possible, but imaginable. The one of the few people who believed in me. Believed in my story. This is another strange paradox to writing. She criticized me *because* she believed in me.

O! Muse,

There were, of course, more critiques and criticisms. There were more revisions. They became fewer and farther between. Then the manuscript was locked and sent to the copy-editor to ensure all spelling, grammatical, and punctuation errors were corrected. He researched all of my mythology to insure that I was consistent throughout the book, that any terminology that wasn't original with me was correct and consistent. Any factual data was accurate, except when for supernatural or plot reasons, it didn't need to be accurate.

I had read in the delightful "Note on the Text" of *The Lord of the Rings*, that the compositor working for the Houghton Mifflin Company had made "well-intentioned 'corrections' to [Tolkien's] sometimes idiosyncratic usage. These 'corrections' include altering of *dwarves* to *dwarfs*, *elvish* to *elifsh*, *further* to *farther*, *nastutians* to *nasturtiums*, *try and say* to *try to say*, and ('worst' to Tolkien) *elven* to *elfin*." How is that for a kick in the pants? To have "invented languages and delicately constructed nomenclatures" only to have a compositors "errors, and inconsistencies impede both the understanding and the appreciation of serious readers."

I would have been just as horrified as Professor Tolkien if my novel reached the shelves "corrected". My own novel was like Professor Tolkien's in that they were both fantastical in nature and I had invented my own terminology and albeit simple languages (when compared to Professor Tolkien), and I encountered these very same "corrections" from my own copy-editor. I understand the art of the copy-editor and their passion for the English language, but sometimes their precision impedes the imagination.

O! Muse,

The galleys and proofs came in today. I had been sent various sketches and compositions of cover ideas to get my feedback and selections. The skills of these artists and graphic designers is beyond comprehension. The fonts chosen, the images drawn, even in their rough state, were exquisite. And when I opened the package with the final cover galley and an honest to God copy of the book, the proof.

Muse, you can't possibly understand the excitement and giddiness that comes from holding the book, your book, in your hands. You've seen it on the computer screen. You've seen in printed in manuscript form. You've seen the manuscript bloodied like Mary Kelley. And now, I get to see the book as the readers to see the book.

Suddenly. This. Was. Real.

The weight of the hard-cover book just felt... right. I don't know. When the editor and her superiors were debating whether my novel, being a first novel, deserved a trade-cloth (publishing speak for a "hard-cover" book) release or just a trade-paperback (that bigger non-"mass market paperback" paperback book). I had hoped for the former, as did my editor, but this was a decision more up to the accountants than anyone else. And in the end, my editor had prevailed. My book would receive a trade-cloth edition.

I sat in bed, with my legs bent, and propped the book up in

my lap. And I read it. I read *The XII Labors of Alistair Strange* for the very first time. That overwhelming feeling of narcissism came flooding back. I felt a sinful pleasure in the enjoyment of my own novel. And it had been so long since I had any real contact with the text of my own novel, after completing the revision process and the manuscript was locked. I had that Writer's Amnesia, but magnified to the n-th degree. I couldn't believe I had written even a single word of that beautiful, graceful, poetic prose. It was the most wonderful kind of experience.

I. Pray. All. Authors. Feel. At. Least. Once.

Chapter Nineteen

Polygamist Contracts– The Sister-Wives Scandal

—Transcription of a Meeting—

Christopher Hanson: We find ourselves in an untenable situation. The elation we felt by the overwhelming success of our release of *Alistair Strange and the Weight of a Feather* has been deflated. *The Weight of a Feather* had millions of pre-orders. The midnight releases as successful, if not more so, than previous midnight releases for *The Clash of the Olympians*, *The Dark Seas Sleeper*, and *Those Whom the Gods Detest Should Not Be Unearthed*. These reasons for my desire to publish the so-called "fan-fiction" novel by Alex K.C. Sterling are numerous, but the primary focus was solely the continuation of the Alistair Strange series. Abigail K.C.

Sterling had become a recluse. She missed deadline after deadline after deadline. She refused to any form of communication:
email, telephone, or in-person. I feel this is strange considering
how early in her career, she embraced her fans, whom call themselves Strangers. She held a midnight release party for *The Dark
Seas Sleeper* at Madison Square Garden, which has gone into the
Guinness Book of World Records for largest midnight novel release party. Because of this lack of communication, I was advised
that we were within out rights to continue the series without the
participation nor input of Ms. Sterling.

Brett Walton, Esq.: We are within our rights according to the legal and binding contract that was signed between Ms. Sterling
and our publishing house. The wording while ambiguous has
proven to be iron-clad. There has been no response from Ms.
Sterling's lawyers, who must have realized the meaning and ram-
ifications of the same wording as we have and have chosen not to
pursue legal action. I believe Ms. Reilly, the editor of the Alistair
Strange series, has received no communications from the author

Iris Reilly: No emails. No phone calls. No in-person meetings. Until the publication of *The Weight of a Feather*, there has been no
contact from Ms. Sterling in over eight years.

Hanson: I must reiterate our frustrations at a lack of a manuscript.
Iris has set repeated deadlines for Ms. Sterling to meet for the
delivery of a manuscript and each deadline has come and gone
without a manuscript in our hands. We are not alone in our consternation. The Hollywood studio that holds the film rights to
the series has put the pressure on us to force Ms. Sterling to
deliver a manuscript, so that a screenplay could be adapted and
production begin on the fifth film in the series.

Walton: I have reviewed the contract granting the film rights and
the wording benefits Ms. Sterling, for the most part. Their film
rights at first glance seem to be limited to stories written and
published by Abigail K.C. Sterling, this includes the previous
four novels and the numerous short stories published in various
magazines in cooperation with our publishing house. This is the

key phrase in their contract with Ms. Sterling. "In cooperation with [our publishing house]". If the work in question is authorized for publication by our publishing house, they hold the film rights to said work. This now includes *The Weight of a Feather*.

Reilly: I hate to be the bearer of bad news. But the loud silence from Ms. Sterling has been broken. I received an email last night from a verified account. The email contained no message, only an attachment: a Word document for <u>her</u> fifth novel in the Alistair Strange series. I have gone completely without sleep. I spent the entire evening and most of this morning reading her manuscript. Because of her extreme reclusiveness, we began to doubt her mental faculties and her ability to write another novel. In her silence, we began to believe she has hesitant for whatever reason to write her novel. Perhaps, she had the worst case of Writer's Block in modern history. Perhaps, the fame and fortune she acquired had compelled her to withdraw from modern society completely. We simply don't know. But now that I have her manuscript and have read much of the novel in a binge-reading session that has left me weary from lack of sleep. I can state, emphatically, that this novel is her greatest achievement. It is spell-binding. It is beautiful. It is graceful. It is poetic. She is at the height of her powers.

Hanson: Where does this leave us? Legally speaking.

Walton: We were completely within our rights to publish *The Weight of a Feather*, with or without the permission or input from Ms. Sterling. Legally, we are sound. She could, of course, sue us and we would be forced to defend ourselves in a court battle that could last for last years. If we were to secure a trial by judge, we would be on much more stable ground, but if she and her lawyers insist on and receive a jury trial, we would be susceptible with the whims and emotions of a jury of her peers. This includes any Strangers in the jury box.

Hanson: For the time being, Ms. Sterling is continuing to be reclusive, despite having delivered her manuscript. We haven't heard a word in actual communication from her. What does she think of our publication of *The Weight of a Feather*? Why has she waited this long to deliver her manuscript for her own fifth novel in the series? What is her motivation and intentions for emailing that manuscript

Walton: We don't know. We won't know until she decides to communicate. Until then, we must keep knowledge of this manuscript between the three of us, the secretary not withstanding. No one else can know that she has not only written but delivered a manuscript no matter how late said delivery is. The fanbase has already been split into Teams Dracarys and Griffindico. If Team Dracarys were to learn that Ms. Sterling has written and delivered the manuscript, we would be placed in an untenable situation.

Reilly: This is the Internet age. Not even the government can keep secrets with the tweet happy world we know find ourselves in. It only takes one Tweet from Ms. Sterling to expose our duplicity in keeping this knowledge from the fans. No. We cannot hide this knowledge. We need to let the literary world and Team Dracarys know that Ms. Sterling has written the long-awaited fifth novel in <u>her</u> series.

Hanson: Are you mad? We cannot let the literary community know that we published a continuation novel when Ms. Sterling had already written her novel.

Walton: We were within our rights to publish that novel. She hadn't delivered the manuscript. She missed deadline, after deadline, after deadline. We didn't even know the manuscript for her fifth novel even existed.

Hanson: That won't matter in the minds of public opinion. In the eyes of the Strangers, they will only see that we weren't patient enough. That we should have waited until Hell froze over for Ms. Sterling to deliver her manuscript. And now that she has? What is our best course of action.

Walton: We keep this between the three of us.

Reilly: We publish Ms. Sterling's novel.

Hanson: What?

Walton: Have you lost your mind?

Reilly: It is our only course of action. I expedite the editing of her novel. We accelerate the designing of her book, get a marketing plan in place, sales representatives and publicists preparing for the flood of media attention.

Hanson: And what do we do with *The Weight of a Feather*? We have published it. We devoted months of attention to its promotion. There are millions of copies in print. Less, of course, the millions we sold at the midnight release and over the past few days. But there are still millions of copies still unsold sitting on the shelves and back-rooms of bookstores and in warehouses around the world. Do we just destroy them all? We have spent millions of dollars promoting it as the one true fifth novel in the series. And now, we tell the entire world, the fans, the critics, and our book-stores-partners that was all a lie. There is *another* one true fifth novel. Do we say, "Oops"? And try to let bygones be bygones? The fans and media will crush us, crucify us We have not only betrayed Abigail K.C. Sterling, but in their minds, we betrayed *them*!

Reilly: We are in a situation not unlike what HBO finds themselves in with the *Game of Thrones*. George R.R. Martin, like our own Ms. Sterling, has waited years, missing repeated self-imposed deadlines to deliver the manuscript of *The Winds of Winter*, the sixth novel in his *A Song of Ice and Fire* book series. Due to the uniqueness of HBO's contract with Mr. Martin, they are, some-how, able to continue the television series beyond that of the book series. The fans of *A Song of Ice and Fire* have had, up until this point, had the advantage over the television series audience. They knew that Ned Stark was killed in the first book back in 1996. They knew every plot-line, every betrayal, and every death of a main and beloved character. Now the television audience for the *Games of Thrones* is getting the advancement in the story that the book readers will still have to wait for.

Walton: But those are two different mediums: novels and television adaptations. Television rights often give more freedom to the

Hollywood producers to expand and continue the story beyond that of the source materials. *We* published someone else's continuation novel. Now, we have Ms. Sterling's own continuation novel. We are caught between a legal rock and a hard place.

Reilly: But the readers still don't know what the story of *The Winds of Winter* is. How much of story has been outlined by Mr. Martin. The producers of the *Game of Thrones*, no doubt, has access to this outline and are in constant communication with Mr. Martin, but there will be differences. There were already numerous deviations between *A Song of Fire and Ice* and the television series in the later seasons of the *Game of Thrones*. The television show will end long before the sixth book is published. It's like there are two parallel, alternate reality story lines happening simultaneously. Which is canon? Which takes precedence? This will be up to the television and book audiences to decide amongst themselves.

Walton: But we can't publish two different fifth novels in the Alistair Strange series. That will cause confusion and chaos.

Hanson: No. No. I kind of like where Ms. Reilly is going with this.

Walton: I beg your pardon.

Reilly: Ms. Sterling already introduced an alternate parallel universe storyline in, what was it, the *Those Whom the Gods Detest Should Not Be Unearthed?*

Hanson: Yes! I see the wheels turning, Iris. This is getting exciting.

Reilly: We can spin the real world chaos between the two authors, the two books, and use the continuity of the world of Alistair Strange to justify the publication of two different novels. Two different alternate, parallel story-lines playing out simultaneously. One fifth novel following this parallel universe storyline by Alex K.C. Silver and the other fifth novel following another storyline by Abigial K.C. Sterling. We will give the readers the best of both worlds.

Walton: And what if our two contracted authors do not agree with our decisions to publish both books.

Reilly: If the contract with Ms. Sterling is ambiguous enough to allow us to publish *The Weight of a Feather* without her permission, then I doubt there was any wording in Alex K.C. Silver's contract that would hinder us. Their contracts only guarantee the publication of the novels they have written. So, we will publish them both.

Hanson: Iris, begin working with Ms. Sterling's manuscript immediately.

Walton: And what of the sixth novels? Are we going to dedicate ourselves to publishing two sixth novels? Two seventh novels? Two eighth novels? Are we going to cannibalize our own audience.

Hanson: I actually don't see why we can't have our cake and eat it too. If the sales of Ms. Sterling's previous four novels and the overwhelming response to Alex's *The Weight of a Feather*, there is an insatiable appetite for novels set in the world of Alistair Strange. This situation that we have found ourselves in through Ms. Sterling's reclusiveness and Alex's passion and devotion to the series that inspired the writing of *The Weight of a Feather*, have put us in the position to double our profits within the same literary series. Imagine how ecstatic the Hollywood studio will be when they discover they can have twice as many Alistair Strange films.

Walton: This is without precedence, Mr. Hanson.

Hanson: Aren't lawyers always dreaming of setting precedence? We are in uncharted waters. We can make the most out of this situation.

Walton: And if Ms. Sterling decides to turn down our offer to publish both fifth novels simultaneously? She would be within her rights to remove the book from publication.

Reilly: She has submitted her manuscript to us. She has fulfilled her obligation to us. According to the wording of her contract: *[reading]* "Publisher has the right of final approval of Author's manuscript. Publisher may assign an editor to work with Author in making revisions. The Author will be notified prior to any and all substantial changes, which will be made only with the Author's approval and participation...Publisher may make corrections of typographical errors without Author's consent." If we accept her manuscript as she wrote it, we are free to publish it as submitted. Wouldn't we be within our rights to continue the publication process <u>with or without</u> Ms. Sterlings permission or input?

Walton: My own words have come back to haunt me. But yes. We would be within our rights.

Transcribed by Patricia Stone

"I've been imitated so well I've heard people copy my mistakes."
    –Jimi Hendrix

Chapter Twenty

Shakespeare by any other name

To my Constant Critic,

You have been in my corner for the entirety of our friendship. You have been my mentor, my editor, and my Constant Critic. You do not delight in editing my stories with such brutal honesty, but you understand the necessity of having another set of trusted eyes on a book. Other friends and my family read my stories and I get half-hearted congratulations about how wonderful and excellent a writer I have become.

I don't want that. I don't need that.

What I do need at the moment is some of your the wisdom you have imparted to me over the years of your mentorship. We are both immense and devoted fans of Alistair Strange. You

yourself
first introduced me to Ms. Sterling's world. You were
the first of our friends, despite being well into your
fifties, to cosplay at the midnight book release party
for *Clash of the Olympians*. You've accompanied me to
the midnight premieres of the films with the rest of our
friends, whom also count themselves as Strangers.

I wrote my entire *The Weight of a Feather* novel in
secret and seclusion. I didn't even tell you that I was
writing it, until it was almost too late. I had almost
uploaded the file to the fan-fiction website when I decided to come clean. You read it without criticism that
I was writing "fan-fiction". You edited my manuscript
until it screamed bloody murder and then over the
course of several rewrites, it began to truly sing. You
never once criticized my decision to write within the
world of Alistair Strange, nor my intention to publish
it on the Internet.

What concerns me most at the moment is. I know
that I haven't stolen someone else words and passed
them off as my own. I have instead stolen someone
else's character and their world, making it my own.

Am... I... A... Plagiarist?

Sincerely...

My dear friend,

What's in a name? That which we call Shakespeare-
by any other name would smell just as sweet? This
thing that you call "fan-fiction" is a far older and far
wiser and far more respected vocation than anyone in
this digital Internet age comprehends.

I personally think the Earl of Oxford wrote Shakespeare. If you don't agree, there are some awfully funny

coincidences to explain away... I'm not alone in my feelings. Freud was adamant about it. Olivier and Gielgud, arguably the greatest Shakespearian actors of my generation, believed as I do. Mark Twain, for criminy sakes wrote a book about it! Emerson? Whitman! How could you possibly not?

There is an argument made that Edward de Vere took the *nom-de-plum* William Shakespeare and presented plays as such? Why? Is it because as a member of the aristocracy, an Earl of Oxford couldn't been seen writing something as common as plays?

But a *nom-de-plum*? Heavens, no. I'm not suggesting anything of the sort. Not a "pen-name". Mercy. Not even a pseudonym. An allonym. This is a completely different literary creature all together. A wicked little fraud and deceit utilized by many of the greatest philosophers, wordsmiths, statesmen, and, yes, apostles. This is what allonymous is all about.

A pseudonym is writing under a fictional name not your own and anonymous is writing under no name. Allonymous writing is writing under an actual historical person's name.

Why would anyone want to publish under someone else's name? Since you asked, Alex, I will answer. Are you a plagiarist?

Heavens, no. It's the exact opposite of plagiarism. Plagiarism is taking someone else's words and claiming they are your own. Allonymous is taking your words and claiming they are someone else's words. They can't be any more different.

Then it's more akin to forgery, huh?

Again, you can't be more wrong. Forgery is taking, say, the Mona Lisa and painting another Mona Lisa and passing yours off as the original Mona Lisa. Allonymous is painting something new and exciting and saying, "Look! This could be an entirely new Leonardo

DaVinci."

In the opinion of many, it's worse than plagiarism and forgery.

Oh, ye of little faith! It is grand and glorious. And it is far more common than one would think. After Plato's death, his students continued writing philosophical tracts in his name. No one in their time or for hundreds, nay, thousands of years, thought this was in any way deceitful. They were carrying on Plato's own tradition by continuing his thought... in his name. This is writing allonymously.

Alexander Hamilton, one of the founding fathers of our country, wrote with a couple of compatriots, the *Federalist Papers* under the name of the Roman official Publius. This gave the *Papers* and, ultimately the young nation, an air of historicity it desperately needed. Are these great men frauds and their words fraudulent?

Was William Ireland a forger for publishing *Vortigern and Rowena* and *William the Conqueror* as authentic Shakespeare? If Shakespeare didn't actually write Shakespeare, how can we fault Ireland for writing "Shakespeare"? There were many plays written during Shakespeare's own lifetime that people of his day thought were actually written by Shakespeare. There was no doubt whatsoever in the minds of audiences and critics that these suspect plays were written by William Shakespeare. These plays are now considered "apocryphal" because scholars say they may not have been actually written by the pen of William Shakespeare of Stratford-upon-Avon. Ironically, there is some scholarly movement lately concerning *Two Noble Kinsmen* and *Edward III*, which says that these two once apocryphal plays are actually part of the legitimate Shakespearean canon. Hilarious.

Who is to say, who wrote what? Scholars? Bah. Did Moses write the Torah or was it some Hebrew priest hundreds of years after the fact? Did Matthew write Gospel of Matthew? Or Luke Luke? Many scholars… hmmph… think a disciple of Paul actually wrote at least one of the letters attributed to Paul. Is the Word of God any less the word of God because of the writer? Is Shakespeare any less Shakespearean if written by Edward de Vere? The words are the words are the words.

Some people have a stick up their butt about authenticity. Is Hamlet any less magnificent if written by the Earl? Or a woman as some others suppose. Scholars claim that if Shakespeare didn't write Shakespeare than all is for naught. The plays are brilliant no matter their authorship. Shakespeare or de Vere? Apocryphal or canon? Casey or Alex? It does not matter.

Always your friend

"Create your own visual style... let it be unique for yourself and yet identifiable for others
—Orson Welles

Chapter Twenty-One
H for Hoax
An Introduction

Hoaxery (not exactly a word, but are we splitting hairs over faking a word?) requires intuitive forethought with a premeditated and conscious effort to deceive. Not the least of which require the skills of:

- CONFIDENCE MAN: The art of the "long con", as grifters like to call it, begins long before the mark ever meets him and essentially and effectively ends the moment the mark truly believes that the idea is actually theirs. The hoaxer knows intuitively that he will be believed because of (not in spite of) the believability and/or ridiculousness of his idea.
- MASTER FORGER AND COUNTERFEITER: The forger and counterfeiter agonize over the slightest imperfection of the color or

texture of the paper, the chemicals used to age and otherwise affect the paper, and every stroke of their pen or en-
graving in their silver plate. Likewise, the hoaxer obsesses
over every minute detail of his hoax, attempting as best he
can to foresee every possible challenge to his hoax and have
an appropriate rebuttal.

- FORTUNE TELLER: The hoaxer, not unlike a fortune teller,
feeds off of the eagerness of their victims to believe and
provides them with the precise story they are most willing
to accept as true.
- PARLOR MAGICIAN: Both the parlor magician and hoaxer
use misdirection to make their audience believe they have
seen what they haven't actually seen and will have claim to
have seen until their dying day.
- STAGE ACTOR: The stage actor uses suspension of disbelief-
the audiences' willingness to lay aside their logic and rational intellect to believe every word occurring on a stage only
a few feet away.
- CAREER POLITICIAN: And finally, but certainly not least,
just as a career politician spends a lifetime pandering to
his constituency, the hoaxer gives his marks everything they
are looking for and more, leaving them, the majority of the
time, satisfied and completely unaware they were duped.

Hoaxes, as a matter of definition, also require a victim, known
to the above professions by such colorful and poetic names such as
mark, dupe, or pigeon. Each victim has certain personality traits
that "mark" him as a "pigeon"; which are known to include an
over eagerness to believe, being easily susceptible to suggestion, a
willingness to suspend their disbelief, or an innate need to trust.

Literary hoaxes have a long and storied history. My own, *The
Autobiography of Howard Hughes*, is still whispered about in literary circles and is hailed as the supreme example of a hoax that was
nearly successful due to the subject's obsessive reclusiveness. I had
almost pulled it off. Other literary hoaxes are successful because
the "author" is dead; many years, decades, or if the hoaxer has
chooses his subject well, centuries dead. This may have been my

downfall. How was I supposed to know that a notorious recluse who had not spoken in public for decades would denounce me so publicly?

The Hitler Diaries were a contemporary of my *Autobiography* and both were ridiculed as obvious forgeries. This point I take offense to. Konrad Kuto, a hackneyed forger from Stuttgart, made little to no attempts to forge anything. "With the exception of imitating Hitler's habit of slanting his writing diagonally as he wrote across the page," Kenneth W. Rendell noted, "the forger failed to observe or to imitate the most fundamental characteristics of his handwriting."

Where is the art of the forgery? I slaved over that copy of *Newsweek* magazine, sweating blood over every subtle penstroke. Because of, not in spite of, my choosing a contemporary celebrity figure, I didn't have to stalk antique book stores, like a tomb robber, looking for blank leaves from historical manuscripts from the era of my hoax, nor did I have to manufacture inks with the same chemical signatures as inks used during said time-period. All I needed was a pen, some fine stationary, and a great deal of artistic and literary skill to perpetrate my hoax.

The publisher and editor of Alistair Strange series has confessed to me, in their letter, that they have acquired a work of "fan-fiction", but they wanted a hoaxer's opinion of its "hoaxery" (this word again, but theirs not mine). Their questions and concerns are:

- Is *Alistair Strange and the Weight of a Feather* effective enough in its language and style to succeed as a hoax?
- If so, should the novel be published as an authentic work of Abigail K.C. Sterling or under the pseudonym of Alex K.C. Silver?
- What are the legal and moral consequences of hoaxery, fraud and forgery?
- Is it worth the consequences to publish this book?

I fear they prefer to hide behind the term "allonymous" which they consider to be their second best option in publishing this novel. "Allonymous" is a word I thought they made up, until I looked it up in an older and admittedly heftier dictionary from my library. Now that I understand the historicity of "allonymous" works, it fits entirely into their marketing. It is certainly the safer road. This I know all too well.

They will not claim that this is an "authentic" Abigail K.C. Sterling novel, which is their right, but this is cowardly. They should have the will to proclaim to the world that they have finally received the fifth, long in gestation Alistair Strange novel.

If the works of William Shakespeare were indeed written by the Seventeenth Earl of Oxford-Edward de Vere, Francis Bacon the statesmen and poet, or by playwright Christopher Marlowe, then the works were actually written allonymously. William Shakespeare was a contemporary of them all, who is known to have worked in the theater as a lowly actor and minor theatrical entrepreneur. But the claim is that there little to no proof he had the education nor the literary talent to write the plays attributed to him. If de Vere, Bacon, or Marlowe had actually written *Hamlet*, *Julius Caesar*, or *Henry the V*, they published their plays, not under the pseudonym "William Shakespeare", but the allonym "William Shakespeare". It is splitting literary hairs, but entirely plausible. I am an indentured Stratfordian; Shakespeare wrote Shakespeare. There is no doubt in my mind about that.

But in the realm of hoaxery, it is an exquisite story. I didn't write allonymously. I had the courage to put my own name on the cover of my *Autobiography of Howard Hughes*. I didn't hide behind the literary hokum of allonyminity. As if this absolves the author, editor, and publisher from the charges of forgery. When caught, I accepted by fate and spent my time in prison. They want the notoriety of a great forgery, but don't want to suffer the legal consequences.

Cowards.

As to the "hoaxery", it fails on a few counts, but succeeds on many more. I will say, "Bravo!" to the author for having the audacity to write a fifth novel in the Alistair Strange series. A series in which the author is still alive and kicking. This is both bold and audacious. Whoever she is, she is a master mimic. Bravo!

In the end, I declined their invitation to write an introduction for their impressive, but ultimately little book. I told them, if they are so bold, they can write their own damn introduction and put my name on it: allonymously. Let's see if they have the *cojones*.

> *"Writing is like sex. First you do it for love, then you do it for your friends, and then you do it for money."*
> —Virginia Woolf

Chapter Twenty-Two
I Want a Divorce!

O! Muse,

The pain! I don't know if I can take the pain! It is suffocating. It is blinding. I can't– I can't–

I thought I had put away the feelings of rejection behind me over fifteen years ago when I finally sold *The XII Labors of Alistair Strange*. I had survived the long drought caused by rejections from agents and editors, then I weathered the storms from blustery reviewers to reach the pinnacle of the literary community. I thought the days of rejection were behind me. And now? I have been betrayed. I have been rejected, cast aside, in favor of a new, sweet, young thing. I have been betrayed by the person I trusted more than any other– my editor.

The relationship I have– had– with my editor was as trusted as any marriage. I trusted her to help raise my children. I trusted her to protect them at the cost of her very life. We had a contract that bounded us together in the bounds of holy publication.

"I, Abigail K.C. Sterling, take thee, Iris Reilly, to be my editor, to write for and be edited by, with glowing blurbs and scathing reviews, on *New York Times* bestseller lists or in bargain basement remainders, forsaking all other publishers 'till I have fulfilled my seven book deal do us part."

And– "I, Iris Reilly, take thee, Abigail K.C. Sterling, to be my writer, to be edited by me, with glowing blurbs and scathing reviews, on *New York Times* bestseller lists or in bargain basement remainders, forsaking all other publishers 'till you have fulfilled your seven book deal do us part."

I was faithful to her. I didn't look to other publishers to care for my children. I gave her my name. My reputation. And now I discover her adultery on Twitter! She has been seeing another author behind my back. I know I have been distant. I know that I have not been the partner that I could have been in these last several years. I have not given her the children she desired. Now, she has given this adulterous slut my name, my children.

Casey, you're being melodramatic.

Am I? I don't think I am overreacting enough. If I wanted out of my seven book deal, they would have stopped me in my tracks. And army of attorneys would have descended from the heavens to unleash the wrath of the gods. They would have used my iron-clad contract to keep me enslaved to them until the day I fulfill the writing and submitting of book number seven. Instead, Iris went behind my back, armed with legal loopholes and technicalities that allowed her to publish someone else's Alistair Strange novel.

The Strangers have chosen a "fan-fiction" novel over something written by me. Why was I so reclusive? Why did I not write faster? It wasn't like I had other irons in the fire like George R.R. Martin. While his fans wait for the *Winds of Winter*, at least he has published a untold history of Westeros and the *Game of Thrones*. At least he has published a collection of Dunk and Egg novellas.

I haven't done do-diddily-squat. For. Nearly. A. Decade!

Sure, I have a collection of character descriptions, biographies, potential location and set-pieces, storylines in the past and in the future and running concurrently, that I can use in future stories, but as for future stories, I don't have anything. I don't know what to do with his information. I've written a lot of words in these– I don't even know what to call it– reference documents. *Urgh!* That sounds awful. It has to more than just a collection of characters descriptions, biographies, and potential storylines, it the source of everything I've written. Without all of these words, I would never have created a three-dimensional, five-sensational world of Alistair Strange. My world would have been a drab and boring place without having written all of these words, all of this– I don't know what it is or what it is good for! What do I call it? What do I do with all of this information? It isn't doing me any good at the moment. Would my Strangers be interested in getting a peak behind the curtain or will they be disappointed that I'm not always the Great and Powerful Oz and sometimes, I'm just an old humbug hiding behind the very same curtain I don't want peaked behind. I should just delete each of the reference files off of all of my hard-drives and back-up hard-drives, and flash-drives. It's just useless information anyway.

Sure, I've written short-stories and novellas that I have published in various magazines the world over, but I don't want to publish a greatest hits collection. That smacks of desperation. Do I want to tide my Strangers over with a greatest hits collection? I don't think my publisher is interested in publishing anything of the sort, or they would have already pressured me into publishing such a collection the short stories.

I don't know what to do anymore. The Strangers have spoken. They want more from Alistair Strange than I can give them. Should I bite the bullet and allow HBO or Netflix to develop television series of prequels, and sequels, and side-quels? I'm sure they'd pay a pretty penny to develop and produce stories in my Strangeverse. But I can't let go of the control. I need to write the stories. I can't let other screenwriters, an entire writers room of sceenwriters and showrunners to develop Alistair Strange stories.

Even if they set their stories in far flung corners of the world that *I* built, it would just be too weird to have other writers dilute my Creation.

He's mine. He lives because of me and only me. If I had my druthers I would just murder Alistair Strange and have it all done with.

Casey, you kind of already did that at the end of *Those Whom the Gods Detest Should Not Be Unearthed.* Alistair Strange is already dead.

Until I choose to resurrect him. It is my choice, not their's. I will resurrect him or I will leave him rotting in the ground of my unpublished manuscripts! I am the god of my third-person omniscient world and I will destroy it all!

Alistair Strange, I am the Lord thy God of your third-person omniscient world, which have brought thee out of my own mind. Thou shalt have no other gods before me. Thou shalt not make unto thee any graven image, or any likeness of any thing that is in heaven above, or that is in the earth beneath, or that is in the water under the earth. Thou shalt not bow down thyself to them, nor serve them: for I the Lord thy God am a jealous God of your third-person omniscient world, visiting the iniquity of the fathers upon the children unto the third and fourth generation of them that hate me; And shewing mercy unto thousands of them that love me, and keep my commandments.

Muse, why do I always turn to blasphemy? Please, somebody pray for me!

That is a level of betrayal that would unrealistic in a Hollywood movie. The critics would complain endlessly in their certified rotten reviews that their would never possibly be any wording– any legalese– that would allow a publisher to do what they did. No agent would ever allow such wording to slip by her and into her client's contract. The reviewers would further criticize the moviemakers because no publisher in the really, real world would ever betray their best selling– top selling– author in such a fashion.

There would be no amount of lost revenue that would cause a

publisher to betray their top selling author. No matter how many deadlines she may have missed, the world she has created is her world. Little, Brown would never have dared to take the Wizarding World of Harry Potter away from J.K. Rowling. Bantam would never have hired another author to complete *A Song of Ice and Fire*, without the input and approval of George R.R. Martin, no matter how many deadlines he may have missed, or how many further deadlines he will have missed before finally submitting his manuscript for *The Winds of Winter*. HBO, no doubt, has worked with, not against, George R.R. Martin using the author's own outlines to plot and plan the subsequent seasons of *The Game of Thrones*.

Such a betrayal would not only betray their top selling author, not only every other under their publisher's umbrella, but every future author the publisher would ever attempt to sign. Why would any unpublished author, no matter how eager to see their novel in finished book-form, sign a contract with a publisher who would act in such a fashion. Every agent, with a lick of professional sense, would blacklist every editor at that publisher. Every author, every other editor, would mutiny over such a treasonous act.

It would be an act of professional suicide.

And yet, they have suicidally betrayed me. I may not have yet crossed the billionaire threshold like J.K. Rowling, but I have the millions of dollars– hundreds of millions– necessary to hire the top entertainment lawyers in the industry to sue my publisher into bankruptcy.

Murder! Mayhem! Death!

O! Muse,

That bitch!

I sent her my manuscript of *Alistair Strange and the Orchardist of Yggrasil* to prove that I had been producing quality work over the course of the last seven –eight? nine?!?– years. I needed to prove to her that despite my seclusion, I had been toiling away on the *Orchardist* all this last decade. Is the novel I submitted to her finished? Is it the "Final Draft"? Dear God no! I am still polishing it! And she decided to use the same goddamned legal loopholes she used to publish that "fan-fiction" abomination to publish my own novel against my will. Apparently, my contract allows them to accept my submitted manuscript as I wrote it. Apparently, they are free to publish it as I had submitted it. I hadn't finished polishing it until it positively sings! It wasn't in a state that I consider publishable. It is still stillborn!

But apparently they are within their rights to continue the publication process with or without my permission or input! They have set a publication date. They are in the process of designing a cover and laying-out the interiors as we speak. In their twisted reasoning, they will give my Strangers a choice between two follow-up novels to *Those Whom the Gods Detest Should Not Be Unearthed,* one my *Orchardist of Yggrasil* and the other, that trollop's *The Weight of a Feather.* Two "fifth" novels in the Alistair Strange series?

They are going to confuse the hell out of my passionate fan-base with this heresy!

O! Muse,

That smooth-talking so-and-so. I'm trying really, really hard to be mad at her, but the conversation we just had, that I illegally wire-tapped– you know, just in case, there is a legal case– has me temporarily convinced– somewhat smitten– that my publisher only has my best interest– the best interest of Alistair Strange– at heart.

I would like to transcribe the conversation to you, Muse, you know, for the record, but I can't repeat what I said to that so-and-so. It wouldn't be fit for public consumption. I'll just leave it to your overactive imagination!

Chapter Twenty-Three

A Casey 4...Right Now! 4 Realz? 4 Realz!

by alistairstrange#1fan

ORIGINAL: OMG! I can't believe they know who I am? OMG! How did they find me? I'm crying! I'm dying! Casey's publisher sent me– ME– an advance copy of her fifth novel. Not Alex K.C. Silver's "fifth" novel, BUT Abigail K.C. Sterling's fifth novel! I can't believe its real. I can't believe Casey actually wrote the fifth book! I know, I know. Around the first of the year, her official Twitter account announced that the manuscript had been delivered to her editor, but I DIDN'T BELIEVE HER. Why couldn't I have believed my beloved Casey?

I didn't believe her because of the publication of that heretical *The Weight of a Feather* at Christmas. How could our "Casey for Christmas" tradition be sullied by an "AleX for Xmas". How ridiculous was the desperation in the marketing department to shoehorn Alex's name into that sacred slogan? IDK what season that abomination should celebrate, though. I really don't know.

And the title is so much better than that fan-fiction. ALISTAIR STRANGE AND THE ORCHARDIST OF YGGRASIL! Oooh! There are so many possibilities on WHO the Orchardist it! And you actually have to Google Yggrasil to find out what it is! And when you do Google it, the mind just explodes with possibilities! Nothing is tamed or for the timid!

The Weight of a Feather lazily picks up from that cliff-hanger, and if you are a devoted Stranger, you know, THAT CLIFFHANGER! And titular *Weight of a Feather* is a plot-line that is resolved in the first freaking chapter! Where is the mystery in that? Yeah, yeah. I know Alistair "died" at the end of *Those Whom the Gods Detest Should Not Be Unearthed.* The possibilities on where the next book would take us could have been endless. Instead, in the very first chapter Alistair has his heart weighed against *The Weight of a Feather* in the Halls of Two Truths... and failed. Done. Over. The mystery posed by the title has been solved. The title is now meaningless. Alistair must now spend the rest of the novel journeying through the seven (why only seven?) hells in order to return to life?!? Arrgh! How lame!

Casey is an author with the creativity, skill, and devotion to her craft to keep WHO the Orchardist secret and what his plot-line is in the righteous cause of suspense. This is a journey the Strangers actually want to go on, because Casey is OUR guide, and not some journey through the seven hells that the publisher wanted us to go on. And let me tell you, reading that schlock was worse than journeying through a freaking hundred hells, let me tell you.

I'm going to go away, Strangers, and make a cappuccino and curl up on the sofa and read. READ!

UPDATE 1: OMG! OMG! OMG! There are literally no

words. IDK! IDK! What to say! I need time, Strangers. I really do. Srry.

UPDATE 2: K! K! I'm ready! Let's get into this! My initial, kinda-"official" review of *Alistair Strange and the Orchardist of Yggrasil*!!!!!!

[No spoilers, I swear!]

Alistair Strange and the Orchardist of Yggrasil is the culmination of everything Casey has been planting the seeds for in the first four novels. Seeds? Planting? A World Tree? Yes! While not every plotline, subplot, and question has been answered, enough of the seeds she has sewn have sprouted and grown into the wondrous, wonderful fifth novel *Yggrasil*! AND the Orchardist plants enough seeds in this one novel alone to sprout several more novels.

Enough of the arborist metaphors. This novel is Casey at the height of beautiful, graceful, poetic powers. While she began to dabble in rather heady philosophies and spiritualities beginning with *The XII Labors*. Her fifth novel, though disguised as a young adult novel, poses questions about the 21st Century that rival those of Plato and Aristotle about Ancient Greece, Immanuel Kant, David Hume, Rene Descartes and John Locke about Europe. Even the philosophies of the antagonists rival those of the more controversial philosophers Friederich Nietzche and Niccolò Machiavelli. She sugar-coats nothing, yet her beautiful, graceful, poetic plot is never once gets bogged down. The pacing of the novel is exquisite. It's lightning quick were it needs to be, but never afraid to slow down and really savor and satiate the intellect.

Casey really ups the ante by questioning everything about the 21st Century! Religious devotion in a scientific age, the Internet cultism of and on social media, the explosion of information readily accessible by even the common man from the information superhighway, the literal shrinking of the world beginning with airline travel and culminating with the worldwide-web. Is there really a Doomsday clock? Modern religions, even those of the Egyptians, Greeks, and Norse, are warning of the end times: Ragnarök, climate change, peak-oil. Even the pantheons cannot escape religious cultism, extremism, and terrorism. Is our 21st century global, Internet-connected civilization about to collapse? There is rampant crime and social alienation and political extremism. The fuse has been lit and the world is about to explode!

This is THE novel FOR the 21Century, OF the 21 Century.

Chapter Twenty-Four

FANDOM CIVIL WAR:
First Shots Fired

by alistairstrange#1fan

COMMENTS SECTION

IHeartAlexSilver: Why did our beloved Casey wait until her publisher published someone else's "fifth" novel in the series to even bother herself with submitting her manuscript? I went to the midnight release party for Alex K.C. Sterling's *Alistair Strange and the Weight of a Feather.* There were hundreds of Strangers in attendance. We were cosplaying. We were excited to read the continuation of the Alistair Strange sage– I mean, saga (curious little typo). Now, a few weeks later, Casey goes on Twitter to announce she is finally, after nearly A DECADE! going to grace us with a new Alistair Strange? Now, we have two "official" fifth novels?!? I know that I'm supposed to relish the coming months before the release of Casey's own fifth novel, but I am dreading every moment of it.

>**VampressFromMars:** Dreading it? This is a momentous moment. After nearly a decade, we are going to find out how she chose to continue the story.

>**IHeartAlexSilver:** CHOSE?!? Why should we care anymore where she CHOSE to take Alistair Strange? Casey chose, SHE CHOSE, to sit on her hands until she was forced to act by HER publisher publishing Alex's novel. I'm sure she didn't believe that a so-called "fan-fiction" novel was a threat. I'm sure she didn't believe that her publisher would stab her in the back by publishing someone else's Alistair Strange novel.

>**VampressFromMars:** They did "stab Casey in the back". They had not right, no Copyright! to publish someone else's Alistair Strange novel, no matter how popular it was on the seedy, unseemly fan-fiction websites. She OWNS her own story. She CREATED it. She only sold the publisher the rights to publisher HER stories.

>**IHeartAlexSilver:** But SHE FORCED THEIR HANDS by missing deadline after deadline after deadline. George R.R. Martin has been open and fine with HBO continuing the *Game of Thrones* above and beyond what he has written. Why couldn't Casey have been so gracious?

>**VampressFromMars:** GRACIOUS! That was a betrayal of Biblical proportions. Judas would look up from Dante's Ninth Circle of Hell and say, "Damn! That's cold, man!" The publisher married Casey, but decided to have an affair with that whore, Alex K.C. Silver.

IHeartAlexSilver: SHE wasn't contributing to her own world. She missed deadline after deadline. We, THE FANS, had every right to go to the "fan-fiction" community to discover Alex K.C. Silver's own fifth Alistair Strange novel.

VampressFromMars: RIGHT! What right did you have? Did Alex have the COPYRIGHT? Of course not! Did you have the COPYRIGHT to download that INFRINGEMENT! Of course not! As a fan of Alex's, you are a criminal. You committed a crime by downloading that "fan-fiction".

IHeartAlexSilver: I'm the criminal?!? What was criminal was waiting nearly ten-freaking-years to continue her story. What was criminal was depriving her publisher of the money that could be made when the next Alistair Strange novel was published. Can you imagine millions of dollars that was felt languishing in the pockets of Strangers, when that money could have been put to better use, like buying an Alistair Strange novel. I bought an "OFFICIAL" copy of Alex's novel. I PAID my money to her publisher. The publisher and author got their share of MY money. I'm no pirate. I stole nothing!

VampressFromMars: You're worse than a criminal. You're an infidel! You have chosen worship a false prophet.

IHeartAlexSilver: Oh! Sh*t! We're going to get all into religious symbolism, are we? I can play that game. When your god abandons her people, we have no choice to worship the golden idol. And you know what. It worked. She got Casey to come down from her haughty mountain-top to deliver her "fifth" novel. But at this point, I couldn't care less. I've already read continuation of the story. I enjoyed the hell out of it, despite being a devoted Stranger and fan of Casey Sterling. When I heard that her publisher had selected Alex's novel as the "official" fifth novel in the series. I rejoiced. But now that they are pushing a second "official" fifth Alistair Strange novel, I'm disappointed..

VampressFromMars: Disappointed? We should be rejoicing. @ALISTAIRSTRANGE#-1FAN has read it. She says its glorious. It's been worth the decade wait.

IHeartAlexSilver: Oh, lah-de-FREAKING-da!. A blogger has been selected from on high to be bequeathed the new "OFFICIAL" fifth novel and she loves it!

DarthStranger: I don't know why we can't have both. It's like we're getting two alternate but parallel realities. Why can't we enjoy Casey's novel when it is published and enjoy Alex's novel, too? Wasn't Alistair Strange briefly sent to our reality where the Abrahamic religions of Moses, Jesus, and Mohammad dominated and supplanted the pantheons of the Egyptians, the Greeks, and the Norse? Now, we can follow the Alistair, who had his heart weighed against a feather and has to journey through the seven hells in order return to life. And we have the Alistair, who must journey through the roots of the world tree, Yggdrasil, and eventually reach the branches of the heavens to return to life. It's like the best-of-both-worlds. Literally.

VampressFromMars: Oh, be quiet.

IHeartAlexSilver: Yeah, shut up! THERE CAN BE ONLY ONE!

VampressFromMars: I for one can't wait for Casey's novel to finally be published. From what @ALISTAIRSTRANGE#1FAN says in this article is could very well be a truly transcendent experience, where Alex's novel was just... commonplace.

DarthStranger: I can't wait, either. I just finished all of the Alistair novels leading to up and I can't wait to read another. I am a true Stranger now, aren't I?

IHeartAlexSilver: COMMONPLACE?!? If I want a transcendent experience I'll read the Holy Bible, or I'll watch that torture-porn film, *Martyrs*. I don't read popular fiction for a transcendent experience. I read to be entertained. And Alex's novel was very entertaining. I enjoyed every single word of it. I don't need to be philosophized at. Sometimes I don't want to think.

VampressFromMars: Well, that's obvious.

IHeartAlexSilver: What I'm trying to say is I don't want Alistair Strange novels turning into something written by Ayn Rand. Our political system is already a tinderbox and any spark can set it off. I don't want that spark being a stupid, insignificant (in the scheme of things) young adult novel. Christians already don't want their children reading Alistair Strange or having the books in public school libraries because there's no "Christ" in it. Any book that imagines a world where Jesus and Christianity didn't become ascendant must inherently be Satanic. It's nothing but pagan-gods-this and pagan-gods-that. Now, Casey wants get into this heady, haughty stuff that @ALISTAIRSTRANGE#1FAN is fawning over in her article. Not in my popular entertainment, thank you very much.

VampressFromMars: I for one want to be challenged when I read. And it's not like Casey hasn't touched on sensitive issues. Like you said, the very imagining a world where the Egyptian, Greek, and Norse gods are still worshiped and WALK AMONG US!!! was controversial. And still is! You can't say that didn't set off your precious tinderbox. That happened fifteen years ago! And the world survived perfectly fine. That is one of the reasons Alistair Strange is so popular with an adult audience is Casey MAKES YOU THINK. Which you obviously don't like to. Hurts your precious little pudding head.

DarthStranger: Can't we all get along?

IHeartAlexSilver: Shut up @DarthStranger! And shut up @VampressFromMars! So what if I just like reading for the shear enjoyment of it. That doesn't make me any less smart. I'm read the classics in school. I've read all of the required reading: *The Odyssey, To Kill a Mockingbird, Animal Farm, Night, Lord of the Flies, Anthem, The Outsiders, Huckleberry Finn, The Giver, Of Mice and Men, Fahrenheit 451, A Raisin in the Sun, The Scarlet Letter, The Great Gatsby, Brave New World.* Just because I don't choose to read any of those for ENTERTAINMENT doesn't make me an imbecile.

VampressFromMars: No, it just makes you uncultured.

DarthStranger: Please...

VampressFromMars: There is no reason young adult novels can't or shouldn't make you think. *The Giver* is a young adult novel and Lois Lowry makes you think. *A Handmaid's Tale* is a harrowing young adult novel and -*gasp*- Margaret Atwood makes you think. *A Wrinkle in Time! Animal Farm! The Lion, the Witch, and the Wardrobe! The Never Ending Story* (not the movie)! and *Ender's Game!* They all MAKE YOU THINK! And that is why they stand the test of time.

IHeartAlexSilver: I would much rather be a popular novelist, selling millions of copies, getting on *The New York Times* bestsellers list, and getting Hollywood movies made of my books.

VampressFromMars: Thousands of books are published every year that are just entertainment. Yes, many become wildly successful *New York Times* bestsellers and get optioned for a movie. But most sit relatively unsold, ending up on the bargain basement remainders shelves. Many, if not most popular novelists will be utterly forgotten about in a generation or two. The books that make you think will stand the test of time. I dare you @IHeartAlexSilver, go into any used book store and look at their paperback section. Do you recognize many of the names of the older books?

IHeartAlexSilver: Stephen King. James Michener. Scott Turow. Tom Clancy. Michael Crichton, Peter Benchley. James Clavel. Robert Ludlum. Sidney Sheldon. Jackie Collins.

VampressFromMars: I'm not talking about those authors. Those are the exceptions that prove the rule. I'm talking about the thousands of paperbacks from authors you've never heard of. Authors of the paperbacks that the used bookstores can't give away, because nobody has ever heard of them. The books that have yellowed with age or have colored edges. The mysteries. The romance novels. The westerns.

The pulp novels that aren't even worth pulping. Most of the authors, even those with hardcovers you see at Barnes and Noble right now will be completely forgotten about in a generation. That is why the publishing industry churns out as many books as they do. They are looking for the next Stephen King. The next Tom Clancy. The next Abigail K.C. Sterling. Some popular authors from my parents' day like James Michener, James Clavel, and Colleen McCullough are still remembered decades past their heyday. But they are truly few and far between.

IHeartAlexSilver: And Alex. K.C. Silver will be counted in among the remembered. All because of *Alistair Strange and the Weight of a Feather.* She has earned her spot.

VampressFromMars: She hasn't earned anything of sort. She is a writer that piggy-backed on the characters and story of a much more established author. If it wasn't for Casey, Alex would still be nobody. If fact, Alex, still is a nobody because she chose to use a name that is such an obvious knockoff of Abigail K.C. Sterling! We don't even know Alex's real name. She is still a nobody. She is an imposer claiming the fame of another. Until she writes something without the name "Alistair Strange" on the cover, until she writes something ORIGINAL, she is less than nobody. If it weren't for the crimes of Casey's publisher, she would still be home writing "fan-fiction", dreaming of one day having an agent, having an editor, having a book published.

IHeartAlexSilver: E.L. James is a best-seller. A *New York Times* bestseller. She was sold 125 MILLION copies of *Fifty Shades of Grey.* She is a phenomenally successful author who made "Mommy porn" an established and popular genre of fiction.

VampressFromMars: Again the exception that proves what I'm talking about. If it weren't for her UNDERGROUND success as an author of erotic *Twilight* fan-fiction, she wouldn't have adapted her own copyright infringing erotica into -urgh- *Fifty Shades of Grey*. And what as she done since? Nothing.

DarthStranger: Can't we all get along?

IHeartAlexSilver: This exactly why I am dreading the next several weeks– months?!? Dear God– until Casey's novel is finally released. @ VampressFromMars, you and I are having a flame war in the comment's section of a stupid blog and neither of us have read the freaking book. You are defending Casey's actions and eight years of INACTION and the only word we have on the quality of the book is a BLOGGER!

VampressFromMars: You and I both have come to this blog of our own free will. You have to have been curious to read a review of *The Orchardist of Yggrasil* because you're commenting on such an article. The review must have affected you emotionally otherwise you wouldn't have commented on it in the first place. You felt you needed to defend your precious Alex under the weight of such praise for Casey.

IHeartAlexSilver: Exactly. And that is why I'm dreading every moment of the next several months. This is what Twitter is going to be like. This is what Facebook is going to be like. This is what reddit is going to be like. I won't be able to go onto the Internet and not be part of a stupid flame war between Team Alex and Team Casey.

VampressFromMars: Then why are you still talking?

AlistairStrange#1Fan: Burn! Locking this thread.

> *"You must stay drunk on writing so reality cannot destroy you."*
> –Ray Bradbury, *Zen in the Art of Writing*

Chapter Twenty-Five

Book Signing Writ In Her Blood!

O! Muse,

I don't know why I read that *Playboy* interview conducted with that trollop Alex K.C. Silver. I knew that it was akin to stalking your ex's new lover on Facebook, reading her posts, looking at her photos, seeing how many friends she has, etc. *ad nauseum*. I wouldn't learn anything worthwhile in that interview and yet I read it anyway.

And now I can't forget the image the interviewer painted of Alex. It has been seared into my mind: that early twenty-something giggle, the tossing of her unnaturally pink hair over her shoulder, brandishing of her Horde (whatever that is) tattoos, and the computerized flick of her dresses that make her look like she's been plucked straight from a video-game.

I don't know why I agreed to do a duo-book-signing with Alex K.C. Silver. Our– my– MY– editor believed that splitting the fan-base– MY– fanbase– would be detrimental to the property and that by both of us signing at the same exact time and at the exact same event would be a great service for our– MY– fans. Secretly– okay, not so secretly– I wanted to prove once and for all that I alone an the creator, the curator, and ultimately the destroyer of my literary universe. That once that books were counted, it would proved once and for all that I am the best-selling author in the *Alistair Strange* universe. And the usurper to my throne would be proven to be a pale, pink-haired imitation.

I was ushered in through the back-door and into the employee's lounge to wait for the signing to begin. I ate stale donuts and drank God-awful coffee and sat and waited.

And waited and waited for Alex K.C. Silver to arrive so I'd have an opportunity to interrogate– talk to the pink-haired Millennial video-gaming nerdette. I wanted– desperately needed– to look her in the eye. But she wasn't there when I arrived and as the clock impossibly slowly ticked towards the appointed hour of our joint book-signing, she was a no-show. There was a part of me excited to see her bale on the joint book-signing. In my mind's eye, she panicked at the very thought of meeting me, the creator of the literary universe she had chosen to usurp. Who would want to stand face-to-face with the woman from whom you stole your entire career– your entire identity as a writer– from. I smiled at the thought that she had told the driver of the car that had been sent to pick her up at her hotel to "keep driving" as the car pulled up at the back-door of the bookstore.

I smiled and smiled and smiled more and more like the Cheshire Cat. I was so freaking giddy. She. Was. Going. To. Be. A No. Show.

When the appointed hour came to make my entrance into a veritable sea of my Strangers, the store manager made his announcement over the loud-speakers. When I emerged from the back of the store and made my way to my table, where copies of my latest novel, *Alistair Strange and the Orchadist of Yggdrasil,* sat stacked along with copies of the previous four novels, I was caught off-guard by the whispers, murmurs, and hushed rumors.

"Is that really Casey?"

"Is that the real Casey?"

"I don't know.

"Nobody's seen her in over a decade."

"She hasn't aged well at all."

"She doesn't look anything like her dust-jacket."

"Life hasn't been at all kind to her."

"Is this what life secluded to a dark room does to people?"

"No, I heard she lived in an haunted house with hundreds of cats."

"There could be a dark room in her haunted house."

"I really thought she had died."

"Yeah, she died. Isn't that why it's taken so long to find her replacement? Like Paul McCartney."

"Paul *who?*"

"*Replacements.* Alex and then the other Casey."

"Why do we need another Casey when we have an Alex?"

"I don't think that is Casey."

"Holy crap!"

"You're right."

"That isn't Casey."

"They hired an actor to sign our books."

"Who's 'they'?"

"Her publisher."

"The film studio."

"Maybe the bookstore."

"Why would they do something like that?"

"Because she really did die."

Arrragh! I screamed ever so silently.—

—And when Alex K.C. Silver walked into the bookstore, all of the Strangers– MY Strangers– turned to catch their first glimpse of Alex making her– HIS grand entrance, Alex (if that is, in fact, his name) was a wonderfully tall man in his early-to-mid forties, with salt-and-peppered naturally bed-headed hair with a curious little cow-lick at the crown of his head. He possessed striking green eyes, behind his wire-rimmed glasses, that pierced through the crowd seeking out only one person's gaze, my own. He was not only tall, but lanky, like a cool breeze would fling him across the street and through the plate-glass of a dress shop's display window. He saw me from across the room, he waved his monkey arms awkwardly and smiled, wrinkling his proud Roman nose. He was... so... I don't know.

I could easily imagine him still living in his elderly mother's basement, sitting at his computer, wearing headphones, hollering into a microphone over the infinite gulf of the world-wide-web, full of consternation at fellow raiders for standing in fire (whatever that means), as he tried to heal them of their–often self-inflicted wounds– as the D...P...S... (?!?) battled impossibly powerful raid bosses that pounded on one of two "meat-shields" he proudly kept alive with Power Word: Shields, Smiting enemies while healing allies with Atonements in *World of Warcraft*.

What-the-hell-did-I-just-type?

This could not possibly be the person I have held in such contempt for the last several months.

I was struck by the oddest thoughts as my preconceived notions vanished like a fart in a whirlwind. As I sat at my table with my books stacked beside me and his heretical books stacked on the table beside my table, I was able to begin to comprehend the truth that Alex. K.C. Silver was– nay, nay, nay– is– had always been a man. Whatever spiteful hatred exists between women– chatty, catty hatreds– simply don't exist between women and men. Whatever chatty, catty hatreds I had previously directed at the pink-haired phantasm are now discovered to be nothing more than a tempest in a teapot. I don't know whom to date–hate, hate!– anymore.

Oh, the odd thought. The odd thought was this, Muse– if Zooey Deschanel had been born with a Y-chromosome instead of a pair of X's, this is exactly how she would look. So freaking adorable.

Don't digress, Casey. Don't. You. Dare. Digress!

I stewed in my own seething hatred for this woma– man– who had the audacity to write a novel set in my literary universe, dared to put words into my characters' mouths, and steal the affections of MY Strangers!—

—I was, however, absolutely destroyed by the Beatles-esque screams, shrieks, and torrent of tears from not only the teenagers in attendance, but also the middle-aged mothers of those teenagers as well. Their screams suddenly and irrationally sounded like fingernails on the chalkboard. I really, really want to hate this man as much if not more than I hated that pink-haired feminine phantasm I originally pictured in my mind.

And with a grand wave of his monkey arms, the sea of screaming, shrieking women patiently and peacefully parted like he was Charlton-freaking-Heston parting the God Blessed Red Sea.

Their shedding gallons of tears were as maddening and illogical as the flood that nearly drowned Alice during her adventures in Wonderland. A flood of feminine futility. I've never been one of those women, whether it was our mothers with Elvis the Pelvis or the Beatles or the Rolling Stones, or our sisters with New Kids on the Block or the Backstreet Boys or 'N SYNC. The shear deluge of emotions is something that is so alien to me even when directed directly at me. And now that Alex has revealed herself– HIMself– to all the Strangers in attendance at our– MY– book-signing, that inundation of affections is now so keenly directed directly at him, this usurper, this pretender to MY throne.

OFF WITH HIS HEAD!

He sat down at his table to sign copies of *his* book. The weeping and wailing as the girls and women handed *him his* books that *they* had purchased. They wanted *his* signature on *their* books. *Aarrgh!*

Blood boiled in my eyes and I didn't hear the nice little girl speaking to me. She held out a copy of my *Orchardist* in her little hands as if she were offering her child to the preacher for baptism. I seized her book, rather violently and slammed the book onto the table. I opened the cover, cracking the book's spine– that wonderful creak of a brand new, hard-bound copy of a novel. I grabbed my pen and stabbed it into... my ink well.

Yes, Muse, I sign my books with an old-fashioned calligraphy pen and ink well filled with the finest India ink. I consider my novel– all novels no matter their genre, even romance novels– to be works of art and the artist signing them should show respect for the special contract between author and reader. Who in their right mind would want their book signed with a Sharpie. There is no art to a Sharpie.

For as many Strangers who offered me their cherished copies of my books, I couldn't help but seethe with every single sacrilegious book signed by Alex, with every selfie taken with giggling girls or weeping women.

While I signed completely on auto-pilot, my writer's imagination began to run wild like a stalker in a Hollywood horror movie. I imagined his table was not a table but a rack used during the Spanish Inquisition– "Nobody expects the Spanish Inquisition"– damn Monty Pythons– and from a vein in his left arm a tube drawing out his life's blood dripping drop by drop into my inkwell. I dipped my pen into the well and signed each and every copy of *Alistair Strange*– both *mine* and *his*– in his heretical blood. At the end of the evening, when my hand began to cramp from signing hundreds of copies of books, I imagined him having been bleed to death!

Damn, Casey. Get a grip on yourself.

You aren't a monster. You aren't a sociopath. You don't write horror novels. You're not Stephen King, for pity's sake.

> *"A rose by any other name would smell as sweet."*
> —William Shakespeare, *Romeo & Juliet*

> *"Just erotic. Nothing kinky. It's the difference between using a feather and using a chicken."*
> —Terry Pratchett, *Eric*

Chapter Twenty-Six
the graham norton show - segment one

Abigail K.C. Sterling: Ophelia, that is a particularly *interesting* nom de plume, you've chosen for yourself.

Ophelia [Censored]: *Nom de plume?* Pen-name? What makes you assume that it isn't my Christian name?

Casey: Surnames by their very nature, particularly British surnames, more often than imply either a familial relationship or a profession: Smith, Bishop, Parker, Fletcher, Foreman.

Ophelia: It could very well be an occupational surname. Or haven't you read my book?

Casey: But your pseudonymous surname is a swear word. A particularly vulgar swear word. An exceptionally anti-feminist swear word.

Ophelia: What? I can't hear you.

Casey: [*Uncomfortable laughter*] Oh... Oh! I see what you did there. Hidden behind your pleasant, lady-like British accent, you swore at me. Twice! You asked a seemingly normal question, "What? I can't hear you", and yet you swore at me... twice. The words surely sounded like "what" and "can't", but those weren't the words you actually vocalized? Were they? You called me two vulgar names for women's private parts. That is very un-lady-like of you.

Alex K.C. Silver: Ladies. Ladies. Let's not get off on the wrong foot, shall we? I've– we've got to survive a very, very long segment together and we've just begun. Ophelia. That is a surprisingly Shakespearean name, isn't it? Very poetic. Very punny, if I'm not mistaken.

Ophelia: Thank you so very much for noticing. My name is the first part of a sentence, "I'll feel your..."

Graham Norton: Now. Now.

Ophelia: "... for a dollar."

Alex: That sounds very much like a line The Bard himself would have– um– *could* have written. It is very...

Casey: [*Interrupting*] ...Profane...

Alex: ...Poetic...

Casey: ...Poetic profanity. But profanity nonetheless.

Ophelia: [*Sincerely*] Thank you, that means so very much to me.

Alex: I read a copy of your play on the flight to England. *Marquis de Sade's* A Midsummer Night's Wet Dream?

Ophelia: You did? Oh! Oh, so lovely of you to read it. You'd be surprised the number of people whom haven't read it.

Casey: I wouldn't be all that surprised if I were you.

Ophelia: Were you able to read it? I tried to desperately to get the feel for how Shakespeare would have written erotica. The Jacobean English. You know the *iambic pentameter*. The rhyming couplets. It wasn't impenetrable, was it?

Alex: The way you were able to weave in-and-out of the lines originally written by William Shakespeare and the lines that were original with you, was really... something, I must say. There were times when I couldn't tell which lines were original with Shakespeare and which lines were original from you.

Ophelia: Oh, thank you, thank you. That means the world to me. It really, really does.

Alex: I know what inspired me to write in the world created by Casey, that wonderful, wonderful world of Alistair Strange, the world that I have been thankful to have been invited to participate in. What inspired you to adapt *A Midsummer Night's Dream* into erotica?

Ophelia: Inspiration is a mysterious creature; mischievous and prankish in nature just like Robin Goodfellow. Ask any writer where they get ideas for their novels, plays, or movies and the answer is the same: we simply have no idea how or why we get the ideas we do.

Casey: *[Interrupting]* Alex surely does.

Ophelia: Inspiration often rears its ugly head at the most inopportune times. The idea for erotic Shakespeare came to me while rehearsing for a production *A Midsummer Night's Dream* many, many years ago when I was ill prepared as a writer to receive such a revelation.

Graham: As a novice, an ingénue, were you shocked at the implied eroticism found in the play?

Ophelia: Beyond belief. My drama teacher disagreed with me, often vehemently, concerning the erotic nature of this comedy. She held the opinion that the Bard had written a playful comedy, not a play filled to the brim with sexual aggression, cruelty, and violence. To me, Shakespeare implied any number of erotic fetishes that he, in his age, dared not write, blatantly. Even in our age, many of the fetishes Shakespeare alludes to cannot be written, spoken, or performed on the stage.

Graham: My theater instructor back in grammar school went against the grain in her solidly anti-British thoughts that Shakespeare was the dirtiest of dirty old men. A man likely to expose himself to the queen herself to win a bet over a shilling. She, like you, saw bawdy Bill hiding his eroticism through innuendo and poetic trickery. Instead you, in the bright uncensored lights of the 21st Century, can project to the entire English-speaking world.

Ophelia: Although I was a neophyte to the world of Shakespeare, and theater in general, I immediately saw homosexuality, bestiality, and countless other fetishes. Every rehearsal reinforced my belief in the mysterious and hidden world of eroticism in the play. Lysander's line, "You have her father's love, Demetrius/Let me have Hermia's. Do you marry him?" implied a homosexual relationship between Egeus and Demetrius.

Graham: You made Hermia's father and her own betrothed homosexual lovers?

Ophelia: Wherever Shakespeare hinted at an eroticism hidden from the Master of Revels, Edmund Tylney, that is where I took my erotica. When Theseus proclaims near the end of the play, "midnight hath told twelve lovers to bed.'Tis almost fairy time," I interpreted this to be a wanton orgy. And the entire Bottom and Titania love story screamed bestiality. Was I the only one who has noticed this?

Graham: You would have Mrs. MacTavish squarely in your corner, Ophelia. She'd exclaim to all who would listen like a town crier, "See I was bloody right the entire while." Who would you picture acting in a motion picture of your *Wet Dream*?

Ophelia: A motion picture? I don't really think my play is filmable. Not in the slightest. It would have to be rated 18 at the least. Or banned outright.

Graham: Very well then, what about the stage? Whom would you cast in a Royal Shakespeare Company of the *Marquis de Sade's* A Midsummer Night's Wet Dream produced on the stage of the reconstructed Globe Theater herself?

Ophelia: My. Let me think. What would my dream cast– *wet dream* –cast be? If I had my druthers, I'd say...

- Ian McKellen as Egeus?
- Patrick Stewart as Nedar?
- Kenneth Branagh as Oberon?
- Emma Thompson as Titania?

- Alan Cumming as Puck?
- Emma Watson as Hermia?... or dare I say, 'Helena'?!?
- Eddie Redmayne as Lysander?
- Chris Hemsworth as Demetrius?
- Brian Cox as Theseus?
- Gillian Anderson as Hippolyta?
- Al Pacino as Bottom?...
- or Tom Hanks as Bottom?!?

Graham: Do you really think all– any of these accomplished Hollywood and/or Royal Shakespearean actors would dare act in your "erotica for EVERY fetish"!

Ophelia: Perhaps I need to look less to the Royal Shakespeare Company, West End, Broadway or -sigh- Hollywood and more to the San Fernando Valley, shouldn't I...

- Sasha Grey as Helena!
- Nina Hartley as Titania!
- Jenna Jameson as Hippolyta!
- Joanna Angel as Puck!
- Ron Jeremy as Bottom!

Graham: That's quite the cavalcade of porn stars. I do realize your *Wet Dream* could have easily been a porn parody of *A Midsummer Night's Dream*, but at what point in the process did the idea of writing your eroticization in Shakespearean verse occur?

Ophelia: First, first, I'd like to add one more to my dream cast. And this last one isn't a pornstar, quite on the contrary, she is a glorious, gorgeous Hollywood actress– I'd love to see Candis Cayne as Penelope, a transgender Oberon!

Graham: Wow! Just wow! I want to go down this little road for a moment. There has been a lot of controversy in Hollywood for white-washing, the practice of casting white actors in roles that are traditionally ethnic in origin. There is also a lot of talk about whether or not a cis-gendered male should play a transgender character and here you're saying that your cis-genedered character could be played by a transgender actress. I don't quite get the reasoning.

Ophelia: When I was writing *Wet Dream*, this was before the American Supreme Court legalized gay-marriage, I didn't see Oberon as transgender. I don't know if I do even now. But in the years since, as the tides are changing not only Hollywood, but the world at large, I can now see Oberon as a trangender-character.

Graham: But "Penelope"? Where did the name come from? Out of the ether?

Ophelia: I made a promotional video for *Wet Dream* using a 1905 silent film of *A Midsummer Night's Dream*, but I replaced the dialogue cards with my own eroticized dialogue and the finished film is surprisingly pornographic.

Graham: That is a rather clever promo. How does that relate to "Penelope"?

Ophelia: For some queer reason the director didn't include Oberon as a character, but instead cast a woman as Oberon's mistress, Penelope. That is the source of the name "Penelope".

Graham: A director in 1905 gender-bent his casting? That's amazing. Thank you for indulging me my little digression. Now back to my original question: it must have seemed like a daunting task to rewrite Shakespeare in *iambic pentameter*.

Ophelia: I started reading the play with an Internet page open here the entire Shakespearean text had been digitized. I stared blankly at an empty Word file on my computer, having absolutely no idea what to do. I could take the beauty of Shakespearean poetry and bastardize it as prose and fill in the paragraphs with description, but I couldn't will my fingers to type. Then that mischievous and prankish inspiration toyed with me. "Write the erotica in Shakespearean verse", Puck said. I so I did.

Graham: Puck could not possibly have been a schizophrenic hallucination of...

> Robin Goodfellow, that merry wanderer night,
> Who jests to Oberon and makes him smile
> When I a fat and bean-fed horse beguile,
> Neighing in likeness of a filly foal:
> And sometime lurk I in a gossip's bowl,

In very likeness of a roasted crab,
And when she drinks, against her lips I bob
And on her wither'd dewlap pour the ale.
The wisest aunt, telling the saddest tale,
Sometime for three-foot stool mistaketh me;
Then slip I from her bum, down topples she,
And 'tailor' cries, and falls into a cough;
And then the whole quire hold their hips and laugh,
And waxen in their mirth and neeze and swear
A merrier hour was never wasted there.

Ms. MacTavish would be so proud I remember my lines after all these decades. Are you convinced that Robin Goodfellow, Puck himself, auditorily instructed you on the fairy wiles of erotica?

Ophelia: I know it sounds strange, but sometimes the author's inner-voice seems, somehow, disembodied, like a phantasm. Sometimes the voices were so loud and so persistent, that I feared if I didn't have a secure relationship with my family, that if I didn't have the, albeit limited, financial freedom to devote hours on end to my writing, that I could, I very much could, see myself as a transient wandering up and down the lanes of shops with a trolley filled with all of my personal belongings and arguing with my characters as an undiagnosed, unmedicated schizophrenic.

Casey: Oh, my. I shudder to think of writer's relationship with our glorious Muse as a mental disease. But to the outsider, the layman who toils in a traditional nine-to-five, that has never wrote a short story or began a novel, to them the very idea that characters speak to their author, actively deciding whether they would say this or do that sometimes overruling the author themselves. To the rest of the world, it would seem like all writer's suffer from a mental disease. But I certainly prefer to think of it just as an extremely loud internal monologue that won't shut the heck up. But you truly feel it was schizophrenic?

Ophelia: Most certainly. I don't believe that I am schizophrenic, but to the psychiatric community whom deal with these diagnoses on a daily basis, I could see them mistake something that is so innate to the writing experience as hearing our characters and allowing them their own free will as, well, schizophrenia, however, not paranoid schizophrenia, but perhaps a new category, creative schizophrenia.

Graham: When a film is made of a popular book, the readers of the book almost universally criticize the film as not being as "good as the book". You didn't adapt Shakespeare into a film or even a novel, you chose to adapt *A Midsummer Night's Dream* into another play. It was almost one-to-one.

Ophelia: Not exactly one-to-one. The amount of my trimmings was painfully small. I had taken one of the shorter plays written by Shakespeare through my revisions and additions was able to make it as lengthy and hopefully as epic as *Hamlet*.

Graham: Is there an art to the adaptation?

Ophelia: Certainly. The screenwriter hired by a studio to adapt a popular novel for the screen has a particularly difficult task. A novel is written to be read, while a play is written to be staged with as few locations and scene breaks as possible. And yet the screenwriter must tell the same story, often rewriting dialogue to be enunciated properly and editing or cutting entire scenes and plot-lines to make a palatable two-hour motion picture. And when a film is adapted in the inverse direction as seen with popular Disney musicals being produced on Broadway in front a live audience, concessions have to be made given a restriction in the number of sets and characters.

Graham: And what about adapting films or plays into novels.

Ophelia: Oh, the novelization: the bastard offspring of a movie and book. That is an unholy creature. Few novelizations of a screenplay ever survive on the bookshelves beyond the release schedule of the motion picture. I'm sure in the past, cinephiles were forced to own the novelization of their favorite movie if they wanted to recapture that experience of watching their favorite film in the days before VHS, DVD, and Blu-ray. While my initial and poorly chosen decision was to write my *Wet Dream* in prose. I didn't think that I had the talent to write Jacobean English in *iambic pentameter.* When was the last time anyone attempted such a thing.

Graham: I was just about to ask you the very same questions with the very same wording.

Ophelia: Four-hundred years, I'd assume. But thankfully, I knew from that first line of *iambic pentameter* I wrote that I could write blank verse worthy of The Bard. I also made a covenant with myself that wherever William Shakespeare led I would go, no matter how depraved. That is how Egeus and Demetrius became lovers.

Alex: Why did you feel the need to write this play with "erotica for EVERY fetish"?

Casey: Actually, the question we should be asking you is, "How does it feel to have written erotic fan-fiction?"

Ophelia: I afraid I don't quite understand your question.

Casey: The gentleman sitting between the two of us, with his bed-headed adorkable cow-lick, is more than aware that there this disgusting, ignoble little genre of fiction called erotic fan-fiction. Because of the shear plague of fan-fiction set in my beloved Alistair Strange literary universe, I waded deep into the nefarious under-belly of the world-wide-web and discovered to my dismay– my horror– this sub-culture that delights in eroticizing our favorite literary, cinematic, and television characters.

Ophelia: I... I... I...

Alex: Casey, why don't we...

Casey: No! I really want to know where the joy is in eroticizing our most beloved characters. I am one who is wont to understand the history of this seedy sub-culture and so I did some research. It appears to have been birthed in the 1960's with erotic fan-fiction "shipping" Captain James T. Kirk and Commander Spock. I'm sure it is much, much older, perhaps going back to 19th century fan-fiction set in Jane Austen's novels. How far back does this go, Ophelia? Do you really want to know?

Ophelia: I... No... I... don't.... really...

Casey: It goes back to the days of the Holy Bible. To the decades after Jesus walked on this very earth. Does that surprise you? Shock you? There was this little Gnostic Gospel called *The Gospel of Mary Magdalene*, a little pamphlet of a gospel that first eroticized our Lord and Saviour Jesus Christ. Why would somebody do that? I ask you, why would *you* eroticize our Lord and Saviour Jesus Christ.

Ophelia: You... you... actually... read... my... play?

Casey: Of course, I've read it. It was a particularly long plane-flight and I was curious to know whom I'd be sitting on this dais with. What pleasure did you get from taking this "wise and humane drama" writ by the most beloved wordsmith in the English language and turning it into debased and reviled erotica?

Ophelia: I... I... I...

Alex: Casey...

Casey: That would Shakespeare think of your having written fan-fiction– erotic fan-fiction– of his play.

Ophelia: I... I... think he'd be proud!

Casey: I beg your pardon. As an author whose most famous creation, Alistair Strange, has been forced against his will to star in homoerotic fan-fiction, I take offense...

Ophelia: *[Interrupting]* He'd be so proud of me! William Shakespeare had to write his sexuality through allusion, metaphor, and *entendre*. He couldn't write the blatant eroticism that I have been able to. I think that every little hint he gave– like Egeus and Demetrius between homosexual lovers– was what he had intended to write, but was forced merely hint at. He could not write a homosexual or pedophilic or bestiality storyline like I know he desired to between Egeus and Demetrius, Oberon and the Indian Prince, and Titania and Bottom. This self-censorship was because he had to deal with Edmund Tylney, the Master of Revels, whom wielded the righteous hammer of forbiddance over every play written during his years writing for the stage. Shakespeare wouldn't have been able to write what he wanted to write. Likewise, I wouldn't have been able to write what I wrote without the evolution of pornography. Henry Miller wrote his erotica in the 1930's, but his novels were almost instantly banned and weren't republished for decades until the political and social environment of the 1960's began to change. Without Lenny Bruce being arrested on obscenity charges time and time again, there wouldn't be many– any of the modern comedians.

Casey: That's a nice little justification. But there isn't justification for having written fan-fiction– erotic fan-fiction.

Ophelia: It's not fan-fiction. It's an erotic adaption.

Alex: Casey... this isn't her fight... it's mine...

Casey: *[Ignoring Alex]* You're mincing words, little miss-priss.

Ophelia: I'm not. William Shakespeare was not the most original of authors. That may not be the most English thing to say out-loud, but he bloody-well stole virtually every plot he ever wrote. *Romeo and Juliet* was "adapted" from Arthur Brook's English translation of Matteo Bandello's own adaptation of Luigi da Porto's *Giulietta e Romeo*. That's a whole lot of adapting. Who stole what from whom? Raphael Holinshed's *Chronicles* is the source of nearly every one of his English historical plays: *Henry VI* parts two, three, and then one, *Richard III*, *Richard II*, *Henry IV* parts one and two, *Henry V*, *Henry VIII*, *Macbeth*, *King Lear*, and *Cymbeline*. Was Shakespeare writing fan-fiction set in historical England? I don't think so. Did he quote Holinshed to a ridiculous word-for-bloody-word degree? Yes. Oh my God, yes! And he stole *Julius Caesar*, *Timon of Athens*, *Antony and Cleopatra*, and *Coriolanus* from Plutarch. Of course, he did. So, yes, he had sources for most, if not all, of his stories, but he didn't write fan-fiction and neither did I!

Casey: Oh, now the pot is calling the kettle–

Alex: Casey!

Casey: I don't have to listen to some twenty-something girl giggling.

Ophelia: I'm not laughing. Who's laughing? I'm the one being assaulted.

Casey: Tossing her unnaturally pink hair over her shoulder.

Ophelia: What does my hair have to do with anything?

Casey: Brandishing of her Horde tattoos.

Ophelia: What in the bloody-hell is a "Horde"?

Casey: The computerized flick of her dress that make her look like she's been plucked straight from a video-game.

Ophelia: Why is she speaking to me in the third-person? Like I'm not bloody here!

Alex: Casey... you really aren't fighting with Ophelia here.

Casey: I'm not? What are you, clairvoyant?

Alex: Casey, you're picking this fight with me. Alex.

Casey: I beg your pardon!

Alex: These are all of the talking-points for an argument with me, not young Ms. Ophelia here.

Casey: But you didn't eroticize Alistair Strange, turning my poor, little boy into a homosexual lover.

Alex: And neither did Ophelia. You aren't upset with Ophelia for eroticizing William Shakespeare, you're angry with me for writing fan-fiction of Abigail K.C. Sterling. I wrote a novel in your literary universe!

> *"I am the greatest, I said that even before I knew I was."*
> –Muhammad Ali

Chapter Twenty-Seven
The Fight of the Century

by alistairstrange#1fan

Oh ma gawd! I don't know what the in the ef I just watched. I've never even heard of Graham Norton, nor have I ever watched his talk-show on BBC America, but when I heard that my beloved Casey and that em-fing impostor Alex would be interviewed together and on the same couch, I ran to on-demand and lo and behold it was there in its complete, nearly un-censored, wonderfully uncomfortable glory.

The gloves came off! The gauntlet was thrown down! They were stand-ing toe-to-toe, fighting tooth and nail! (I don't know many fighting idioms so that's all I've got) But it was the FIGHT OF THE CENTURY (appar-ently, I know one more).

Chapter Twenty-Eight
the graham norton show - segment two

Abigail K.C. Sterling: What?

Alex K.C. Silver: Ms. Ophelia here did not eroticize Alistair Strange. She isn't one of the fan-fiction authors whom transmogrified a beloved teenaged character into a homosexual "twink" whom was seduced and sodomized repeatedly by Zeus, his own great-great-great-great-great-great-great-great?!?-grandfather. She didn't write fan-fiction set in the DC Universe where Alistair Stranger was Batman's fifth– sixth?– seventh?!? Robin, the Boy Wonder.

Casey: It's true. I shouldn't be picking on the poor girl. Ophelia didn't write the fan-fiction where Harry Potter discovers his Alistair Stranger is his long-lost twin brother from an alternate dimension, whom teams with Ron Weasley and Alistair's soon to be paramour Herminone Granger-Weasley against Lord Voldemort, whom has been permitted to leave Hades due to an illicit, and illegal accord with Hades, Alistair's own distant uncle, did she? I particularly despised that one.

Alex: Nor did she write the fan-fiction where, in a galaxy far, far away, Alistair Strange accepted Emperor Palpatine' offer to be murderously replace Darth Vadar as Darth Strange, Lord of the Sith, destined to fulfill an ancient Sith prophecy to rend the Force asunder by ridding the galaxy from the midichlorian infestation.

Casey: *[Laughing]* That one was so stupid. Without the midichlorians, there wouldn't be a Dark Side to the Force either. So stupid.

Alex: *[Laughing]* Without the midicholorians and their asinine ancient prophecy of the "One Who Would Bring Balance to the Force" some of the *Star Wars'* prequels might have made sense.

Casey: *[Laughing]* Boring political intrigue. Fan-favorite characters as children. Death by losing the will to live, *ugh*.

Alex: *[Laughing]* Outside of a couple of cool lightsaber fights, George Lucas' prequels are worse than the worst *Star Wars* fan-fiction.

Casey: *[Laughing]* His own fans know what *Star Wars* should be more than he does– more than he ever did.

Alex: *[Laughing]* The writers of the licensed novels and comic books know what *Star Wars* should be more than Lucas does.

Casey: *[Laughing]* It boggles my mind how the very original creator of *Star Wars* can get this own universe–his own fans– so very, very wrong.

Alex: *[Laughing]* He sells his baby– the cinematic universe he crated– to Disney for four billion dollars and yet he considers *The Force Awakens*, *Rogue One* and the as-of-yet untitled episodes VIII and IX– hell– all future *Star Wars* movies to be nothing more than glorified fan-fiction. How sad is that?

Casey: Do you have four billion dollars, Alex? You really, truly want to own my literary universe and have carte blanche to do with her as you please? You can have Alistair Strange for– I'll give you a good price– a fire sale, if you will– *[dramatic Dr. Evil pause]* one–

billion– dollars. And not a penny less. *[Laughing]*

Alex: It's good you're laughing. Casey, remember, this isn't her fight, it's mine.

Casey: Yeah, you're right, Alex. I'm so, so very sorry, Ophelia. I shouldn't have been picking on you. You didn't eroticize my Alistair. You did not commit any crime against me other than assaulting– torturing– me with damn near every disgusting fetish and paraphilia imaginable in your weird, stupid little play.

Ophelia [Censored]: Hey! That was uncalled for.

Casey: *[Laughing]* So stupid.

Ophelia: Bloody-hell!

Alex: You should be mad at me.

Casey: I'm not mad at you. *[To Ophelia]* I should never have gotten upset at you.

Ophelia: Apology accept–

Casey: Just because neither of you thieves have given birth to anything original.

Ophelia: –withdrawn.

Graham Norton: What is next for you, Alex? I know that Casey will, no doubt, has already started working of the soon to be sixth novel in the Alistair Strange series. But what's next for you? What is your follow-up novel going to be.

Alex: Well, since both Casey and I have both written what are considered by our publisher and fans alike to be canonical fifth novels in the Alistair Strange series, our editor has decided that each of our different alternate universe storylines will both continue to play out in two sixth novels.

Casey: That's certainly news to me.

Alex: My sixth novel will pick up right after the ending of *The Weight of a Feather* and Casey's will continue the story from *The Orchardist of Yggdrasil.*

Graham: This is such exciting news for all of the Strangers. You never seen two *Star Wars - Episode VIIs*, or two *Matrix Reloadeds* from different writers and directors. This is really really cool, exciting news. To be following two different branches of the worldtree, Yggrasil.

Casey: I take offense to that notion.

Alex: It's going to prove to be a glorious undertaking. While I'm definitely proud of my *Weight of a Feather*, it kind of pales in comparison to Casey's *Orchardist*. But despite it's problems, I'm so, so proud of my *Weight of a Feather*.

Graham: As you should be, it was a really, really good novel.

Alex: Casey's *Orchardist* is a certainly more mature take on the Alistair Strange's death and journey toward resurrection. You can really tell that I'm newer to her– our universe, and while I have written several of my own novels, *The Weight of a Feather* is the first one that I've even gotten close to "authentic" publication.

Graham: You're written other novels besides *The Weight of a Feather?* Are we ever going to see the publication of those.

Alex: As for their publication, that is entirely up to Ms. Reilly. But yes, of course, I've written over books. One doesn't just jump into writing fan-fiction without have written other stories.

Casey: You shouldn't really say that. There is no doubt in my mind that most, if not all, fan-fiction writers don't possess the talent to create their own original stories. That is why they choose to write in other authors' universes, with stories starring other authors' characters. There is little– no, no– there is no creativity to be found in fan-fiction.

Alex: We'll have to agree to disagree. There are many, many stories on the fan-fiction websites that are certainly worthy to be placed side-by-side with the original novels.

Casey: If they exist– and I'm not going to quantify their existence– they are, no doubt, buried under a glut of stories by talentless hacks.

Alex: Those sites have good metrics to weed out stories that aren't well written. Those that are are rewarded with "reviews", "favs", and "follows". It is a really good peer-review system to discover which books are popular with the fans and which are, to acknowledge Casey's unnecessary hostility, "talentless hacks".

Casey: And this is exactly why I don't agree, nor accept, the decision by *my* editor Iris Reilly to publish two sixth novels in the Alistar Strange series. The publication of Alex's *The Weight of a Feather* was an interesting little experiment—

Alex: Interesting... little... experiment?

Casey: — But there really, truly is only one canonical fifth novel- mine- *The Orchardist of Yggdrasil.*

Alex: You don't really mean that, do you?

Casey: You had a nice little run there, Alex, but in the end there can only be one canonical Alistair Strange series- mine.

Alex: But... but... I've been published. Your editor chose to publish my novel first.

Casey: I'll freely admit that you really kind of forced my hand to finally deliver my *Orchardist* to Iris- see, we're on a first name basis and always will be. And I thank you for that.

Alex: What? You do?

Casey: This little experiment- justify it however you will- whether your journey to Alistair's resurrection in your *Weight of a Feather* took place in a parallel universe apart from my own journey to Alistair's resurrection in my *Orchardist of Yggdrasil*- certainly snapped me out of my reclusive funk. And I thank you for that.

Alex: I don't know what to say.

Casey: Say that you're moving onto other greener pastures populated with characters and storylines that are of your own creation and not mine. I am giving you the greatest gift that I can. Now that you have the ear of an editor at a major publishing house, you can write anything your heart desires.

Alex: I'm afraid I can't do that.

Casey: I beg your pardon. This is the greatest gift that I give to you. And you're going to refuse me.

Alex: The fans have spoken. By purchasing my *Weight of a Feather* and putting me on *The New York Times* Bestseller list, they have chosen me as the heir to the Alistair Strange universe. Where some Robert Jordan fans may have rejected Brandon Sanderson's attempt to complete *The Wheel of Time*, the fans of Alistair Stranger- your fans- have chosen me as the rightful heir: the

Once and Future King.

Casey: You impudent little snot.

Alex: Have you never read the essay, "The Death of the Author" by Roland Barthes?

Casey: You're just trying to deflect—

Alex: No, I'm not actually. I'm trying to explain the actual nature between the author and their readers.

Casey: You're just trying to justify your own actions– crimes– against me.

Alex: You really don't understand, do you? The author doesn't own their own writing. "The Author is supposed to feed the book – that is, he pre-exists it, thinks, suffers, lives for it; he maintains with his work the same relation of antecedence a father maintains with his child". You nourished him in the womb of your intellect, gave birth to child, and sent him out into the really, really world. You no more own Alistair Strange than you would any natural children. Alistair's life is separate from your own. The writer must die in childbirth, because "the birth of the reader must be ransomed by the death of the Author." You don't own Alistair Strange any more or any less than I do. The readers have married Alistair Strange, they have chosen to share their lives devoted to him.

Casey: I find that a gross distortion of the true Author-Reader relationship.

Alex: No, it's not. J.K. Rowling gave birth to Harry Potter. She nourished him *in utero* for seven glorious novels, dying in childbirth to Harry Potter, not once but seven different times. But she refused to die. She refuses to allow Harry Potter, in the words of Solomon, to *leave his father and mother, and shall be joined unto his wife, and they two shall be one flesh* (Eph. 5:31). Instead, Joanne allows herself to be put on life support on Pottermore.com, constantly and consistently interfering with the life of Harry Potter has with his fans by stating that Dumbledore is "actually gay" amongst other heresies. She refuses to die and is ruining the relationship the readers enjoy with Harry Potter, robbing them of their own interpretations of just who Harry Potter is. J.K. Rowling SHOULD stay dead.

Casey: Nice essay. You write that in Lit Crit class? And what are you in the ridiculous analogy? The wicked step-mother? How do you have any more sway over Alistair Strange than I do. I'm his mother! You... you... aren't just a—

Alex: A fan! I was– I am– I will always be a fan. I'm the one that is destined to inherit Alistair Strange. He no longer belongs to you.

Casey: You think he belongs to *you*? What makes you so special? You think you're the Chosen One because Iris Reilly selected your book to publish? If in her mind, she was able to justify her legal treacheries because I hadn't delivered *The Orchardist* to her in the timely manner. She could have chosen anyone in the entire world of publishing to continue the Alistair Strang series.

Alex: But she didn't, did she? Ms. Reilly chose me. It was my novel that she chosen to publish. Mine.

Casey: She could have chosen anyone in the entire world. There are a host of writers who would have given their eye-teeth to continue my series. And if Iris was able to justify in her own mind, her publishing your heresy as canon, then what is going to stop her from selecting another writer to usurp the usurper? Isn't this how every Roman Emperor died? They were all assassinated.

Alex: What?

Casey: When another author, one with an actual library of published novels comes along with an idea for a second alternate parallel literary universe, you will soon see your own parallel universe completely obliterated in a literary Ragnarok. Iris won't hesitate to put a knife in your back as readily as she did mine. *Et tu, Brute*

Alex: You don't see it, do you? You really don't see the future of the publishing industry, do you? Yes, I was the Chosen One discovered on a fan-fiction website. I was the One Chosen for publication. I was the first and I certainly won't be the last to be discovered among the fans. The fans! I welcome the second alternate parallel literary universe. And the third. And the fourth. And the fifth.

Casey: I don't believe you. You want the power that comes with sitting on the throne.

Alex: Whose throne? There shouldn't be any throne. That monarchy crap of inheriting power and wealth because you won the sperm lottery. You think because your created Alistair Strange that you are entitled to something? I read the reviews when *The XII Labors* was released. Alistair Strange was considered a blatant carbon-copy of Harry Potter. You were accused of stealing the Greek and Norse gods motif from Rick Riordan. The Old Gods were birthed by H.P. Lovecraft, not you. Nothing about your literary universe if original with you.

Casey: It's my right! My children's right!

Alex: Children? All the estates of the most esteemed literary figures want is to reap the financial rewards of the characters created by the deceased. They want their inheritance, even though they contributed nothing to it. And they will stop at nothing to prevent anyone else from wresting control of these characters held hostage by copyright. Tom Clancy's estate holds the keys to his espionage kingdom. Robert Jordan's widow hand-selected Brandon Sanderson to finish *The Wheel of Time*. Christopher Tolkien has milked the filing-cabinets of his father for every drop of creativity found within. Brian Herbert, at least, has the audacity to actually write in his father's universe. Then you have an estate, generations removed from the death of its creator, Sherlock Holmes, who refuses to let go of their birthright, their control, nearly a century removed. And Disney, oh, don't get me started on the Mouse. They will do everything within their billion-dollar power to keep copyrights over the Mouse.

Casey: And why shouldn't I have this same control? Why shouldn't any potential offspring I may or may not have earn this right.

Alex: Because they haven't *earned* it. They didn't create it. Sherlock Holmes lives on, and should live on, in novels, short-story collections, and the BBC and CBS television series. This is what was always meant to happen. Sir Arthur Conan Doyle didn't own Sherlock Holmes. His fans did, and always did. He murdered Sherlock Holmes at Reichenbach Falls and the fans wouldn't stand for the assassination of the beloved literary creation. They made such a stink that Doyle had to resurrect Sherlock Holmes. They brought Holmes back to life, in spite of the wishes of his creator And if he hadn't his estate wouldn't own do-diddi-ly-squat, because it would have fallen into the public domain decades ago. Doyle acquiescing to the fans, not only returned Sherlock Holmes to life, it gave his estate decades of ownership it otherwise wouldn't have had.

Casey: Why would any writer create any characters if they didn't inherently have intimate control over them?

Alex: Copyright is a completely 20th century industrialist creation and problem. Writers have been writing for centuries without any so-called copyrights. The *Illiad* and the *Odyseey* were not original with Homer. Those stories were passed down from poet to poet over the centuries. Homer was just the first to write them done using that newfangled invention, the Greek alphabet. Nothing stopped Shakespeare from stealing his plays from others and nothing stopped Ophelia from stealing hers from him.

Ophelia: Hey! I resent being pulled into this little cat-fight.

Alex: And nothing stopped Twain or Stoker or Melville or Austen from writing their great literary works. Hell, even Bram Stoker wrote a stage version of *Dracula* in a crude, rudimentary means of copyright protection, because the right to prevent unauthorized stage adaptations didn't yet exist under British law. And nothing stopped Universal Pictures or Hammer films from flogging that undead horse.

Casey: You're nothing but a thief– a horse thief. And you know what they do to horse thieves.

Alex: You going to have me hanged in an old oak hanging tree?

Casey: I wish I could. The only reason you are saying any of this– bullshit– is you haven't actually created anything. You don't know what its like to have these characters spring to life in your mind.

To have these characters live in your thoughts and your dreams. To have these characters speak to you and be guided by you. To see them through the exposition, the rising action, the climax, the falling action, and the resolution. I've done that. And every other author in the history of publishing as done the same thing. They created. They gave birth. I've created. I've given birth.

Alex: And like every author worth their salt, you should have died in childbirth.

Casey: More Lit Crit bullshit.

Alex: I wrote *The Weight of the Feather*. I heard Alistair Strange speaking to me, too. The characters have lived in my thoughts and my dreams, as well. Don't you see? Your characters don't just exist in your thoughts and dreams, but the thoughts and dreams of every reader of your books. While they anxiously await you to bestow upon the eager flock the next book, they dream of Alistair Strange. They yearn for him. They take the hints and foreshadows you are so adept at creating, and they create fan-theories to explain this or that. They are tireless in their devotion to Alistair Strange.

Casey: Theorizing? Why is that even a thing? I've seen the Internet explode with theories about *Lost*, about *Game of Thrones*. And it's getting worse with each and every passionately devoted series. Do they so desperately want to be seen to be clairvoyant, that they alone "saw that coming" so they can brag with their fellow Internet geeks? Why does every plot-point need to be dissected? Analyzed? Is nothing left to mystery? Suspense? Why don't the fans just wait until the decision is made by the creators.

Alex: Because they care. Because they feel a sense of ownership over what they love.

Casey: But they don't really own anything, do they? Does Hollywood write a check to the fans? No. Hollywood expects the fan to buy the increasingly outrageous tickets see the film adaptations. Did Hollywood write you a check? Do you get royalties from the Alistair Strange film empire? No, I do!

Alex: Maybe I should. You certainly weren't delivering them with a novel to adapt. I am the one who delivered a finished novel. It was my fifth novel that made Hollywood all twitterpated and rushing to get a screenplay written.

Casey: But are they? Are they really going to devote a hundred million dollars to filming and marketing a film adaptation of *The Weight of a Feather*, when they can just as easily spend that hundred million dollars filming *The Orchadist of Yggdrasil*. They only–I mean, the only f-ing– reason you are a *New York Times* Bestselling author is because I was too reclusive to give Iris my novel.

Alex: The fans love my novel. The fans love me. There is an entire community devoted to Team Griffindico– to me!

Casey: And if Iris decides it isn't worth the headache– either from the fans or my lawyers– there will be no sequel to *The Weight of a Feather*. And where will your devoted Team Griffindico go when the sequel to *The Orchadist of Yggdrasil* is published. They will return to the fold– to Team Dracarys– like the faithful little sheep they are.

Alex: Is that how you see your fans? As sheep? As faithful little sheep to be herded here or there? You don't appreciate– you don't understand– your Strangers. You sit hidden away in your million dollar mansion and have forgotten who put you there. The Strangers put you there. And they can take that away from you just as easily. If you disrespect them– call them your "sheep"– you can find yourself without any fans, without any book sales. You will find yourself imprisoned in that mansion of yours, reclusivity be damned.

Casey: You—

Alex: There could just as easily be a revolt from Team Dracarys to Team Griffindico. Your arrogance can cost you the throne you so desperately sit on. I am the rightful heir.

Casey: —You ungrateful, impudent little SHIT!

Alex: Ungrateful? I am eternally grateful for your having given the world Alistair Strange, but America is a democracy, not a monarchy. And yet we are ruled over by the most undemocratic, most oligarchical, law– copyright! You've had your time governing the

world of Alistair Strange. The fans has spoken– they have voted– for me. Your reclusivity has proven that you don't want to be
the god of your little third-person omniscient world. That's fine.
Abdicate! Pass the torch to a more worthy successor. Me! Alex
K.C. Silver!

Casey: You– YOU– are the first heretic in the history of the printing press to stolen their novel, their characters, their very lives
from someone else– me and had the royal seal of canonization
emblazoned on your pseudepigrapha, your spuriously attributed book. The fifth novel should never have been *The Weight of a
Feather*. That was a crime. That was heresy. The only fifth novel
is *The Orchadist of Yggdrasil*. And there will not be two sixth novels. There will be a sixth novel when I am damn well ready to deliver it. Mark my words, Alex. Heavy is the head that wears the
crown. You should have killed me when you usurped my throne,
because soon, the conspiratorial dagger that will be plunged into
your back will be mine!

Graham Norton: Casey! Alexander! Enough! You're making for a
very, very interesting and entertaining show!

Chapter Twenty-Nine

A Conspiracy
of DUNCES

—Internal Memo—

To: Iris Reilly, editor
From: Christopher Hanson, Publisher

Just got finished watching clips of *The Graham Norton Show*. Every entertainment/news/tabloid Internet rag from TMZ, to EW to E! to People, has embedded the YouTube video of two of our biggest literary superstars battling like the *Battling Bickersons*. A certain amount of animosity is good for business. And while the old axium still holds true: that the only bad publicity being no publicity, this side-sho isn't good for business. If we are going to continue the *Alistair Strange* series into a sixth, seven, eight etc. and beyond– we need to end this war and end it now. You got into bed with both Casey and Alex and if your polyamorous relationship is going to work, you need to get them into bed with each other and they need to kiss and make up.

—Internal Memo—

I sent that last memo before I realized how vulgar that last sentence sounds. Please disregard the *double entendres* and double-down on getting Tinseltown to release a double-feature of Casey's and Alex's movies, before they realize there is a double indemnity cause in their contracts for having double-billed *Alistair Strange* to double the authors, creating a double-standard that is going to doom our publishing house. Do this before one or the other double-crosses us and jumps to Doubleday.

Christopher Hanson, Publisher

—Internal Memo—

The Hollywood studio has been filming *Alistair Strange and the Weight of a Feather* <u>and</u> *Alistair Strange and the Orchardist of Yggdrasil* back-to-back with much the same cast including the role of Alistair Strange himself. They have rented a stage at the San Diego Comic-Con in order to release both of the trailers for the two motion-pictures at the same event. There is going to be a panel with the cast detailing the unique challenges of filming two different fifth movies in the series. I would like to get both Casey and Alex on the dais for their own panel.

Alex is prepared to talk about his sixth novel in the *Alistair Strange* series, which he is prepared to deliver the manuscript to me by the time the event takes place this July. I am convinced that I can convince Casey to speak at the Con. After Alex announces his sixth book, Casey will want to write her sixth novel, and given Casey's predilection for reclusivity, she may already have it fully written, and could surprise us all: Alex, you, me, everyone at the Comic-Con, and the entire world.

But your *double entendres* has given me a delightfully wicked little idea. If we can get Casey and Alex together and I don't mean together on the dais at the same time, but if we can get them together together, then can you imagine the possibilities? The celebrity gossip rags would have a field day with news of the two embittered and embattled authors are in bed together. Paparazzi would give our publishing house all the free–*free*– publicity that we could possibly ask for. We turn TMZ, EW, E!, and People from gossiping hens into the official publicity department of our publishing house. And just think if they were to co-write the seventh book, not books, in the *Alistair Strange* series, therefore uniting the two divergent parallel realities into a single, unified, canonical *Alistair Strange* novel the number of books we could sell.

Iris Reilly, editor

—Internal Memo—

You have got me standing at attention. Do you think one of our romance novelists would be willing to write a playbook on how to get them together? Surely they already have an outline for this sort of thing. There has to be a formula that they follow. And it's occurred to me that we can get the same romance novelist to write an memoir–an exposé– of their budding romance. Let's do this!

Christopher Hanson, Publisher

—Internal Memo—

We already have the makings of the perfect romance novel. Girl creates fictional boy, girl loses fictional boy, girls get real boy. Our heroine and love interest are flawed, not perfect. They are two people our audience, the Strangers, want to be together, need to be together, even though they don't realize it yet. Strangers have already fallen in love with Alex, and yet they sympathize with Casey's plight as the wronged woman. There is already an inherent obstacle (a key ingredient to any romance), a conflict to their being together, that keeps the story moving forward: she hates him. She feels betrayed by one of her beloved Strangers. She feels like this usurper, however adorkable, has stolen her life's work from her. Our love interest admires her, but doesn't see anything romantic in their relationship. This is something we as the authors of this story will need to change. We need to get them together in the same room; we need to get them conversing, perhaps over dinner, hell-even if the evening ends with her throwing glassware in the restaurant, at least that is conflict! While in San Diego, we need to appear focused on the Comic Convention and our panels, but in reality, we need to keep their relationship as the main focus of our attention. In the end, what are our heroine and her love interest willing to sacrifice on the altar of love? Can she put aside her loathing for a chance at a satisfying ending? Then and only then we will get our pay-off at the panel when they embrace in front of all of the Strangers and write happily-ever-after!

Or they could end up killing each other and we end up with a police procedural on our hands.

Either way, as publisher, we'll have a *New York Times* Bestseller.

Iris Reilly, editor

> *"Things can get out of a black hole, both to the outside, and possibly, to another universe. So, if you feel you are in a black hole, don't give up. There's a way out."*
> —Stephen Hawkings

Chapter Thirty

The San Diego CONman & the CONtessa

by Bray Radbury

Casey loved, absolutely adored attending Comic Conventions in those wonderful years before she had faded into reclusivity. While she had never stepped foot on the convention floor as an attendee, she simply loved every aspect of the conventions.

Where else in the world could fans of the geek culture, those who collected comic-books, read genre fiction, and devoured Hollywood films, could gather in a single location to meet their favorite creators, experts, Hollywood actors, and most importantly themselves, those fellow geeks who had also devoted their hobbies, their past-times, their very lives to their chosen franchises.

She delighted in the cosplayers who had

devoted so much money and so many hours expertly crafting screen-accurate reproductions of the costumes of their favorite super-powered comic book heroes or the diabolically-powered villains, Hollywood characters from a variety of franchises: *Star Wars, Star Trek, The Lord of the Rings, Harry Potter, Aliens, Predator, Evil Dead*, Disney princesses, video-game characters, and Japanese Anime. Even the gender-bending of characteres, or taking a character and changing its gender, seethed with creativity.

As an invited, featured celebrity, she loved sitting for hours on end signing every manner of memorabilia: hardcover, paperback, and even first-edition copies of her books, collector's editions of the DVD or Blu-ray editions of the Hollywood adaptations, posters, photographs, fan-art, and for the hardest of the hardcore autograph-hounds, simple, blank 3"x5" index cards.

How far the conventions had come since their inception when they were simply limited to the buying, the selling, and the trading of comic-books. Casey wished she knew the moment when it all changed, or was it a step-by-step evolution from Con to Con? When were the first "superhero masquerades" or costume contests that reward those devoted cosplayers who dared to recreate their favorite characters?

When did Hollywood first discover the importance of the Con and geek culture in general? Now, Hollywood studios plan the announcements of the tent-pole, summer-blockbusters and the release of trailers around the San Diego Comic-Con, featuring panels with their actors.

Even the video-game creators and publishers have created their own convention ecosystem like *E3* to announce their new IP (intellectual property), sequels, reboots, remakes, etc. *ad nauseam.* How is it possible that simple coders are revered as celebrities? She didn't know, but she thought it was delightful.

At her very first Con as an invited featured celebrity guest, she thought she could safely walk around the convention floor, but she couldn't. Even though her celebrity as *The New York Times* Bestselling author was newly-founded, she was mobbed by Strangers. At her second Con, she decided to cosplay in wonderful anonymity as Princess Leia. She reveled in the utter concealment of her identity, despite choosing the shockingly revealing costume of Jabba's slave-barge metal-bikini. Now, her Strangers only wanted to take pictures with the Slave Leia cosplayer, not Abiligal K.C. Sterling.

Iris Reilly had invited Casey to dinner on the eve of the annual San Diego Comic-Con International. There was a three-star Michelin steakhouse, one that featured multiple James Beard Award-winning chefs, one floor below her penthouse suite at the hotel. Casey hadn't seen her editor in person since the entire debacle with Alex K.C. Silver and the publication of his heretical *Alistair Strange and the Weight of a Feather*. She still to this very day considered Iris Reilly to be her own personal Judas Iscariot.

She took the single flight of stairs down to the restaurant, instead of the elevator (add minor claustrophobia to reclusivity in the list of her certified nerosies). She walked up to the Host's podium and said she was meeting a Mrs. Iris Reilly. The Host said, "Follow me," and Casey did. The Host showed her to a table set for two next to the plate-glass window. Casey, whether she liked it or not, was forced to take in the picturesque panoramic view of the San Diego skyline, including the moonlight sparking ocean. She sat in the chair offered to her by the Host and she seized the edge of the table (add acrophobia to the list).

Across from her, as she waited for her editor, was another table set for two, which was currently unoccupied. Soon, the Host returned, not with Iris Reilly, but with a guest he was seating at the empty table across from her. She glanced up and saw to her horror it was Alex K.C. Silver being seated.

They sat across from each other in complete and utter silence just long enough to realize that Iris Reilly was about to no-show not one but two tables. The waitresses each came to each of their tables simultaneously and took their drink orders and offered them menus.

"Well, this is a fine coinkydink, isn't it," Casey said breaking the tension as thick as arctic ice.

"We've been set up," Alex said, and Casey agreed. After a few tense heartbeats that thundered in both their ears, Alex offered to join Casey at her table, since that was the end-game of one Mrs. Iris Reilly. This time Casey only reluctantly acquiesced to the kind invitation. "I wonder what she's up to sitting us at adjacent tables?" Alex asked.

"My guess, and it's only a guess, is she doesn't want any fireworks at the Alistair Strange panel Saturday evening," Casey said. "And she wants us to bury the hatchet. Not literally, of course, in each other, but figuratively."

"I know the difference between literal and figurative. I'm not a complete illiterate despite my reputation as an author of fan-fiction. I happen to join you in this pet-peeve,' he said as he joined her as requested. "I wonder if she also wants us to kiss-and-make-up while we're at it."

"I don't think that will be happening this evening, Mr. Silver, if that really is your last name."

"Actually, it's Mr. Brown. My name is Robert Dwight Brown."

"So you do have a Christian name, instead of stealing mine."

"I didn't steal your name. I chose a pseudonym that would lend me a aura of authenticity in the fan-fiction sub-culture."

"You aped my good name in the most gratuitous fashion, Mr. Brown."

"You don't yet realize what an honor it is for someone like myself to devote my own creativity to the world you built."

"Ah, you finally admit that it is a world that *I* built."

"Of course, no one in their right mind would assert that you didn't create the wonderful world of Alistair Strange."

The two waitresses returned with their drink orders and looked monetarily confused that the two tables had coalesced into one. The first waitress handed Casey a white Chardonnay and the second waitress sat a glass of a curiously green concoction. "Diet Mountain Dew," Robert said in a moment of clairvoyance.

"I was just about to ask what you were drinking. You read my mind."

"I've lived inside your mind for as long as I can remember, Casey– Ms. Sterling– but that wasn't actual clairvoyance. People, everywhere I go, ask what I prefer to drink."

"But Diet Mountain Dew?"

"I have ulcers, so I don't like alcohol. In fact, I don't like most intoxicants, despite, or perhaps in spite of the fact that I live in a state where marijuana is legal. And yes, I voted, 'Yes' on that ballot measure even though I loathe being high or drunk or otherwise intoxicated."

"My father is like you, Mr. Brown. He's not too fond of al-cohol, the Devils' brew, but if you ever meet the man, keep your liberal voting record to yourself."

"Are you inviting me to meet your family, Ms. Sterling?"

"Don't be presumptuous, Mr. Brown. I'm only sitting here at the moment because I haven't eaten since breakfast and I'm charging my– our– dinners to our publisher."

That is when they noticed both of their waitresses were still standing there, ready to take their dinner orders. Casey ordered the Filet Mignon, medium-well and Robert selected the surf-and-turf, Maine Lobster and he took his steak medium-rare. Once the waitresses had retreated to the kitchen to put in their dinner or-ders, the two writers continued their conversation.

"Why did you choose to write fan-fiction? Of all things, Rob-ert, fan-fiction? Surely, someone as intelligent as you seem to be, why choose to write in my world?"

"It's not just your world, Ms. Sterling."

"Please, Casey."

"Casey, it wasn't just the world of Alistair Strange that drew me to write so-called fan-fiction. I have always been fascinated with the works that famous authors *didn't* write. Why didn't Wil-liam Shakespeare write a play about the Passion of Jesus Christ? Why did Charles Dickens only tell the story of the haunting of Ebenezer Scrooge, when it was so obvious his own father was also visited by Spirits? As a Catholic, why —dear God— why did the Holy Bible just stop? Why weren't there Biblical books about the deaths of the Apostles or the destruction of Jerusalem, the Pret-erist fulfillment of Jesus' own prophecies? Were these and other great works lost to history forever, just because their authors never wrote them? Of course not. What was needed was an author with the skill of a forger, but the honesty of a saint. As a master-mimic, I have decided to devote my literary career to writing the works the original authors didn't. I haven't just published in your name, Abigail K.C. Sterling, but the names of Charles Dickens, William Shakespeare, and even God Himself!'"

"That is truly a strange muse you have, Robert."

"So I independently published *The Gospel According To Shakespeare: The Passion*, imagining that I was the Bard whose patron had requested and paid for a Passion play as only William Shakespeare could deliver. I wrote *The Hauntings of Jeremiah & Ebenezer Scrooge* as if Charles Dickens had been more thoroughly inspired by a single throwaway line. Inspired by my own father's predilection for exaggerating even the most commonplace personal anecdote into wondrous bullshit, I re-imagined Orson Welles' radio-drama, "The War of the Worlds", as if it were a screenplay telling the most absurd conspiracy theory ever: that the radio broadcasts heard that night that panicked America were real, that we were being invaded by Martians and Orson Welles conspired with President Roosevelt and William Randolph Hearst to cover up the invasion."

"That's a remarkable imagination you have. But why write someone else's stories in their name?"

"Because they didn't write them. These are great stories. If author's are limited to only writing books that they themselves would write, then we are limiting creativity."

"But you can't just go about writing in other people's names," Casey implored.

"Why not? It's been done since time immoral," Robert said. "There are essentially four different ways an author can be attributed to any given work: 'orthonymous', 'homonymous', 'anonymous', and 'pseudonymous'. Orthonymous is writing in your own name. Homonymous is when you share the name of another more famous author (i.e. if your name was Joanne Rowling). Anonymous is writing under no name. And pseudonymous is writing under a fake name. But there is a fifth means to attribute a work, one that was shockingly common in the ancient world: 'allonymous'."

"You made that word up."

"No. 'Allonymous' is defined, in older, heavier dictionaries, as writing under the name of someone else, particularly someone much more famous than yourself. You can begin to understand the historicity of 'allonymous' works with the knowledge that students of Plato continued the write in their mentor's name long after his death; or *The Federalist Papers* by Roman aristocrat Publius was actually written by American revolutionaries Alexander Hamilton, James Madison, and John Jay; or some epistles attributed to St. Paul were not written by his 'God-breathed' pen, but were simply written in his holy name by another less holy, but still 'God-breathed' author."

"That's an interesting English lesson, Robert. But where are these books. The books that you wrote?"

"The only book of mine that actually made it to an honest-to-God editor and publisher is a fan-fiction novel that I uploaded to a fan-fiction website. The rest of my books are wallowing in the obscurity of the Ingram Content Group catalogue. I was able to independently publish—"

"You self-published?"

"It's more than just that. You have to wear many hats, Casey, author, editor, graphic designer, marketer, publicist, the list goes on and on. But unfortunately, I'm really only an author, editor, and graphic designer. I never mastered the professions of marketer and publicist. I would publish my Shakespeare play and think that everyone wanted to read it, but when nobody was really interested in a Christian Shakespearean play, and when I couldn't get any press, I moved on to the next book. When nobody wanted to read *Orson Welles' Lost* War of the Worlds *Screenplay.* I moved on. I thought that writing a sequel to the Old and New Testaments would be a surefire publicity onslaught that would make my name, but nobody cared that I wrote a Holy Bible Trilogy. Or that I wanted to retell *A Christmas Carol.* All of my books are unknown to the general public. This is where I failed as a marketer and publicist. I'd rather just write.

"Why didn't you use your notoriety with *Weight of a Feather* to better get your books sold?

"Because nobody cares about 'Robert Dwight Brown', they only care about 'Alex K.C. Silver', the stupid, uninspired pseudonym I chose to upload my fan-fiction with. Nobody gives a flying blue– ah– um– about me as an author. They only care about me, because they care so much about you."

There was a long, pregnant pause in the conversation, which seemed to wither and die on the vine. Casey decided for their sake, she needed to say something. Anything.

"So, what do you think Iris is doing at this moment?" Casey asked.

"Besides listening to the police scanner to see if we've killed one another. I don't know."

A guffaw escaped Casey's lips, much to her embarrassment.

"Yes, I can picture her looking out of her hotel-room window waiting for the flashing red-and-blue lights of the police cars, ambulances, and fire-trucks when the 911 calls rang out that two authors were stabbing each other repeatedly in the neck with their dinner's steak-knives."

"I was imagining the same exact thing, curse our writer's imaginations."

"Yes, it certainly is a curse, isn't it?" Casey said agreeing whole-heartedly.

"Yes, it's one thing to be paranoid, but it's another thing for your own imagination to run wild with plots and story-lines about how an evening is going to play out, before it's had a chance to actually play out."

"Even if the fantasy ends in mutual murder?" Casey asked.

"For our own sakes, let's hope it doesn't, Ms. Sterling."

"Either way, this evening probably will end in headlines, if Iris has anything to say about it."

"There is definitely something under-handed about this entire situation. You and me, here in San Diego for the Con, and here at this steakhouse. It isn't a coincidence, is it?" Robert asked.

"Certainly not. I just don't know what Iris wants out of all this. I don't think she wants us to kill each other. The posthumous sales would be nice in the short run"

"That's morbid," Robert said.

"But that spike in sales would not, could not be as nice as continual sales from future volumes of Alistair Strange."

"Unless, she plans for the series to continue without *either* of us. If she's proven one thing, is that if you're replaceable, then I'm most assuredly replaceable."

"Christ, that is a horrifying idea. I'm never going to get Alistair Strange away from her, am I?" Casey said, "I signed my soul to the devil. A literal succubus whose going to bleed me dry. Even dead, she'll just find another Abigail K.C. Sterling, won't she?"

"With both of us dead at each others' hands, she could just create another K.C., Abigail, Alex, or Adrian or Avery or—"

"I shudder at the very thought of that. I wish there was a way that I could just free myself from her devil's bargain. How is it possible that a simple publishing contract could cost me my very soul."

"You hear about musicians, all of the time," Robert said, "getting stuck in awful contracts. You'd think that your publisher would have your best interest at heart, but they only think about the bottom-line. How can they profit by you at all costs. Prince had to change his name to an unpronounceable symbol to circumvent the music industry."

"What could be done to free Alistair Strange from Iris' yoke? You say you care about Alistair—"

"I do. I love Alistair Strange as if he were my own creation, you know that I do, Casey. Don't ever think anything else. I would die before I let anything happen to Alistair Strange"

"Then what can we do? I've got to get my boy away from that wicked, wicked women."

"You give him away."

"What?"

"You give him away. You let anybody and everybody write in the Alistair Strange literary universe. If everybody is writing them, then Iris would bankrupt the publishing company suing literally everybody."

"But I can't just give my boy away like that," Casey had absent-mindedly reached into her shoulder-bag and removed her precious MacBook Air, which she went no where without, even a meeting with her editor, and she absentmindedly clutched the computer to her chest, "He's mine. He's my only."

"Like any other child, Casey, some day you have to let them go. Isn't there a Bible verse about that."

"*Therefore shall a man leave his father and his mother, and shall cleave unto his wife: and they shall be one flesh* (Gen. 2:24)"

"Give Alistair Strange to the Strangers. Let them create– let us create– the future of the Strangeverse."

"But the Strangers don't know everything that I know."

"You've already given the people all the tools they need to create an limitless number of Alistair Strange novels."

"But they don't. They really, truly don't know the entire story."

"Then give them the entire story."

"Wait, what?"

"Surely, you've written a bible."

"A Bible? I wouldn't. I couldn't write a Holy Bible."

"Not a Holy Bible. A series bible."

"A what?"

"A series bible is if a reference document written by a television series creator that can be used by future screenwriters with information like characters, their descriptions and biographies, any series locations and set pieces, storylines and arcs for the first season and beyond. The series bible has everything that a screenwriter needs to write for that series. Surely, you're written something to tells you where you're going and remind you where you've been?"

"Yes," Casey said, "yes, I've written stuff like that down over the years. I just didn't know what it was called. A series bible. I kind of like it."

"You release all of that information you've accumulated—

"—Created—"

"—I stand corrected— created of over the years. You release, you publish, all that information and you will have set Alistair Strange free."

"Free?"

"Truly free."

"Will you help me figure a way to do this?"

"We've got all evening. That is the gift Iris has given us. The gift of time, the gift of togetherness, the gift of leaving us the hell alone."

"Tonight," Casey said, setting the MacBook Air on the table between them. She reached her hand out and together his in hers, "tonight, we set Alistair free."

Casey stood off stage-right, looking at the dais where the panel table had been set up. Technicians from the Hollywood studios were busy putting the finishing, the final touches on the screen and their projecting set-up. Normally, she would have been excited to see the movie trailer for the latest Hollywood adaption, but this Saturday evening, she couldn't get excited about anything. The dread she felt about what she– what she and Robert– were about to do was far too palpable, far too real. She couldn't breathe and yet her heart pounded in her ears.

She peaked out of the curtains and saw that the doors were now open and the Strangers would flooding into the room, taking their seats, and eagerly awaiting the news, any news, any exciting news about the future of Alistair Strange. They were anticipating seeing the movie trailers for not only *Alistair Strange and the Orchardist of Yggdrasil*, but also the trailer to the simultaneous release of *Alistair Strange and the Weight of a Feather*. Perhaps, they would get news on the Alistair Strange MMO of which rumors had been swirling around for years. But most assuredly they would get announcements of the sixth volume in the series. Both sixth volumes, if they were lucky. It was only July, but they couldn't help but hope for a Casey (and Alex) for Christmas!

The Hollywood panel got underway and they did, just as the Strangers had anticipated, show both of the trailers for both of the fifth Alistair Strange movies. The same cast, who acted in each of the fifth movies, sat on the dais and talked about what it was like to follow their characters down two completely different, yet parallel paths. How they were able to create a new, yet ever so different, version of their own characters. How they looked forward to the two sixth movies and two seventh movies.

Casey had to stifle the tears knowing that there wouldn't ever be two sixth movies or two seventh movies. She was about to blow up the Hollywood franchise and hers and Robert's literary franchises with a weapon-of-mass-destruction. She clutched her shoulder-bag to her chest. What she possessed in her bag had the power of a suitcase nuclear weapon that was going to destroy everything and everyone in that room leaving a radio-active crater that would poison San Diego for the half-life of plutonium.

When the time came for Abigail K.C. Sterling and Alex K.C. Silver to take the stage, she started to panic. She wanted to bolt. She wanted to flee. The fight or flight instinct was buried somewhere in the lemur D.N.A. that evolution had kept in her chromosomes after millions of years.

Then Alex took the stage, much to the cheers and adulations of the Strangers. There was no backing out now. She just had to step up the four steps to the stage and the rest would be literary history. But she couldn't move a single muscle. She couldn't will herself to utterly and revocably destroy the literary universe she created. Yes, Robert insisted that they were setting Alistair free, but she couldn't help but think of it as literary genocide.

Robert– or was it Alex– did she even know at this moment– Robert was waving Casey onto to the stage and she took the first step, then the second, and before she realized it, she was on the stage. She didn't hear her Strangers cheers and adulations. She didn't see the flashes of the cell-phone cameras. All of her very being was focused on what she was about to do.

She took her seat at the table and looked out into the audience and saw Iris Reilly, her treasonous editor, and Christopher Hanson, her duplicitous publisher, and Brett Walton, Esq., their ignominious lawyer, sitting together in the front row.

Alex stood and addressed the room. She couldn't hear a word he was saying– that is, until a cute little thing ran onto the stage and she handed him a novel. A completed novel. A bound-and-printed novel. She strained to hear what he was saying, but the pounding in her ears was too loud, but she finally heard—

"I'd like to show you the cover to the sixth novel in *my* Alistair Strange series: *Alistair Strange & Alistair Strange: Through the Multiverse.*" He paused to the allow the eruption of applause to swell, to peak, to plateau, before the applause began to quiet a bit, then he continued, "In the novel, you will meet a third Alistair Strange. The first created by our esteemed Ms. Sterling, the second created by myself, and the third created by the winner of a contest at last year's San Diego Comic-Con! I have brainstormed with the winner,– please show yourself, stand up!"

And a young woman, shyly stood up from the audience and waved to everyone in the room. She dipped her chin a bit, uncomfortable with all of the eyes trained on her.

"This young woman and I created an entirely new Alistair Strange universe and this is a universe you are going to be able to explore– today. Look under your seats!" And the audience began looking under their seats and as the realization of what they were finding dawned on each and every one of them, they erupted into cheers and screams. "You will find first editions of *Alistair Strange & Alistair Strange: Through the Multiverse* under each and every seat in the room! And not just any first editions, unique first editions, unique to the San Diego Comic-Con!"

After the cacophonous eruption of cheers and adulations died down and Alex took his seat on the dais with Casey, he leaned over and said, "Now, it's your turn."

Casey sat unable to move, unable to think, unable to breathe.

"Casey, it's your turn. Give your announcement."

She still sat unable to move, unable to think, unable to breathe. She was so furious, utterly blind with rage at the announcement by Alex K.C. Silver of a third Alistair Strange. How could he have kept that from her? Where was she when this contest was being won? Why didn't she know this pretty little thing in the audience had the audacity to create a third Alistair Strange.

"Casey– please, you're embarrassing me– us– all of us. Please—"

Casey clutched her shoulder-bag to her chest. The timer on

her nuclear weapon of mass destruction was ticking. She needed to open the bag and detonate the bomb and destroy her precious little Alistair Strange universe.

Casey stood, slowly stood, painfully, excruciating stood. She checked to see of the microphone was still curled around her jaw. She felt for her ear-piece which would allow her to hear herself. They were both exactly where the technician had placed them earlier. She walked around the dais and passed Robert. She grazed the back of his neck with her fingers. She secretly hoped she pricked gooseflesh all over his body.

"Ladies, gentlemen," she croaked. She cleared her throat, trying to swallow the Tolkiensian frog in her throat. She was afraid she'd sound more like Gollum than Sméagol. Finally, she opened her mouth, just as she was setting her precious– her *precious*– shoulder-bag on a table placed there for just such a purpose.

"Ladies, gentlemen, Strangers all," Casey finally said, "I'd like to thank you all for coming. Ever since I created Alistair Strange in that coffee shop all those many years ago, when Alistair Strange, a very, very minor character in the very first, very terrible first draft of the book, poked his head up and said that this was his story now and he was going to tell it his way. Well, I have listened to Alistair Strange more intently over the past nearly two decades, and I have served him as well as I know how to. But I can't protect him. I can't protect him anymore. I don't know how to protect him under the weight of all of this attention."

The audience murmured amongst themselves.

Two paths stood before her, one of two decisions that would alter the course of her life. Which would she choose? She understood, intimately, the relationship between artist and Muse, but who were the Fates, those three mysterious sisters, Clotho, who spun the thread of our lives, Lachesis, who alloted our time, and Atropos, who wield a pair of scissors to cut our lives short?

The very fabric of Space-Time woven by the three sisters shimmered, then shuddered, and finally tore. The tiniest of rips, most infinitesimal, would either unravel the tapestry of her life into chaos, or be woven into something new, something wonderful.

〜〜〜〜〜〜〜〜〜〜〜〜〜〜〜〜〜〜〜〜〜〜〜〜〜

"I have been betrayed. You all know I've been betrayed. You all have been complicit in this betrayal. Every single one of you, who bought Alex's heretical Alistair Strange novel have been complicit. Every one of you are my personal Judases. And for the creators of this heresy, you betrayed my trust, you betrayed your profession, you betrayed every one of the Strangers who trusted you with the future books in the Alistair Strange series.

Everyone in attendance, Robert Dwight Brown, Iris Reilly, Christopher Hanson, Brett Walton, and the entire Stangerverse didn't notice the pretty young woman enter from stage-right, dressed to the nines in a business suit and skirt, with heels so sharp they would be worn by a female assassin in an espionage thriller. A young African-American stood at the front of one of the aisles, dressed impeccably in a $3,000 Italian suit, just behind the row where Iris Reilly, Christopher Hanson, and Brett Walton, Esq. sat.

"The author-publisher relationship is a sacred one, a legally binding one. A marriage, holy, ordained by God that no man may tear asunder. I could have remained virginal and pure. I could have self-published *The XII Labors of Alistair Strange*. I could have been everything I needed to be myself: author, editor, graphic designer, typesetter, marketer, and publicist.

"But I chose a different path. A different path. An equally difficult path. I chose to find an agent to represent me and my book. I trusted my book, my child, to her that she may find the perfect home for Alistair Strange. Then I met Iris Reilly and I entered into a relationship with her, a professional relationship, yes, but a relationship that was somehow more, something far more intimate, the author-editor relationship, a relationship worlds are built on, and characters live through."

Casey nodded to the young woman with the stiletto heels, and the young man standing in the aisle.

"You have been served," Casey said, as the young woman on the stage handed a document to Mr. Robert Dwight Brown, his legal name, and the young man standing in the aisle handed Ms.

Reilly, Mr. Hanson, and Mr. Walton nearly identical documents. "I am suing you for breach of contract. I am suing you for copyright infringement. I am suing you for anything and everything that I can legally throw at you.

"You betrayed the author-editor relationship. I entrusted my child, Alistair Strange, to you and you betrayed me, you stabbed me in the back, you murdered my creation, creating instead that unholy abomination, that Frankenstein's monster crafted from the corpse of *my* Alistair Strange. You will no longer have any say about the future of Alistair Strange. He's mine now.

"Iris, from this day forth, you'll keep your filthy hands off my child, you bitch!

The audience gasped at Casey's use of the word. It was a harsh word. It was a profane word. It was a wholly appropriate word. The audience had been stunned into an awkward silence, but soon the murmuring began. The quiet hum sounded like the summer serenade of the cicadas, but soon, the hum amplified into a buzz, then soon it was a riotous clamor.

Casey raised her hand and put a single finger to her lips as if to shush them as misbehaving children, and the audience behaved.

"I have an announcement for my Strangers. There *will* be a sixth novel in *my* Alistair Strange series. Yes, you hold in your hands Alex's heretical sixth novel, a novel that proves my betrayal at the hands of Mr. Brown and Iris. But I will be publishing the sixth novel in *my* series on my own.

"I always looked at self-published authors as cowards. I suffered in the creation of my child. I sent query letter after query letter to any and every agent who had a policy of accepting unsolicited query letters. I knew that the process would be difficult. I knew the process would be time consuming. I thought, I knew, that I had a special book on my hands. How could they not see this? I received my first rejection letter and it was like a getting punched in the heart. I couldn't breathe. But I persevered. Every rejection letter was a badge of honor. I wallpapered my writing room with each and every rejection letter. I allowed all of these agents to lord over me, glaring at me with their disapproving eyes.

But I trudged on until the day that an agent accepted me and the pursuit of an editor, a honest-to-goodness publisher who would publish my book and put it on the sacred shelves of a bookstore.

"Self-published authors are cowards who took the easy way out. They were and are too afraid to suffer through and ride wave after wave of rejection letters from agents and editors until finally your novel is accepted by them and published by real publishers, by authentic publishers. How good could these authors be is they can't get an agent, any agent to read and represent their work. They all just had to be hacks. They all just had to be illiterate non-writers.

"But now, I see the light! I do.

"They choose a different path. But it is an equally difficult path. They do not have a team of professionals who are paid top-dollar to take a book from mere manuscript to finished, polished, published novel. They are walking a lonely road. A different road. An equally difficult road.

"They are more than just authors. They are more than just self-publishers, or how they prefer to call themselves now, independent authors. They are not only authors, but editors as well; they are graphic designers, and typesetters, and marketers, and publicists. They have to do it all. And they are stronger for it.

"Sure. Their sales may not be what they may hope. But their work is their own. They live or die by their own bootstraps.

"I thought of Lightning Source and the print-on-demand publishing world as an abomination. Why wouldn't you want a real publisher to publish thousands of copies of your novel, warehousing them until they could be shipped to the Barnes and Noble and independent bookstores where the readers of the world actually buy their books. On the shelves of bookstores. Those sacred shelves. I am not discounting Amazon.com buyers. Jeff Bezos has proven that virtual bookshelves sell just as well as physical bookshelves, but there is something special to standing in that sacred space amongst all of the books on the shelves of a real, honest-to-goodness brick-and-mortar bookstore.

"But print-on-demand publishing is an interesting, fascinating alternative. Lightning Source makes your book available in the In-gram catalogue and onto Amazon.com where any reader can find your book. When a reader orders your book, Lightning Source prints the one single copy and ships the one single copy to the bookstore, or the Amazon warehouse, where it will be sold (or mailed) to the reader. I don't have to print and warehouse hun-dreds, if not thousands, of copies of my novel in order to produce a quality work. The print-on-demand printer accepts the order, prints the copy of the book, sends the copy of the book to the bookseller, who then pays Lightning Source, who deducts the printing costs of the book, and pays you the rest.

"It is a wonderfully simple process.

"Yes, it may not be the most perfect relationship. An author would hope to have an agent who loved their book enough to rep-resent it to the editors they have cultivated a personal and profes-sional relationship with. An author would hope to have an editor who loved your book enough to help you make it the best book it could possibly be and see the process through until the manuscript makes it through the traditional process of copy-editing and cover selection, until the book finally reaches that illustrious Promised Land, the bookstore.

"But what if you can't trust your editor, your publisher, their lawyer," Casey said, glaring in the general direction of Iris Reil-ly, Christopher Hanson, and Brett Walton, whom all, no doubt, blushed and turned their heads away.

"I would like to announce, here at the San Diego Comic-Con, that I am the master of my own domain. I have self-published, I am an independent author of a new Alistair Strange novel. A final Alistair Strange novel: *The Utterly Irrevocable Destruction of Alistair Strange*.

"He was mine when I created him. He was mine as I taught him to speak. He was mine when I offered him to you. He is still mine. You, my publisher, you thought you owned him outright. You, my editor, you though your controlled him, that he only lived because of you. You, my Hollywood producers, you thought you owned even the littlest a piece of him. You, my wonderful little Strangers, you think that own him through your adulation and worship. You are all wrong. He's mine. He's mine alone. I gave birth to him. He's mine alone to murder. He lives because of me. He breathes because of me. And he will die at my hands.

"I once thought that fan-fiction would be the death of my Alistair Strange. I didn't understand the desire and need of my Strangers to read the non-canonical works about my beloved creation. I know I've said this before, but– Alistair Strange as the villain? Alistair Strange as a girl? Alistair Strange and Luke Skywalker in adventures in a galaxy far, far away? Batman and Alistair Strange, the new dynamic duo? Why explore plot-lines that even I haven't had a chance to fully explore? Why feature a minor character as the protagonist? Why write sequels to the first book that ignore where I took the second and third books? Why the prequels? Distant sequels when they're all adults? Why is there such a thing as a side-quel? Why can't my readers wait until I have finished the fifth book to discover where I take my own characters? Why so much needless speculation? Why so such theorizing? Can't they just enjoy the books for the sake of enjoyment? Can you give me any answers to any of these questions?"

There is hushed murmuring in the audience.

"Why!

"I don't see why there is so much interest in reading these– I don't honestly know what to call them that is polite– non-canonical stories, maybe? *Arrgh*. Fan-fiction. This is where I must draw the line. Alistair Strange is my child. I gave birth to him and I'll murder him if I have to.

"And I have."

She opened the shoulder-bag and removed the $30 proof copy that Lightning Source sent her of *The Utterly Irrevocable Destruction of Alistair Strange*. She held the book high so all could see."

The audience stared in awe and wonderment. What was this curious creation they beheld. It sure looked like a book. It didn't appear to be any different than any other book. It was bound like any other book, printed on paper like any other book. The only way you could tell the different between this and any other book was the graphic-design. Did the independent author take the time, energy, and money to design or have designed a professionally looking book? And if so, there was no way of knowing that this book was printed on a print-on-demand printer and not an off-set machine. How was this alchemy possible? How did Lightning Source find a way to transmute base-metals into gold?

"As I stood off to the side of the stage, I used my phone to approve the distribution of *The Utterly Irrevocable Destruction of Alistair Strange*. The book is now live. And living on the many distribution channels of Ingram Content Group. There the last Alistair Strange novel will live on in infamy.

"I have just killed him, because of your undying love for him. Because of your undying love for him, my boy is dead!

"Live with that paradox!"

"You don't have to burn books to destroy a culture. Just get people to stop reading them."

"There is more than one way to burn a book. Ad the world is full of people running about with lit matches."
    –Ray Bradbury

Epilogue
THE WAR OF THE WORDS

by Bray Radbury

Trials of the Century usually involve salacious and newsworthy crimes of rape, kidnapping, and most importantly murder, not something as insignificant in the grand scheme of things as copyright infringement.

One of the first of the infamous "Crimes of the Century" involved Leopold and Loeb, two wealthy students who kidnapped and murdered a 14-year-old boy, Robert Franks. Famed attorney Clarence Darrow's 12-hour-long "masterful plea" at sentencing would be text-book teachings in law-school concerning its criticism of capital punishment as retributive "shedding of blood" rather and transformative justice that may "help human understanding, to temper justice with mercy, to overcome hate with love."

The "Helter-Skelter" trial of Charles Manson

and his "family" of hippy-dippy cenobites for the grisly, horrendous murders of a quite pregnant Sharon Tate and her house-guests, and the murders of Leno and Rosemary LaBianca only hours later, evolved from a Trial of the Century into a circus-sideshow that put 1960's Counter-Culture on trial.

The trial of famed football running-back O.J. Simpson for the murders his ex-wife Nicole Brown Simpson and Ron Goldman captivated a spellbound television audience initially upset at the interruption of afternoon soap-operas ended up becoming a soap-opera of its own right. The acquittal, that stoked the burning embers of racial prejudice that had smoldered since the Civil Rights movement of the 1960's into a firestorm.

But could a case of copyright infringement rise to the level of a "Trial of the Century"?

If John Grisham had delivered a manuscript to his editor concerning his latest legal thriller entitled *Alistair Strange and the Fan-Friction*, he would have been laughed out of the editor's office and escorted by armed security from the publishing house's premises and perhaps committed to an insane asylum for having "lost his ever-loving mind".

The civil case of *Abigail K.C. Sterling vs. her publishing house & "Alex K.C. Silver"* should not have also preempted the beloved day-time soap-operas, but it did; it should not have Trended or set Nielsen ratings records, but it did; it should not have set Twitter ablaze with tweet-storms and flame-wars, but it did; testimony concerning intellectual property rights should not have beguiled and bewitched a spellbound populous, but it did.

In a country divided by a political system that has divvied up every hot-button politic issue equally between the Republican and Democratic parties, either vehemently opposed to something, *anything*, or supporting the fundamentally contrary opinion as fundamental to our rights as a nation. And in the case of Abigail K.C. Sterling against Alex K.C. Silver, the Strangers found themselves in familiar waters, either supporting Abigail devoutly and idolatrously as the god of her third-person omniscient universe and crucifying Alex as a usurper to the throne or supporting Alex as the rightful heir and deposing Abigail as the God-ordained ruler of her literary universe. There were only two sides in the civil legal battle waged as a Cold Civil War on the battleground of the Internet: Team Dracarys and Team Grifiindico.

To the outsider looking in, the legal battle seemed like innocuous fluff. Who cared about who wrote what novel? The outsider simply doesn't understand the passionate faction war between the Alliance and the Horde in *World of Warcraft*, or the battle over Neilsen ratings in the Monday Night Wars between professional wrestling titans W.W.F. and W.C.W., or Team Edward and Team Jacob that waged between *Twilight* super-fans, or the battle of Potterheads versus Twihards over the supremacy of either the *Harry Potter* or *Twilight* literary franchises.

Why our tribal society divides itself so readily into dual diametrically opposed camps will be left to philosophers, political pundits, and legal scholars. What needs to be understood is however small the Alistair Strange literary universe may appear from the outside, those who lived within the world created by Abigail K.C. Sterling considered it was a battle over reality itself.

Before the copyright infringement case between Ms. Sterling and "Alex K.C. Silver" and the breach of contract case between Ms. Sterling and Iris Reilly, her editor, and Christopher Hanson, her publisher, no one would have anticipated the sheer cavalcade of literary and cinematic celebrities whom would be called upon to testify, in open court, over various legal and literary practices.

J.K. Rowling was forced to testify on whether she had the right, the copyright, to continue releasing tidbits about the Harry Potter franchise that never ended up on the page. Did she have the copyright to reveal long after the publication of *Harry Potter and the Deathly Hallows* that the beloved headmaster of Hogwarts was gay, when many of her fans just "can't see him in that way"? Did she have the copyright to reveal this plot-point or that storyline that never even ended up in the finished product? Did she had the copyright to regret killing off this character or that character years, and even decades after maliciously and gleefully murdering them in her books?

George R.R. Martin took the stand to answer whether HBO, who purchased the television rights to *The Song of Fire and Ice* series of novels from George R.R. Martin, had the copyright, to continue the series after the events detailed in the last to be published novel, *A Dance of Dragons*? Did H.B.O., even having access to G.R.R.M,'s outlines and notes, have the copyright to create legal and authorized "fan-fiction" of the beloved series of novels into the previously unknown waters of *The Winds of Winter* and *A Dream of Spring*? Don't the fans of the novels have the copyright, not to have their literary series of novels spoiled by the "fan-fiction" H.B.O. was peddling to enormous ratings and huge subscriber numbers?

George Lucas appeared to answer questions concerning his copyright to sell his own cinemic universe to that corporate behemoth called Disney? Didn't the *Star Wars* fans, this rabid fandom, that has turned, albeit well-made, pulp space-operas into practically a religion, have any copyrights to their revered series of movies, television cartoons, novels, and comic books? When director Rian Johnson seemingly defecated all over the remembrances and idolizations of cherished *Star Wars* characters like Luke Skywalker and Mary Poppins– I mean Princess Leia– the shitshow that erupted all over reddit, YouTube, Twitter, and the rest of the Internet was a tsunami of sewage.

Stephen King testified in open court that the fans, not unlike Annie Wilkes in *Misery*, had no copyright, over their beloved characters. Nobody could force any author, like Paul Sheldon, to write and/or publish any book against their will. The author alone, King testified, is the god of their little third-person omniscient world. If Paul Sheldon wanted to kill off Misery Chastain, then the fictional author in the Stephen King universe had the right, the copyright, to kill off the beloved character.

After deliberating for seemingly minutes, the jury returned the verdict in favor of Abigail K.C. Sterling. The jury upheld several of the exclusive rights afforded by the government to the owner of the copyright: "protection of the work, to determine and decide how, and under what conditions, the work may be marketed, publicly displayed, reproduced, distributed etc., to produce copies or reproductions of the work and to sell those copies (including, typically, electronic copies), to import or export the work, to create derivative works (works that adapt the original work), to perform or display the work publicly, to sell or cede these rights to others, to transmit or display by radio, video or internet".

The jury held that Abigail K.C. Sterling alone can "determine and decide how and under what conditions the protected work may be used by others". They upheld that the negative right of copyright "serves to prohibit certain people (e.g., readers, viewers, or listeners, and primarily publishers and would be publishers) from doing something they would otherwise be able to do, rather than permitting people (e.g., authors) to do something they would otherwise be unable to do".

All unsold copies of the heretical *Alistair Strange and the Weight of a Feather* and unreleased, warehoused copies of *Alistair Strange & Alistair Strange: Through the Multiverse* were ordered destroyed. The original film negatives and computer hard-drives for *Weight of a Feather* were likewise ordered to be destroyed.

Bookstores around the world, from Barnes and Noble to Amazon.com returned every single unsold copy of *Weight of a Feather* to the publisher, whom warehoused them with all of the printed, but as of yet undistributed copies of *Though the Multiverse* at their New York City warehouse. Once every unsold copy was accounted for, the books were picked up from the warehouse and delivered to a vacant lot on the outskirts of the city.

In an act of literary apostasy that would have horrified Ray Bradbury, Abigail K.C. Sterling hired her own "firemen" to stage the epic and theatrical eradication of Alex K.C. Silver from the collective consciousness of the human race. The "firemen", themselves actual firemen, arrived in their firetrucks. They hooked up hoses to the water-hydrants so they would be able to put out the fires they were about to intentionally start.

Strangers came from far-and-wide, from every corner of the country and perhaps even the world itself, to participate. The semi-tractor-trailers arrived with boxes upon boxes of unsold and undistributed heretical novels. The Strangers formed a bucket-brigade passing copies from the boxes in the trucks hand-to-hand along a long line of Strangers, piling the books in a ever-growing pile.

As the pyre of books grew larger and larger, the "firemen" stepped forward, armed with flame-throwers and set the heap of books, both the unsold and the undistributed, ablaze. The flames licked the books, quickly reaching "Fahrenheit 451–the temperature at which book paper catches fire, and burns..." The flamed leapt from one book to the next book, the paper "dust jackets" charred and shank under the intense heat, the cloth covering cardboard of the hardbacks ignited next, the glue binding the books together melted and warped the spins, opening the books as if the flames had intended to read them instead of consuming them. But consume the books they did. The edges of the paper blackened and curled up at the corners as the flames liquefied the ink printing the copyright-infringing "fan-fiction" onto the once authorized Alistair Strange novels.

The Strangers danced around the bon-fire like they were heathen Romans at a bacchanal. Boxes and boxes of still unburned books were carried and placed in a ring around the pyre. The Strangers, eagerly, greedily, seized copies of the books and gleefully flung the books onto the pyre. To the news-crews who had come to record and report on the spectacle, they were horrified by the sheer and unmistakable parallels between this scene in an abandoned field in the United States of America, that bastion of liberty and freedom-of-speech, and the rallies of National Socialist German Workers' Party, or the Nazis, in the stadiums of Berlin. The Strangers made a mockery of the scene, happily burning books, and as the insanity began to peak, they tore at their clothes.

Casey went to the trunk of her car and removed the final and only known print of the Hollywood film adaptation of *Alistair Strange and the Weight of a Feather* and carried the metal cannisters to the edge of the conflagration. She threw reel after reel onto the pyre, the negatives warping and melting, like the infamous cigarette burn in the corner of the picture indicating to the projectionist that the reel was ending and to begin the next one. But the cigarette burns that evening, consumed not only the corners but the entirety of the negatives. Even modern "safety film" burns under such heat and pressures, but tonight, the negatives of the heretical adaption of the equally heretical fifth novel burned with the relative ease of the old hazardous nitrate film that has decayed and even spontaneously combusted, costing humanity much of the early silent film era motion pictures.

But this night, the books and film negatives were burned by the order of a judge in good standing with the state of New York. How had we reached this point in the War of Words between Abigail K.C. Sterling and her case of copyright-infringement against her publisher and Alex K.C. Silver? Were the lessons of the past not learned once again this night? To the onlookers who were horrified by what they were witnessing in person that dark, moonless night and those watching in horror on the television sets, computer monitors, and cell-phones, Casey had become the very thing all writers fear, the censor, the oppressor of the freedom-of-speech. She was worse than the "firemen" of Ray Bradbury's dystopian novel.

She may have been the god of her third-person omniscient world, but she not only utterly razed her Creation to ruin in a Ragnarök that utterly destroyed her literary universe, but her reputation as well. She had intended on saving her titular hero from the ancient evil of "fan-fiction", but in the end, her reputation as a writer, an author continuing in the long line of societal commentary through fiction, was utterly ruined. She became a pariah, an outcast from the fraternity of writers.

She would forever be remembered as The Fireman!

THE
BIBLIOGRAPHY

Bates, J. (2015). *Writing your novel from start to finish: a guidebook for the journey.* Cincinnati, OH: Writers Digest Books.

Card, O. S. (2010). *The Writers Digest guide to science fiction & fantasy.* Cincinnati, OH: Writers Digest Books.

Oswalt, Patton, *Talking For Clapping,* Netflix, 2016

Tolkien, J. R., & Lee, A. (2002). *The Fellowship of the Ring.* Boston: Houghton Mifflin. pg xi

Walsh, T., & Bell, J. S. (2016). *Author in progress: a no-holds-barred guide to what it really takes to get published.* Cincinnati, OH: Writers Digest Books.

Websites

http://blog.janicehardy.com/2013/10/how-to-plot-with-three-act-structure.html

https://josephblakeparker.deviantart.com/art/Three-Act-Outline-Template-522287162

https://ucomm.wsu.edu/what-copyright-protects/

https://www.nytimes.com/2015/04/12/education/edlife/12edl-12mfa.html

http://flavorwire.com/476264/27-writers-on-whether-or-not-to-get-your-mfa

http://www.aerogrammestudio.com/2013/03/04/e-m-forster-the-difference-between-story-and-plot/

https://killzoneblog.com/2014/06/15-questions-for-your-beta-readers-and-to-focus-your-own-revisions.html

http://jamigold.com/wp-content/uploads/2014/08/Beta-reading-worksheet-A-and-B.jpg

http://www.mariavsnyder.com/advice/showvstell.php

https://oregonstate.edu/instruct/comm440-540/criticism.htm

http://aaronline.org/FAQ

https://writersblock.loft.org/2014/01/31/2991/7_essential_tips_for_writing_a_romance

https://en.wikipedia.org/wiki/Copyright

ROBERT DWIGHT BROWN is the author of *allonymously* (yes, its a real word) written classic-fiction, Shakespearean plays, and even a sequel to the Holy Bible itself. He has enjoyed writing the books that other authors *did not* write themselves. Now, he chooses not to write in the name of Charles Dickens, William Shakespeare, Orson Welles, or God Himself, *but* in his own name and in his own voice, except that name and voice is a *pseudonym*: Abigail K.C. Sterling.

www.ingramcontent.com/pod-product-compliance
Lightning Source LLC
Chambersburg PA
CBHW050505260626
47157CB00004B/1191